s l

FACING IT

FACING IT

A Novel of AIDS

PAUL REED

Gay Sunshine Press
San Francisco

First edition 1984
Copyright © 1984 by Paul Reed
Cover design by Timothy Lewis

Excerpts from the *Morbidity and Mortality Weekly Report* (Vol. 30/No. 25)
appear courtesy of the Centers for Disease Control. Quotations from May
Sarton's *A Reckoning* appear by permission of W. W. Norton & Co. "2 Fatal
Diseases Focus of Inquiry" appears by permission of the Associated Press.

The author gratefully acknowledges the following individuals for their as-
sistance in coordinating medical information and for their overall support:
Dr. William J. Kapla, Robert Kirsch, David H., Joseph Brewer, Scott and
Paul, John Karr, Joann Passariello, Julie Wright, Phil and George. Special
thanks to Marvin Bevans and to Cap, who precipitated the writing, and to
May Sarton, for encouragement along the years.

Aside from the news articles excerpted herein and the reality of the AIDS
crisis itself, this work is fiction. Any similarities to persons, living or dead,
are purely coincidental.

Publication of this book was made possible in part by a grant from the
National Endowment for the Arts.

Library of Congress Cataloging in Publication data:

Reed, Paul, 1956–
    Facing it.
    I. Title.
PS3568.E369F3   1984   813'.54   84-13751
ISBN 0-917342-43-7 (lim. hardcover)
ISBN 0-917342-44-5 (pbk.)

Gay Sunshine Press
P.O. Box 40397
San Francisco, CA 94140
Complete catalog of books available for $1.

for Dale and Joe

PART ONE

1   *June 1981   •   New York City*

Had it been some other season of the year, Dr. Walter Branch wouldn't have given the hospital morgue a second thought. But now, in the heat of early summer, late on a Friday afternoon, he remembered that there was, somewhere at least, one cool spot to which he could retreat should the heat get much worse. But there were patients waiting, and more work to be done in the lab, so Dr. Branch opted for just a moment sitting down in his inner office.

On the sixth floor of Manhattan's Mt. Zion Hospital, Dr. Branch's suite of offices and research lab occupied a corner of the oldest wing of the large midtown hospital. Dr. Branch slipped his glasses off and rubbed his eyes. The heat was sweltering, unendurable really, and this corner of the old hospital—built of brick at the end of the last century—was like an oven. The ventilation system, which, to Branch's amusement, some called air-conditioning, failed altogether if the temperature exceeded ninety-five degrees. And it has, Branch thought to himself. Even in the sleek new patient wards—in the highrise wing added in the nineteen-fifties and sixties—it was steaming hot.

Well, on with it, Branch told himself, thinking that surely the heat wave must break. He stood, slipped his glasses back on, and stretched his arms. He was tired today, and he looked it. Long ago, much earlier in the day, he had shed his jacket and tie, despite his position, and was working in a plain white shirt, the sleeves rolled up.

He looked his age—fifty years, with his fifty-first birthday approaching in the fall. He wasn't handsome, but neither was he ugly; his face was kindly, the sort of face that would suit the grandfatherly years. He was tall, not fat. His thin hair, once chestnut, was now almost all gray. The chestnut still showed in his bushy eyebrows, only lightly salted with gray. Deep lines were etched in his cheeks, lines that deepened with every smile. He had the thin lips of a native New Englander, as well as a stiff posture.

Today, the heat and fatigue of his work was beginning to show in his face. Not only did he maintain a frantic pace as an immunological and infectious diseases researcher, he insisted on keeping a fairly large clinical practice, though in recent years he had been forced to restrict his clinical work to the more specialized medical problems that dumbfounded general practitioners. But today he had allowed Meg, his secretary, to schedule a full afternoon of patients, including some of his patients he should have let go to general practitioners; he just couldn't give up his contact with general clinical work.

He stretched again and went back into the outer office. "How many patients are left, Meg?"

She looked up from her typewriter. "Just one, doctor. And then you're through for the day, as far as patients go."

He poked his head around the corner and surveyed the empty waiting room. "Thank God for that," he said. "Even I have to admit that I think I overdid it today, but it's this damn heat."

"Amen to that!" Meg said. She picked up a file and handed it to Dr. Branch. "Andrew Stone is the last one for the day. He's in Room Two."

Dr. Branch took the file and stood looking at it for a moment. Andrew Stone was one of the few patients he saw as a general practice, and that was because Andy Stone was a special young man. Twenty-eight years ago Branch had delivered Andy screaming and kicking in an uptown restaurant in the middle of a blizzard; the storm had been so bad that getting Andy's mother to a hospital would have been too late, so Branch—in his first year of medical school at Columbia—had volunteered to help.

Branch and Andy's parents had become friends then, but when Andy was three they had moved to Philadelphia. It was fifteen years before Walt Branch saw Andy Stone again. Andy was eighteen then, Branch forty-one, and Andy had just left home and moved to Manhattan.

Branch smiled as he looked through Andy's file. He thought to himself that even though he was tired and hot, it was always good to see Andy. He took the file and entered the examining room.

"Hello there, Dr. Branch," Andy said.

Branch was so shocked by Andy's appearance that he hesitated for a moment. "Hi, Andy," he answered, regaining his composure. "It's been quite a while since you've been in to see me. What can I do for you?" Branch was formal as he tried to hide his shock.

Andy related his symptoms to Dr. Branch, and the doctor took a long look at him as he spoke. Usually quite robust and muscular, Andy now looked extremely tired, pale, and much thinner. He had never seen Andy so drawn, with such a pallor. He frowned as he listened to the litany of complaints.

"It's so unusual for me to be so tired," Andy said. "But in the last month or so, I've noticed that I've been really fatigued, really run down. Last month we were in Yosemite, on vacation, and I noticed that I couldn't hike very far or for very long before I got completely tired out. David and I blamed it on the altitude, but I'm not so sure." Andy stopped, his voiced trailing off.

"Anything else?" Branch prompted as he flipped through the pages of Andy's medical chart.

"Well, I'm a little wrecked about it—I mean, it's not like a cold or the flu; it's been longer than that. What really got me to come in was that this afternoon—earlier, at work downtown, I just had the most overwhelming attack of being tired, like I was going to pass out. I got up and went to the washroom, splashed water on my face; you know, trying to wake up and perk up, but it hit me like a wave.

My hands shook, and I felt weak all over. So I called Meg and made an appointment."

"How *are* things at work?" Branch asked. "Any changes there?" Although Branch could see that Andy was ill, he wanted to check if there was a great deal of stress in his life at the moment—stress could cause such symptoms.

"No changes, not really," Andy answered. "I got a promotion, sort of, but it's not stress, if that's what you're asking. I thrive on stress, really. I noticed that I've been having a really low fever in the evenings, too, it comes and goes."

"And you've lost some weight," Branch observed.

"Yes, about ten pounds I think. But I figure part of that is because I've quit going to the gym and my appetite is down. After Yosemite I thought maybe I must have a low-grade infection, you know, so I thought that taking a break from the gym would get it over with."

"But you haven't improved?" Branch asked.

"No, not at all. And then with this afternoon's episode, that's when I knew I'd reached the edge of my patience; I know you don't want to bother seeing general patients anymore, but I'm just so worried..." Andy grew silent.

"No, no, it's not that," Branch said. "I just have to restrict myself mostly to the rare cases."

Branch put the chart down and fastened his stethoscope round his neck. "Let's check you out; take off your shirt." Andy pulled his shirt off and the doctor listened to Andy's heart and respiration. Everything seemed normal there. The doctor looked into Andy's ears, throat and nose. Unremarkable, he noted. He asked Andy to lie flat on his back so he could palpate the liver and internal organs, but nothing presented itself as remarkable.

"You can sit up again," Branch said. Andy sat up and Branch ran his fingers along Andy's neck. "By the way," Branch said, continuing to feel Andy's neck, "how is David doing these days, anyway?"

"He's fine," Andy answered. "A little frustrated about his career, though. He wants to be a writer, a journalist really, but he didn't get the training he should have, so he's at a disadvantage I think. That's just my opinion, though.

I tell him to try writing a book, but no go. He keeps working at the part-time copy-editing jobs from different publishing houses, though, and he *is* turning out a fair number of free-lance features for the gay press."

"It's not easy," Branch said, his exam complete. He was making a notation in Andy's records. "You know that your lymph glands are swollen?" Branch asked.

"Oh, I guess so," Andy answered.

"I'd like to run some tests," Dr. Branch said.

Andy started to put his shirt back on. "What is it?"

"I don't know," Branch said, "but I'd like to do some blood work to check for hepatitis. It often shows up just like this."

Andy looked crestfallen. "Hepatitis? Oh, shit! How the hell did I get hepatitis? I mean, I take care of myself; I don't understand." He was shocked and frustrated. "I don't have time for it, anyway. Don't you have to stay in bed for six weeks or something?"

"Well, you do have to take care of yourself," Branch answered. "And as to where or how you got it, there are about a hundred ways I could name off the top of my head; it's not so rare."

"But it's not fair," Andy protested.

"Now there's a different topic," Branch said. "And it's not worth going into. We'll have to confirm this with the tests, then we'll know. I'll send a nurse in to draw some blood before you leave, and we need to get a urine sample. And then you go right home and get into bed. And stay there for the rest of the weekend and early next week, until we get back the test results."

"Go to bed in this heat?" Andy said.

"It is bad, isn't it?" Branch agreed, noticing that it was just as hot as before. He had become so engrossed in Andy's problems that he had temporarily forgotten how utterly miserable it was. He took his handkerchief and wiped his brow.

Andy asked for a glass of water. Then, sitting sullen and drinking it, he looked up at the doctor and asked: "What are the chances that it is hepatitis? How sure are you?"

Dr. Branch frowned and sighed; the heat was getting to

him again, now that he had been reminded. "I think it's *probable* that you do. So take it easy, please."

"Okay, okay," Andy said, starting to button his shirt.

"And be careful around David," Branch warned.

"Oh!" Andy exclaimed, unbuttoning his shirt again. "I almost forgot; I wanted you to look at these sores here." Andy took his shirt off again and pointed to a number of small red sores in his armpit. "I don't know how I forgot them," Andy said, "because they're pretty painful whenever I move my arm like this..." Andy rotated his arm forward.

Dr. Branch laughed and joked: "So don't move your arm like that." They both laughed at the old joke as Branch leaned in close to examine the sores. They were red and pustular, not many, but enough to be troublesome.

"That's a staph infection," Branch said. "I'll have the nurse do a culture on that to be sure, of course." Dr. Branch frowned again, puzzled. "That's funny..."

"What's funny?" Andy asked, thinking he had missed another joke.

"Oh, I didn't mean funny," Branch explained, sitting down and fanning himself with Andy's medical file. "I mean odd, odd that you should have such symptomatology indicative of hepatitis, and then the staph infection as well. It's odd because you've been healthy these last few years." He was quiet for a moment, pondering; then he shrugged his shoulders—it was too hot to think. "Well, let's see what the tests tell us. And in the meantime, I'll give you a prescription for cloxycillin, for that staph infection. You can take it down as soon as you leave here and get it filled at the hospital pharmacy. It's in the new wing, near the emergency room, open for outpatients until six."

"Okay," Andy said. "Thanks, doctor. When do I call about the tests?"

"I'll have Meg call you when we get the results back from the lab. We'll talk about your recovery then. Take it easy, now."

"Uh, doctor," Andy said, "I have to be at a meeting on Tuesday and another on Wednesday. It wouldn't hurt if I went into the office for a couple hours each day, would it?"

Branch shook his head. "It's okay, but I don't like it. Just go in for your meetings and then go home to bed. I know that hepatitis is something you hear about frequently, but it is a serious illness. You should be careful around David, too. Don't share any dishes or anything like that."

"Fine, thanks," Andy said.

"I'll send a nurse in now," Branch said, suddenly distracted by the scorching heat. He needed to sit down. He left the examining room and sent a nurse into the room to draw the blood. Branch sat on the edge of Meg's desk and wiped his forehead again. She stopped working and leaned back, looking up at him. Meg had been Branch's secretary for almost ten years now. She was forty-two, rather motherly in her way, but still a striking beauty. As a younger woman, she had been exceptional, and much of the fine characteristics of her beauty had deepened with her maturity. In many ways she seemed younger than her years; there was a vibrancy about her that indicated still waters running deep.

"What a day, Meg! I'm glad it's over." Branch took off his glasses and loosened his tie further. He rubbed his forehead and then smiled at Meg. "Was it rough out here?" he asked, not really waiting for the answer. He was still puzzling over Andy. In all his years he had never seen such a rapid and dramatic waning of health in a usually healthy patient. Even if it was hepatitis—which he was sure it must be—there was something else that troubled him. He had quite a diagnostic skill, as well as a native intuition, and he was troubled by Andy's sudden decline. It wasn't just the hepatitis, he told himself; no, there was something seriously wrong, something anomalous that made him suspicious.

"All the same!" Meg said, her answer jolting him back into the present. She handed him a stack of files. "Your records, doctor." Meg laughed and smiled when she saw Branch's look of exasperation.

"It's just too hot..." he said, holding the stack of files unenthusiastically in his lap.

"Now, now, doctor," Meg said. "Why don't you go sit down and get comfortable; plop your big tired feet up on that big tired desk of yours, and get busy dictating these records."

"You're a sadist, Meg," he accused.

"No, you're a masochist, doctor, because it was you who insisted on seeing half a million patients this afternoon."

"Hmmm," Branch grumbled, standing to go into his inner office. "Would you call up Dr. Maguire's office and confirm that appointment with him for Monday morning? Last time I had an appointment with our eminent chief administrator, I waited for over an hour before his secretary told me he was out of town, disappeared for the afternoon again!"

"I remember," Meg said, reaching for the phone.

"And would you get Dr. Leider on the line for me," he added. "I need to talk to him about Andrew Stone."

"Oh," Meg said, waving the doctor back to her desk. She leaned in close. "What's the matter with him, anyway?" she whispered. "He looks like death warmed over."

"Please, Meg," he whispered, frowning. "That's not very professional talk. But it's too much night life I suspect. My guess is hepatitis, but I'm worried about how sudden it is—his whole decline, that is. That's why I want to talk to Dr. Leider for a few minutes."

"That's too bad," Meg said with conviction. She had always been very fond of Andrew. She found him quite affable and very attractive. "Is he still with David?" she asked.

"Yes," Branch said, "and he says that David's doing fine."

"And that's too bad, too!" Meg said, and then, seeing Dr. Branch frowning again, she said, "I'm only kidding, doctor. Its just that Andy's so handsome."

"And half your age, Meg!" Branch said, a wry smile on his lips, his head shaking.

"Just kidding," she said again. She looked up as the nurse came out of the examining room with the vials of blood, Andy following behind. "All through," she said to him. "We'll call you next week."

"Thanks, Meg," Andy said, "I think I'm going to treat myself to a cab ride this afternoon."

"In this heat you better," she said, watching him leave

[16]

the waiting room and go into the hall. She, too, was shocked at Andy's appearance. He was a very handsome young man, she thought to herself; even his illness didn't mask that fact. But my word! she thought to herself, he certainly doesn't look very well, not at all.

*

Dr. Branch, taking the stack of medical records into his inner office, caught a glimpse of Andy leaving the examining room. Branch walked around the perimeter of his spacious private office, going to the long windows that overlooked the small courtyard that made up the hospital's front entrance six floors down. He looked down into that yard at the few shrubs and trees there, noticing that there were a great many nurses taking their coffee break under the shade of the trees.

He stood there, feeling the heat and looking down at the people coming and going. He thought about Andy Stone. Bright young man, always in good shape, no history of previous serious infection—these were the facts that created a sense of suspicion and foreboding. Well, Branch told himself, he would wait for the tests to confirm hepatitis, and that would be that.

He looked away from the windows, breathed a heavy sigh as he saw the unavoidable mess on his desk. He had yet to dictate the day's medical records, and he had hoped to make some notes on the morning's research, but now, as dinnertime approached, he realized that he wasn't going to fit it in today. He had to get home for dinner with his wife Carolyn, and then they were meeting friends for the summer symphony, Mozart's "Jupiter" symphony it was to be.

His eyes lingered for a moment on the framed degrees, certificates and awards behind his desk: Dr. Walter Branch, Professor of Infectious Diseases, Mt. Zion Hospital, New York City. He looked at his Bachelor of Arts from Rutgers, his M.D. from Columbia. Then, two years later, he'd received his PH.D. from Columbia. A very steady climb, he thought, but the thought brought with it a deep frustration, a sudden sense of longing, of something missing.

[17]

He looked at the huge stack of paper on the end of his credenza, feeling the disappointment and sadness more sharply. Another failed proposal, he thought to himself, fingering the stack of papers. At fifty, he was beginning to feel time slip by just a bit faster. Every missed opportunity seemed more frustrating.

Ten, twelve years ago he had emerged as one of the top researchers in infectious diseases, after a long haul of grueling work, research, papers, studies, lectures. He had studied hepatitis for some time, had even helped in developing the vaccine against Hepatitis B; he had worked in leukemia, leprosy, cholera. But he hadn't gone far enough; he had always stuck to traditional methods, revising, considering methodological problems and even epistemology. And it was this academic approach—as well as his stubbornness in maintaining a clinical practice—that had betrayed him lately, allowing others to compete more successfully in the arena of medical politics, the scramble for money.

In part, he blamed his wife for distracting him from his work with her endless round of social engagements, but he knew this wasn't fair. Carolyn had never forced him to join her; he had wanted it all at once—to be the prominent medical researcher, to gather esteem as well as to participate fully in the high social scene. He had, he admitted to himself, been greedy.

For a moment he considered his role in relation to the other top researchers. There were only two, really, who held a place near him. And neither of those two have any problem winning grants, he reminded himself. There was another group he omitted from consideration—a whole new crop of rising young researchers armed with information and training he could never hope to equal: there wasn't time to catch up. He put them out of his mind and thought about the two competitors.

Dr. Maxwell Leider—his close friend and colleague there at Mt. Zion, dispenser of good advice and cheer—had been doing remarkable work in rare, tropical diseases, isolating the bacteria that casued the diseases. In more recent years, Leider had moved into the new field of recombinant

DNA, branching out into areas of applied genetic engineering that were, quite simply, dazzling. And for that reason, there seemed no end to Leider's research funds.

And there was Dr. Alfred Kinder-Mann at the University of California in San Francisco, his old med school buddy, now something of an adversary. Branch and Kinder-Mann had been competitors as long as they had known each other—competing for the same research assignments at Columbia, the same assistantships, the same scholarships and even the same residency post. Now Kinder-Mann was out in California, out of touch with Branch, though Branch was continually haunted by Kinder-Mann's name appearing with such regularity in this or that medical journal.

Branch sat down at his desk and tried to put his frustrations out of his mind. He picked up the stack of medical records, hoping to clear his mind with the work. He drank a glass of water that was sitting on the desk, only to find that it, like everything else today, was too warm. He kicked off his shoes, removed his tie completely, and put his feet up on the big desk.

His phone buzzed. "I have Dr. Leider on line two," Meg told him over the intercom.

"Thanks," Branch said, taking his feet down and sitting up. He found Stone's file, opened it, and picked up the phone.

"Hello there, Max," Branch said, "Have you decided to take a break from vacation and do a little work? I didn't think Meg would find you in the hospital on a Friday afternoon."

"You crazy goy, what's up?" Dr. Leider asked, laughing.

"Just a quick question about a patient I had in this afternoon. It's not too serious, I don't think, but a couple of things have me puzzled."

"Shoot," Leider said.

"Young man named Stone, Andrew Stone..."

"Yeah, yeah..." Leider prompted, impatient.

"Anyway, he's always been okay, a healthy patient, very strong, good condition. He's gay, too, but he's got a steady lover. He showed up today all run down, presenting fatigue, weight loss in excess of ten pounds in two months, low, low fever—a spiking fever, by the way. He says it's been with him for about a month now. Also presents with occasional dizziness and lymphadenopathy...."

"Hepatitis," Leider cut in. "Do a panel of liver function, hep antigen-antibody, see what..."

"Of course, Max, that's what I thought," Branch broke in. "That what I ordered. But what puzzles me is that he also had a series of skin lesions, axillary, full of pus. My diagnosis of the lesions is that they're a staph infection..."

"But what mystifies you is the fact of two different things at once in a usually very healthy patient?" Leider finished for him.

"Yes, exactly." Branch said. "It's not major, mind you, but it has got me suspicious. You've got to understand how sudden and inconsistent this is for Andy."

"Well, Walt," Dr. Leider said, "I wouldn't worry much until you get back the blood panels and all that. I'll think about it, but it's probably just a coincidence. You know how much we're seeing weird things showing up all the time; we live in a chemical soup out there. He's probably got hepatitis, plain and simple, with an unassociated axillary staph."

"Thanks, Max," Branch said, realizing that perhaps he had let his worries run away with him. It was a long, hot day; perhaps Andy's appearance had been as affected by the heat as Branch was sure his own must be. He hung up the phone and made a notation in Stone's file to call Max back when the test results came in.

Branch stood up and noticed for the first time that it wasn't as hot as it had been. The constant film of perspiration on his forehead had begun to dry. He walked to the windows and looked out, to see if a storm were moving in. But it was clear, the late afternoon sun still slanting in the street below.

"Hey, Meg," he shouted. "It's getting cooler. And is my meeting still on with Maguire?"

"Yes, it is," Meg answered, stepping into his office. She had shed her white smock and was turning up the sleeves of her blouse.

"Good, I want to talk to him about this grant," Branch said.

"No," Meg corrected him. "I mean yes it is cooler, but no, your meeting is cancelled. His secretary said that Dr. Maguire's schedule is... let me see, what was the word?... *inflexible* at the moment."

"I see," Branch said, his frustration clearly showing. Not only was his grantsmanship failing, he was pulling less and less weight with the hospital administration. Dr. Art Maguire was the chief administrator for Mt. Zion's Research Division, and as such, his help was invaluable in the winning of funds; but he had begun to shut Branch out.

Meg regarded him with sympathy; she knew what he was thinking. "Oh, come on, now, don't be such a sourpuss. You New Englanders can get so cranky. It's probably the heat, that's all."

Branch frowned; he didn't know what she meant. She shrugged her shoulders; she didn't know either. She turned to go. Branch was studying Andy Stone's file as he heard the door to the outer office shut. He barely perceived that Meg had left. He was absorbed in Andy's file. Something's out of kilter there, he thought; he hoped it was just a case of hepatitis. He made one last notation in Andy's file, then closed it and picked up the next. He began dictating.

2

Andy went home and put Aretha Franklin's new album on the stereo. He needed to sit down and rest, to assess the day and absorb the possibility that he might have hepatitis. He looked around the small living room, at the two small sofas facing each other, at the soft white easy chair and ottoman, the stereo and the two windows that opened out over the street. The sofas looked too cozy, which in the heat meant too stuffy and warm. Andy went to the windows and opened them wide, letting in something of a slight cooling breeze, at least releasing the stuffiness of the room. He pushed the windows wider, traffic noise roaring into the room from the rush hour below. For a moment he stood there without moving, transfixed by the busy street; then he realized he could no longer hear the music.

He went to the stereo and slipped the headphones on, lying flat on his back and propping his feet up on the ottoman. He listened to the rhythm, blocking his worries; he closed his eyes and thought: at least if he did have hepatitis, there was something he could do—rest and take it easy. That would be a relief he knew, much better than simply feeling sick and run down as he had the past several weeks, not knowing what was wrong. He stretched his arms above his head and felt the discomfort of the staph infection. Dammit, he said to himself, realizing he had forgotten to take the first dose of antibiotic.

He got up and unplugged the headphones, turning the volume up high on the stereo. 'Retha swelled around him, flooding the apartment with dancing music, cheering, bright. He went to the kitchen to get a glass of water, then went into the bathroom and swallowed the pills. He splashed water on his face and stared at himself in the mirror. Okay, what do I see? he asked himself, studying his face in a new light. Though he had lost some weight, it had helped define his features more clearly. His jet-black hair offset his steel-gray eyes, which were highlighted by the thick moustache. At twenty-eight, he was one of the most handsome young men in Manhattan, and his looks seemed perpetually to improve, though it was hard to improve on perfection. Or so his lover said. Still, as he stared at his own classically handsome face, there was a remnant of fear. Why was he so tired? Why was he losing weight?

He looked down at his body, its perfection equal to that of his face. He had, in high school in Philadelphia and then later in City College in New York, worked hard as a gymnast; his body had formed the graceful, masculine lines that went with the sport. Now, in recent years, he had switched to training with weights, and the solid definition of his chest and arm muscles, the rippling abdomen, the large, firm thighs—none of it could be disparaged, not even with the weight loss. In fact, the weight loss had pared him down to the essential leanness: he was hard and tough.

He took a towel and patted his face dry, then walked back to the living room. He saw a note from his lover propped on the table by the door, saying only that he was at the library and would return home soon. No time was written, so Andy couldn't determine when "soon" would be.

Seeing the note jolted him into thinking about David in relation to the hepatitis. Would Andy have passed it on to him? And what about work? For a year he had been working to get the gay rights ordinance passed by the city council, and they were nearing a critical juncture; if Andy dropped out of the picture for a few weeks, the thing could truly be jeopardized again. Why the hell had he chosen a career in city politics anyway?

Well, he told himself, he couldn't face any more depression at that moment. He moped around the apartment for a few minutes, doing nothing, finally dozing off on the floor again, his feet propped up, his arms flung above his head. He slept fitfully, dreaming of nothing in particular, certainly nothing that would make much meaning of his life as it had been before or after that afternoon, or as it would become. At that moment, quietly, restlessly asleep on the floor, the summer heat unbreaking, Andy was not aware that he stood on a threshhold between the future and the past.

*

His adolescence had not been easy. When Andy was fifteen, returning home from school on a warm spring day in suburban Philadelphia, things happened in his family, as they do, that changed and directed his life differently. One moment he had been a teenager looking forward to summer vacation; the next moment he had been the object of his mother's ferocious inquisition. She'd swooped down at him from the stairs, coming at him with a purpose, a phalanx of furied motherhood in one woman, waving, gesticulating, flapping the porno magazines he had hidden between the mattress and box springs of his bed; he had bought them downtown only the day before. He stood there, shocked and wondering; she opened the magazines to a two-page spread that featured three young men entangled on a bed: one wore a jockstrap and hard-hat; the other two were completely naked, preparing to finish their business with the jockstrap-clad youth. "Is this the sort of thing you want?" she'd demanded. "Is it?" He shook his head and answered yes. At that instant of his confession her face went blank, then registered a rainbow of emotions: shock, surprise, recognition, and pain. She'd stared at him through the four emotions, her eyes clouded with tears. "How?..." she'd whispered, collapsing on the stairs, sobbing. He went to his room and waited. "Your father will be home soon!" she'd called out after him, and when he did come home, he examined the magazines closely, shocked (he knew about such things, of course; all men did; but he had never seen pictures as lewd nor as graphic) and, disbelieving, he took them to the barbecue out back and burned them.

Twelve psychiatric sessions later Andy heard about the Stonewall riots in New York, and his therapy took a slant his parents had not intended. He began to learn pride and acceptance and a host of other emotions that drew him away from his family; he would go to New York after high school. It took him two years of exemplary behavior in high school to get there, two years during which he studied, achieved what his friends considered greatness on the gymnastics team, and, through therapy, learned about himself and his family and the confounding situation of sexuality and longing, all entangled against the barren landscape of his immediate family.

Andy's mother—Edna—had been raised in Saginaw, Michigan. After graduating from high school in 1949, she and her best friend Claire had taken the train to New York, their first venture into the larger world. They had stayed with Claire's cousins on the West Side, and, one muggy afternoon, when she and Claire were dodging into a café to escape a sudden thundershower, she had bumped smack into Chuck Stone's chest. Her first impresssion of the man who would be Andy's father was of his size. His shoulders were broad, and he stood well over six feet. They had laughed about her clumsiness and apologized, and then he had poured on his reserves of charm and asked her for a date. By the time her summer visit in New York was done, she and Chuck were in love and engaged. They married in October of 1949, sharing his tiny apartment on the West Side. Chuck Stone had been a construction worker in 1949. Two years older than Edna, he was raised in upstate New York. Although too young to fight, the war sparked his imagination about the world beyond upstate New York, so when he was done with schooling, he moved to Manhattan and took up work as a construction laborer. After he and Edna were married, they started a family at once. Their first baby, Margaret, was born the first spring after their marriage. A year later, Amanda followed. Then, two years after Amanda, little Andy popped out during a blizzard. The burden of three youngsters motivated Chuck to use his savings to establish his own business. Just before Andy's fourth birthday, he moved the family to Philadelphia where, with his boyhood pal Floyd, he set up a trucking company that specialized in moving construction equipment. At the end of the first year in Philadelphia, Chuck and Edna had their last daughter, Elizabeth. His first year of business had been better than he could have hoped — so much postwar construction — and they began to expand the enterprise to include leasing the heavy equipment. Within a few years, the business grew to a respectable size, and by the late sixties, Chuck Stone and Floyd Wilson were co-owners of a two-million-dollar business. Chuck took pride in his American manhood: his own business, a loving wife, three daughters, and a son. Until, of course, that afternoon when Edna had found that Andy was not, after all, to be a real man. Chuck Stone had found it hard to accept that his son was gay; in fact, he refused to accept it. Andy was a tough kid — on more than one occasion Chuck had detected the smell of cigarettes and liquor on Andy's breath late on a Saturday night. What had gone wrong? Even psychiatry had been unable to help.

Andy's two older sisters, Margaret and Amanda (Margie and Mandy) were also disinclined towards acceptance. That their little brother was queer, even though he was not, technically, a sissy, was both disgusting and embarrassing. And as time passed and he grew deeper into the therapy, he made less effort to conceal his inclinations, so that the two sisters felt always as if they had to make some explanation. They avoided Andy and he avoided them; dinnertime was always a matter of tension—what would they discuss?

Those two years became a proposition of analysis and hate, avoidance and tension. The world was changing fast around them: drugs and free sex and hippies and violent demonstrations disrupted the calm, middle-class rhythms of family life, and Andy seemed to fall on the outside, while the balance of the family remained steadfast; he was, somehow, a part of all that craziness out there; it was all over the news every night. For Andy, it was, although difficult, an exciting period. He was not alone; there were hundreds of thousands of others who either shared his sexuality or shared his rebellion. A great disruption was under way, and he was, by virtue of his attraction to men, part of it. Each night he studied the newscasts, proud to see this demonstration or that speech; vast numbers of people were rising against the sort of life that his parents had so carefully constructed.

For reasons that Andy was never to understand, his little sister Elizabeth (Beth) was the only truly loving voice of sanity throughout those final two years at home. While the rest of the family withdrew their intimacy, Beth remained loving and close, even charming. After each therapy session she was waiting at home, pumping him to repeat the conversations: What had the psychiatrist said? What had Andy answered? What were they to discuss next week? Any strange or conformist notions would be turned away by Beth; she encouraged Andy to stay himself. When, eventually, the two-year wait was done, Andy had been most troubled by the prospect of leaving Beth, but he had gone on anyway.

New York was the beginning for Andy; it was a sigh of

relief. Things with his family had dragged on so long that when he arrived, finally, in Manhattan late that cold and snowy afternoon in February (he had graduated from high school mid-term) he had a sense of real excitement. He had set himself free of his family—and all their problems—and even though he stood shivering with few plans in the vast space of Grand Central Station, he was inwardly thrilled to be, at long last, free. He had made arrangements to meet the Branches—Dr. Branch, who had delivered Andy, and his wife Carolyn—and they took him in, getting him set up with contacts, tips, and cash. Over the few weeks that he stayed with them, at their grand aerie on Central Park West, Andy told them of the whole scene with his family. "My heavens!" Carolyn Branch had declared upon hearing Andy's stories. "We'll have to go shopping!" And she had taken Andy out and given him a wardrobe, as if to disrobe him of his family and cast him anew.

Eventually he'd found his own apartment and started City College. For the next two years he studied hard, working at the college library to support himself, and kept up gymnastics. He never spoke with his family, except for Beth.

At the end of his sophomore year, his grandmother died. Beth called him and gave him the news. She persuaded him to come home for the funeral, which he did. He tried to impress his folks with the fact that he was enrolled in college, was active in sports, and was working his way through college, but they didn't get the message. The evening after the funeral, as the family sat morosely around the house, Andy tried to talk with his mother and father, tried to get through. "You know," he started, "there's no reason at this point that we can't at least talk, communicate. Don't you think you could just forget about that part of my life and treat me like a member of the family again?" His father had fixed a mean eye on him and said nothing. His mother had started to smile, but when she saw Chuck's tight expression, she let her mouth go slack. "Well?" Andy had prompted. "What do you think, Dad?" And then the shit had hit the fan. Andy presumed that it was the use of the word "Dad" that had sparked the tirade which followed; that, plus the tension of the funereal situation to begin with. His father had let loose a string of obscenities about Andy's gay lifestyle and ordered him never to return to their house until he had married and produced a child. "And ruin my figure?" had been Andy's furious and bitchy response, to which his father had shouted he would never speak to him again and slammed his fist into the treasured Tiffany heirloom lamp.

It had been a lonely train ride back to New York that night. Those were the last words he had had with his father. His junior year was slow going. The year passed, rather lonely, but he kept himself busy and distracted enough not to dwell on his father's absolute rejection. Periodically he would fall into a ghastly depression over it all, and those periods of moodiness were deep and troubling. He knew he shouldn't let it get him down, not really; it was no surprise. It was just their ignorance that was the problem. But why was it like that? Why did it have to be that bad? Why did people's families have to throw them out like an unwanted pet simply because of whom they chose to love? Andy didn't have any easy answers to his questions. It all seemed to him upside down and backwards. It was the fault of some crazy Judeo-Christian system of puritanism or simple macho sexism. It made him angry, and it made him active. He became involved in the gay students' union, helping with workshops; it was then that Andy began to see that he might combine his major—public administration—with gay politics.

Shortly after Nixon resigned the presidency, Andy discovered sex, promiscuous, available sex. He was not a virgin until that point, but something happened that year he was twenty, something that opened his eyes to his own beauty. He let his moustache grow, black and thick. He appraised himself in mirrors, naked or dressed; he learned to use his beauty to win sexual favors.

After college he won an internship with City Hall, learning the inner workings of New York City administration, and as he did, he began to feel more and more committed to some sort of gay activism. He came out of the closet on the job, but what he had foreseen as an act of self-assertion became an exercise in boredom; nobody cared, except for Mitch, the overly-straight man in his office who had a thing about "faggots." Andy ignored him.

It was 1977, a hot, broiling day at the end of June. Andy had stood on the sidewalk with a hundred thousand other gay men and women, cheering and hollering while the gay pride parade passed by. He turned and deliberately bumped into a cute young man, dark brown eyes glimmering, nervous and full of energy; Andy thought: New York Jew Faggot Clone. Apologies for his clumsiness gave way to introductions which yielded to casual conversation. At dusk they were walking in Central Park, and by nightfall they made love in the bushes. When they were done they laughed at their impatience. They introduced themselves more formally, Andrew Stone and David Markman, then went to David's apartment in the Village.

They became lovers then. On a breezy day late in 1978, after a year had passed, David invited Andy to move into his apartment. It hadn't been a difficult decision for either of them. Andy was ready for a lover, and David was ready to settle down. David's sexual history had been something along the lines of shocking. Growing up in Brooklyn, with the temptations of Manhattan just minutes away, he had begun his sex life at the very first opportunity. There had been girls at first, nice Jewish girls from Brooklyn who turned out to be even nicer than he might have imagined. Then, in the heart of Manhattan, he had discovered, at the age of fourteen, that the sight of a man's bare chest on a hot summer day inspired him to new heights of lust, and so, not one to linger over manners or mild points of convention, an entire new world of men opened up to him, and for the next several years, he chose boys and girls with equal fervor. At nineteen he moved to Greenwich Village when a friend of his decided to relocate to Paris, vacating a fine and cheap apartment: one of those hoped-for deals. He had remained there ever since, attending NYU and majoring in anthropology. One warm Saturday afternoon, while visiting his folks in Brooklyn, David had, at the age of twenty-one, come out of the closet to his parents. There had been no scene about it; his father had nodded his head, shrugged his shoulders, and declared: "It happens." Mrs. Markman had put a hand to her throat—awaiting her husband's response—and then let her hand fall to her lap in relief; she had worried there would be a scene, and she doubted she could work up much of a frenzy. After all, she had known David very well; she knew the sorts of things that went on in Greenwich Village. It was nothing, so long as he stayed out of trouble and took precautions against social infections.

When David bumped into Andy that summer of 1977, he was half-way through a two-year master's program in social anthropology. He never really knew why he was in that field; it just appealed to him, and once he had received his undergraduate degree the year before, he had been too lazy to consider anything other than going on to graduate school. So he went, doing only the basic work necessary to float through. But through all of it, David had not been particularly driven. Perhaps it was the sex; perhaps not. Maybe it was the freedom he enjoyed with the money his grandfather had left him; maybe not. He gravitated—during college and graduate school—towards writing, becoming rather overly devoted to work on the college newspaper.

The uncertainty about a career was, for David, at times difficult. For fast and direct as he was, he ofttimes felt he should know with greater precision what his life should be. He kept writing, finally winning a place as a frequent contributor to the gay press—*Mandate, Blueboy,* and the *Advocate*—but he wondered if writing was really a career decision, especially for a New Yorker. Just as he finished his master's degree he invited Andy to move into his apartment. David found work through friends; he became a free-lance copy-editor for several publishing houses, often receiving romance novels and thrillers for fast proofing. It served him well, but he knew that he had it in him to do some good writing. He was waiting for something to write about, something worth the effort; he knew inspiration would hit him in time.

So together, he and Andy set up housekeeping. Andy was promoted to assistant administrator of "Special Projects" for the city late in 1980, and David plodded along, enjoying life, partying, fussing, waiting. Their relationship deepened; Andy became more involved in city government and finally began to overcome his bitterness towards his family—David had been a great help there. By the end of 1980, David couldn't imagine a more perfect gay couple, except, of course, for the small details.

The small details loomed larger as time passed. Andy, in his drive to push an ordinance for gay rights through the City Council, became insufferable and obsessed. And David, in his indecision, became languorous, disinclined to the sort of pace Andy was, by then, addicted to. Though they remained deeply involved, there came to be a tension between them, both angry and hilarious. As they moved into 1981, the standard around which their lives revolved was a private world of evenings together, quiet, Andy working on his politics, David proofreading romance novels. But Andy had become too driven, too nervous:

"Please, darling, would you stop that 'Valley of the Dolls' routine?" David had implored one evening as he observed his lover rummaging frantically for the Valium. "Nothing is worth such frenzy!" To which Andy had fixed him with a nervous eye and said: "Nothing? You think Valium is nothing?" He had resumed his search. David shook his head and turned back to the novel he was proofing: "...and then, with a twinkle in her violet eyes, she was swept fully in the pulsing tidal wave of love's flaming sword..." He'd put his pencil down and lit a cigarette, observing Andy more closely; something was wrong, something imprecise, subtle. He watched Andy pop one of the small blue tablets in his mouth, then sit down heavily in the sofa. "Well, I hope that calms you down," David had said, looking back at the novel. "Listen to this sentence, will you? 'Justin whirled around, full circle, his eyes flaming rage in the vulnerable circle of Letitia's panting need.' Can you imagine that it's going to be a bestseller?" But Andy was not listening (just as David had expected). Andy was fidgeting, jumpy, his mind focused on something else; David didn't know what.

And then it had begun. Early in the spring of 1981, they stood at the door, ready to face the cool evening air on their way to the party, to Rita's party, their good friend Rita Carrera, a lusty, somewhat infamous dyke (she was, and they often joked about her corner on several markets, half Portuguese and half black; she was exuberant and ambitious, though given to wasting her inheritance on throwing wild parties; she had done too much—opened a feminist gallery a decade ahead of its time, written a shocking novel, served as chairperson of a dozen important political groups over the years). They arrived at her place, and she greeted them loudly, waving them in. Andy observed her closely as she moved away from them; she had round, teardrop-shaped buttocks that rolled when she walked, describing an oval hovering horizontally above the floor, undulating slightly up to the right, down to the left; she never wore pants, either, so the motion was always invisible, divined by the observer as an abstract; she always wore dresses, usually very large muu-muus in splashing colors, to which she added a dash of style in the form of a satin sash, a tailored jacket, or smart shoes.

The evening had progressed as all such parties do, though David and Andy were not comfortable, the crowd being a touch too chic for their tastes: too many exclamations, declamations, and whispers. At one point, David had told Andy to "Shush!" so that he could eavesdrop on a conversation beside them: "Oh, darling, those pieces are far too captivatingly modern... I mean *moderne*... no, more to the notion of *mode!*..." "I think I'm going to puke," David had said, to which Andy had cast a warning glance. Finally, Rita joined them again, inquiring about Andy's ambitions at City Hall. He explained that he was about to receive an appointment as administrator to a special task force to push the gay rights ordinance through, and Rita had slapped him on the back. She approved! She promised to stop by with her new friend Jim very soon; David had said, "Oh, yes, please do," even though he didn't care for Rita's new friend. Well, there were more drinks to be had, she concluded, and moved on.

Rather suddenly, then, Andy sat down and let out a sigh, almost a gasp. David interpreted this as a rude comment on the party itself until he looked closely at Andy, his face drawn in a grimace, his pallor suddenly waxen. Is something the matter? David had asked, imploring, but Andy just shook his head and shrugged his shoulders and suggested they leave the party and go to the baths. Which they had done, a typical Friday night in spring.

But as the spring lengthened, Andy's weariness became more evident. He was appointed, after all, as administrator of that group to lobby for the gay rights ordinance, but every forward move began to drag him back, three steps forward, two steps back. As the heat of summer settled in, Andy became more and more tired, until finally, one day, as he emerged from City Hall and stumbled through a traffic jam of cars trying to approach the Brooklyn Bridge in the glaring sun, he stopped, short of breath, and realized that he would have to see the doctor soon if the "bug" didn't pass.

But it was intermittent. Andy enjoyed periods of rest. They vacationed in Yosemite for a week, and after they returned to Manhattan—now steaming in full summer—things seemed, for a bit, once again fine. One night, after watching a movie on TV, they made love without the tension they had come to know; it was like their first year together, all hands and tongues and swellings, pressures rising and fusing. Somewhere outside, an accident occurred at just their moment of orgasm; they could hear the squeal of rubber, the rattled thud of steel against steel, the chimes of breaking glass falling to the street. A young woman screamed, and kept on screaming, her voice failing as a siren approached. David and Andy had shaken their heads and started to laugh, but then put their fingers to their lips and remained silent.

3

Andy woke to the sound of his lover coming home. David's entrance included banging the door against the wall, kicking his shoes off and sending them flying into Andy, slamming the door, and finally, brashly calling out "Hi!"

"Hi, David," Andy said, propping himself up on his elbows and feeling groggy and grumpy; he was sweating heavily, undoubtedly from sleeping in the heat. "Where were you?" he asked, forgetting the note.

"The library," David said, leaning over to kiss Andy's cheek. He sat back on the couch and put his feet up on the wooden table in front of it. "I left a note."

"Oh, that's right," Andy said, wiping the sweat from his forehead with the back of his hand. "God, I've been conked out; let me wake up."

"You look tired," David said. "So you saw the doctor?"

"Yeah, I did," Andy said, "but tell me about the library first." Andy needed to stretch and wake up.

"It's nothing much," David said, lighting a cigarette. "I got a feature for *Blueboy*. Pays two hundred fifty. About drag queens in the fifties. That's all. So the doctor said?"

"You want good news or bad news first?"

"The bad," David said.

"He thinks I might have hepatitis..."

"The good!" David cut in, recoiling his body in a mimicry of fear.

Andy was not amused. "Not funny. But the doctor won't be sure until he gets the test results back."

"Oh," David said. "But how the hell did you get hepatitis? Is he that sure? I mean, I thought..." David paused, at a loss. "I just don't understand it," he went on. "Where could you have picked up hepatitis?"

"I don't know," Andy said. "I asked him the same thing, believe me, but he said there were a hundred different ways to get it. Apparently people catch it all the time."

"From what?" David pushed the point.

"I don't know," Andy said, more harshly. "Eating out,

mountain water, that night at the baths, who knows! I don't like it at all."

David was quiet for a moment; he realized he shouldn't badger Andy, not now that he was sick. He must be supportive and helpful; yes, that was the tactic. His own worries and fears should be put aside for the moment. He touched Andy's side. "What about the sores?"

"Just a staph infection, that's all. I've got these antibiotics to fight it off." Andy indicated the small plastic bottle on the table.

"What kind?"

"It's cloxycillin," Andy answered.

"Strong stuff," Andy said, blowing smoke toward the ceiling. "When do you know? For sure?"

"Next week, I guess early on. He said his secretary would call me. Until then, I'm to keep quiet and rest..."

"Impossible!"

"...keep quiet," Andy went on, "eat right, get lots of rest. You know, standard stuff."

"Sure," David said. He crushed the cigarette and pulled his shirt off. "Some heat!" he declared, running his hand across his muscled chest and belly. "Fucking hot! The library was roasting. Do I look parboiled?"

Andy looked up at David's small, tight body, the tan skin stretched taut over the naturally firm musculature. It seemed that David's looks had changed over the last few months. He didn't do much exercise, yet his body was somehow firmer, more solid. Was it just Andy's perception that was changing? Or David in his late twenties? For just a moment Andy felt mixed about it all. His lover stood there, firm and tempting, yet he was suddenly unavailable because of the hepatitis, or probable hepatitis. He smiled anyway and pushed the unpleasant thought aside.

"You don't look exactly parboiled," Andy said, "but you do look something else..."

David cracked a wry smile and pulled Andy up to him. They hugged, running their hands across each other's back, down along their waists. Andy ran the tip of his finger across David's chest, lightly touching the small nipple.

"We can't fuck, you know," Andy said.

"Of course not," David said. "Don't worry about it; I have my ways."

"I know you do," Andy said, laughing. "Can I watch?"

They both laughed. Then David said, "You don't seem very sick for someone who's supposed to have hepatitis."

"I know," Andy said, "but Dr. Branch thinks that I do. I guess there are different levels of it or something. I don't know; we'll find out next week."

"How do you feel now?" David asked.

"Not bad, really," Andy said. "Now that it's started to cool off a little bit and I've woken up; I felt like shit a few minutes ago when you came in."

"Thanks!"

"No, I don't mean that," Andy said. "But I was kind of nervous about telling you about the hepatitis. I was afraid you'd mind. I was afraid I'd have given it to you maybe."

"Shit," David said. "I'm fine; do I look hepatic?" David was quiet for a second. "It is a pain, of course; a pain for you, for me. But I don't know, let's just deal with it and get you well. I'm okay, so don't worry about me . . . can you see us both lying in bed together for six weeks?" David smiled and shook his head.

"I know," Andy said. "This is a pain in the ass." They both sat down on the couch and lay against each other, listening to nothing in particular, the traffic, their breathing.

"You know," David said, thinking of the word "hepatic" he had just used. "I bet you don't have hepatitis."

"Why do you say that?"

"Because you're not yellow," David answered.

"But the symptoms add up," Andy said. "Besides, what else could it be? It does make some sense."

"Yeah . . ." David said, rising to go to the stereo. He found some jazz, piano and bass. The gentle music soothed them as they relaxed on the couch. David lit another cigarette and sat smoking quietly, Andy saying nothing. It was a long moment of silence, each of them reflecting on the day. Finally, David put out the cigarette and smiled at

Andy. "Let's have dinner and get you into bed," he said, suddenly concerned.

"Okay," Andy agreed.

David watched Andy walk into the kitchen, then followed. In the dim twilight, Andy looked worn and pale. David felt a great sadness as he looked at Andy just then, a deep regret about his illness. His heart went out to his lover in that moment, because in the face of hepatitis — if that is what it proved to be — he realized that nothing mattered much beside the insistent reality of the moment: his love for Andy.

★

After dinner they were startled by the ring of the doorbell. Since no one had called ahead, they were at a loss as to who it might be. But when David went down to the door, he found it was Rita with her friend Jim. "Sorry we didn't ring you up," Rita said as they came up the stairs, "but we were just walking by and decided to stop. Okay?"

"Sure," David said. They walked into the living room and stopped short when Rita declared: "Oh, Andy honey, you don't look so good. Still feeling bad, huh?"

Andy nodded his head and smiled. "That obvious?" he joked, holding his hand up to ward off her greeting kiss. "Wait, Rita darling. I probably have hepatitis."

"Ay," she shrieked, stopping dead. "What's this?"

Jim looked at Andy and frowned. "Hepatitis?" he echoed.

"Come on, calm down," David said. "We don't know for sure until the tests come back, but even so..."

"Well, that's not a pretty sight," Rita said, settling down in one of the overstuffed chairs opposite the couch. Jim sat on the arm of the chair and lit a cigarette. Rita waved her hands about her as though batting at insects. "Such filth!" she declared, lifting Jim's cigarette from his hands and rising to deposit it in the fireplace.

Andy watched them and laughed. "It's a constant war with you two," he observed, noticing that Rita had gained even more weight since the party.

"A constant war is right," Rita agreed. "And you"—she

cast a glance at David—"should try to quit the awful habit, too. It's not very nice."

David shrugged his shoulders. Jim gave him a sympathetic smile.

"Well," Rita went on, "we were going to share some sparkling dust here"; she reached into her pocket and produced a small packet of cocaine. "But seeing as how you are not up to par, I think it best we veto the magic for now. What say?" She raised her eyebrows and redeposited the package in her pocket. "We'll bring more after you're well, and celebrate your recovery," she promised.

"But *I'm* not sick!" David protested, unwilling to let some free toot pass by, to which Rita responded with a shrug. "It wouldn't be fair," she said simply.

"Anyway, moving right along," she went on, "when did you get this ugly news?"

"This afternoon," David said.

"Too bad," Jim said. "But it seems like *everybody's* got *something* these days. Even *me!* I recently fell prey to those *god* awful parasites; I *couldn't* believe it!"

Andy nodded. I can believe it, he said to himself. "They're everywhere," he said simply, regarding Jim with caution. They were friends, though the friendship with Jim was new.

Andy wasn't altogether sure he really liked Jim; there was something in his manner—like the pomposity of inflecting in his comment the notion that even *he* had had parasites. Jim was, Andy thought, typical of the young gay man on the rise. He worked hard in the theatre—management, not acting. He was affable, gym-toned, lonely, very beautiful. But in his success, and in his beauty, Andy detected that weird isolation he so often observed: an armor created by the beauty and success, a lonesome attitude of such haughtiness that to befriend someone less "hot" than himself would be painful. Andy was no stranger to the tyranny of beauty among gay men; he had used his own very powerfully at times. But he realized it was a dead end if pursued; it would kill the soul.

"Shouldn't you be in bed?" Rita asked Andy.

"Soon," Andy answered, his brow still furrowed from his reverie on Jim. "I was just getting round to it."

"Well, I think you should," she said. Then growing concerned, she said: "I swear you boys and your troubles!"

"What?" Jim said.

"You've got to watch out," she said. "I don't mean to preach, but really, bodies aren't disposable bottles." She shook her head.

"You don't mean to preach?" Andy probed. "But look, you're talking to the wrong guys. We're married and ever so faithful." He glanced at David. "More or less," he added, remembering their recent foray into the baths.

"Uh-huh," Rita grunted flatly. "But it's all part of the same package, honey, whether you practice it or not; it's set up that way, the whole system."

"You're pontificating again," Jim said to Rita.

"Yes, I am," she agreed, haughtily. "And for good reason."

Jim nodded in mock agreement. Andy watched in silence, deciding once again that he didn't especially care for him.

"Well, we don't want to keep you up," Rita said, making as if to go.

"No, no, no," Andy protested, standing. "You stay and chat with David; have a drink. I'll put myself to bed now. Don't worry about me. Good night." Andy left and went into the bedroom. He pulled off his shirt, unbuckled his belt and unzipped his pants. He stood in front of the full-length mirror and looked at his body, still so perfect, so lean. He turned front and back and studied his build, approving of what he saw in the mirror; he wasn't *that* sick. He could hear voices from the front room, but he couldn't make out the conversation. He was glad, at last, to be alone. He was glad that Jim and Rita would keep David occupied for a while. He wanted to lie back on the bed, all by himself, and concentrate on his feelings, on the sickness that was draining his body.

He had a cold, quiet feeling as he lay back and felt the cool sheet press against his back, his buttocks, the backs of his thighs. He wiggled his toes and raised his arms above

[39]

his head, felt the heaviness of his cock as it flopped from his thigh down between his legs. He closed his eyes and imagined he was at home, that his family was laughing, heartily, as his father told some joke, or as they watched home movies. Yes, that's it, he told himself, being sick always brings out the trouble, always. It was something he couldn't stand; the flu, strep throat, whatever—it always brought out the anxiety, the stuff that he kept bottled up and shut down most of the time. And here was some of it now, the pain of his family's rejection. When the fuck would it just go away? When the fuck could he block it out for good? He knew any goddamn therapist would tell him not to block it out, but bring out the feelings, just like he was doing now. But dammit, that wasn't any fun; not when it happened over and over again. He felt salt water at the corners of his eyes; he set his mouth in a grimace. He would not cry about this again. There had been enough already. And so he lay still, listening to the muffled sounds of David's voice, Rita's laughter, Jim's low tones. He threw an arm across his forehead and fell asleep.

*

And then the dream returned. It was something of a nightmare, something of a Kafkaesque world of grotesques. There was no theme, no special fear that he could name. When he'd waken, the uneasiness would flee, and he wouldn't remember the details, the odd rooms, dimly lit, the silhouettes of men and women passing along some sort of dark hallway, peering—no, leering—into tiny rooms. What was in those rooms? The dream seemed incomplete without the knowledge of what those little rooms contained, but Andy couldn't see around the crowds at the doorways; he couldn't make out what was happening in those rooms. Then the scene pulled away again, just the silhouettes passing in a hall. He tossed and turned on the bed, his sleep restless, disturbed. He faded in and out of sleep and near-sleep. The summer night was hot; he was sweating.

*

Late that night, when Jim and Rita had gone, David sat by the front window and smoked a cigarette. He didn't especially want to go in to bed, not with Andy having hepatitis. He looked down into the street; it was surprisingly still. It was very late, though, close to three in the morning. The heat had broken slightly, at least for the night. David felt good, calm, but apprehensive. It seemed to him that hepatitis was an odd diagnosis; Andy was not, after all, jaundiced, and the symptoms had been fleeting and vague until very recently. But what bugged him was the retrospect; Andy had begun to weaken and tire more easily perhaps around Christmas. It was something he was sure Andy didn't notice as well as David did, but it was a fact that troubled him. Hepatitis didn't do that, at least he didn't think it did. David just had a funny, sudden fear he couldn't name. Well, so much for that, he told himself, finishing the cigarette and tossing the butt down into the street. He stripped off his clothes and threw them on the couch, went into the bedroom, looked at Andy breathing deeply and sweating profusely. He shook his head, lay down beside Andy, and turned out the little bedside lamp.

4

The morning was brilliant, the start of a new week. Andy and David had spent a quiet weekend at home, listening to records and reading. Andy had slept quite a bit, taking the doctor's advice, while David had gone to the library to track down a book he needed to see.

Now, on a bright June morning, Andy felt better, and so he decided that he would go in to work, at least for a short while. He did go in, but it was only a short time before he began to feel extremely fatigued again, so he spoke with his senior administrator, explaining that he was under the weather and would have to stay in bed for a few days.

On Tuesday, late in the afternoon, Andy was napping when the phone rang. It was Meg, asking him to wait for Dr. Branch to get on the line. Andy shook his head and muttered the word "shit" when he heard that the doctor himself was getting on the phone; that had to mean the test was positive. Negative results didn't mean anything; Meg could deliver that message.

The phone clicked as Dr. Branch engaged the line. "Hello, Andy?" he said. "You there?"

"Yes," Andy answered. "As Bette Davis said in *Dark Victory*, 'I'll have a large order of prognosis negative.' So where do we go from here?"

"Hold on, Andy," Branch said. "You've jumped the gun. The tests read negative. You don't have hepatitis."

Andy was suddenly enormously relieved. He had been bracing himself for the news, realizing that it meant several weeks of staying put. But just as soon as he felt the relief, it was replaced by a deeper anxiety.

"But wait a minute," Andy started. "If I don't have hepatitis, then what's wrong?" He was frowning, his hand shaking just a bit as he stood there in his white terrycloth robe, the receiver in his hand. "This isn't some common cold, I can tell you that."

"Calm down," Branch said, projecting his own fears as much as Andy's into the conversation; he, too, was suspicious. "Frankly, I don't know what it could be. You've got me stumped. You'll have to come in for some more tests if you can make it. Can you come in tomorrow? Or do you have that meeting?"

"Sure, I can be there in the morning. You want me at your office or somewhere in the hospital?"

"At my office," Dr. Branch said. "We'll do a complete workup and blood panels on you. I'm sure we'll get to it then."

"Okay, but now I'm worried," Andy said. He was glad that he could tell David he didn't have hepatitis, but he was still more deeply concerned about what might be wrong. He went back to bed in a dark mood.

5 *July 1981* • *Atlanta*

MORBIDITY AND MORTALITY WEEKLY REPORT
Center for Disease Control (CDC)
July 3, 1981/Vol. 30/No. 25.

During the past 30 months, Kaposi's sarcoma (KS), an uncommonly reported malignancy in the United States, has been diagnosed in 26 homosexual men (20 in New York City; 6 in California). The 26 patients range in age from 26–51 years. Eight of these patients died (7 in New York City, 1 in California)—all 8 within 24 months after KS was diagnosed. The diagnoses in all 26 cases were based on histopathological examination of skin lesions, lymph nodes, or tumor in other organs....

Skin or mucous membrane lesions, often dark blue to violaceous plaques or nodules were present in most of the patients on their initial physician visit....

A review of the New York University Coordinated Cancer Registry for KS in men under age 50 revealed no cases from 1970–1979 at Bellevue Hospital and 3 cases in this age group at the New York University Hospital from 1961–1979.

Seven KS patients had serious infections diagnosed after their initial physician visit. Six patients had pneumonia... and one had necrotizing toxoplasmosis of the central nervous system. One of the patients with *Pneumocystis* pneumonia also experienced severe, recurrent, herpes simplex infection; extensive candidiasis; and cryptococcal meningitis....

The occurrence of this number of KS cases during a 30-month period among young, homosexual men is considered highly unusual. No previous association between KS and sexual preference has been reported....

In addition, CDC has a report of 4 homosexual men in New York City who developed severe, progressive, perianal herpes simplex infections and had evidence of cellular immunodeficiencies.... It is not clear if or how the clustering of KS, pneumocystis, and other serious diseases in homosexual men is related. What is known is that the patients with *Pneumocystis* pneumonia described . . . showed evidence of impaired cellular immunity. . . .

It has been hypothesized that activation of oncogenic virus during periods of immunosuppression may result in the development of KS. . . .

Although it is not certain that the increase in KS and PC pneumonia is restricted to homosexual men, the vast majority of recent cases have been reported from this group. Physicians should be alert for Kaposi's sarcoma, *Pneumocystis* pneumonia, and other opportunistic infections associated with immunosuppression in homosexual men.

6 *July 1981* · *San Francisco*

There had been something of a stir the day Dr. Alfred Kinder-Mann's report to the CDC was released. But it hadn't been much. Three reporters from the gay press had called; one from the straight. Five colleagues had called, only to question him further, not to offer any advice or research directions. Kinder-Mann realized the severity of the trend he was witnessing: formerly healthy young homosexual males appearing with sudden debilitation of the immune system, leading to development of various opportunistic infections. He had never seen the likes of it, nor had he read of anything similar. The slight flurry of attention, then, was not proportional to Kinder-Mann's concern.

Alfred Kinder-Mann, tall, handsome, and youthful at fifty-three, with graying temples and a vaguely pretty face, had been the first doctor to notice that, at a medical convention, he had heard tell of recent cases of Kaposi's sarcoma. It had been only a conversation here, a comment there, but all too soon it became evident to Kinder-Mann that there might be a problem. He had phoned colleagues in New York when he returned to San Francisco from the convention, and what they told him had alarmed him. A little bit of dipping—into registries of disease and epidemiology—had produced the report he filed with the CDC.

And that report had been delayed for some time, until he had had a chance to thoroughly coordinate the few facts and make some attempt at treatment, as well as to monitor the other cases and their progress.

Rather rapidly he had realized—with a growing sense of dismay—that there was an epidemiological trend that was something more than frightening. As one of the country's leading medical researchers, it hadn't taken long before he had shifted everything around to plunge into research; the potential for research in the situation was overwhelming.

As a medical researcher he had few equals, he thought, except, perhaps, for Walt Branch at Mt. Zion in Manhattan. But Branch had never found a research problem to suit his brilliance, nor had he ever found the discipline to abandon less important considerations for the grander picture. And—Kinder-Mann smiled to himself at the thought—that had served him very well.

Kinder-Mann turned these considerations over in his mind as he drove his car to the University of California Medical Center. He was barely aware of the dripping summer fog as he drove and thought. A grim summer dawn was beginning to filter through the fog, and Kinder-Mann continued his reverie. There was, of course, Dr. Maxwell Leider as well, but Max had veered off into recombinant research, so his research was safe from Leider. There were a few others, at Sloan Kettering, at NYU, at Johns Hopkins and UCLA, but Kinder-Mann didn't worry about them. He had snagged this research question at the outset; it was his.

As he parked his car in the lot beneath the medical center, Kinder-Mann again thought of Walt Branch, wondering what Branch had thought of his report to the CDC. He was sure it would be seen; by now, Walt Branch and Max Leider should have already discussed the report over coffee in Mt. Zion's greasy cafeteria.

He emerged from the elevator which brought him from the lower parking levels to the ground level at which the medical center was located. As he crossed the small plaza to the glass doors of the futuristic steel-and-glass facility, he paused and glanced around distractedly. Suddenly he experienced a sensation of foreboding about the outbreak, a sense of fear that was quite beyond what he might expect from himself. The excited questions of a curious medical student—something about infectious rhinitis—distracted him as he proceeded into the building, getting him going for the morning, and putting the sense of disquiet completely out of his mind.

7 *July 1981 • New York City*

Dr. Maxwell Leider walked into Dr. Branch's waiting room, noting that it was, unexpectedly, empty. All through for the day? Leider asked himself, incredulous that Branch was not overloaded with clinical work. He smiled at Meg, who waved him over to her desk.

"Hi, there," she declared, looking him over. His bald head was a deep red, shiny, with short reddish fringes left around the edge. His green eyes twinkled mischievously as he winked at Meg. "Is the old goy around?" he asked, nodding his head in the direction of Branch's inner office.

"In there," Meg said, following his look. "Go on back." She watched as Dr. Leider made his way to the inner office. He looks like a bald teddy bear, she thought to herself, noticing that he was filling out around the edges a bit too much.

"How the hell are you?" Branch called out as Leider walked into his office. Branch motioned for him to sit down in the leather chair by his desk.

Leider sat back and yawned. "Sorry, I'm so sleepy, the heat, you know."

"Have you forgotten that New York in July is a tropical port? And by the way, do you notice that I have the windows closed? The cooling system is somewhere near functional." He waved his hand around, as though to indicate the degree of mildness. "You know, a couple weeks ago it was so bad I envied the pathologists down in the morgue."

"You're in a bad way," Leider said, and then, changing the subject, he added: "Have you seen this?" He tossed the CDC weekly *Morbidity Report* on Branch's desk. "You'll notice that it was Dr. Kinder-Mann, our old friend, who reported it to the CDC."

Branch crinkled his face at the mention of Kinder-Mann's name. "Our old friend," Branch echoed Leider, looking accusingly at Max Leider. He studied the document, leaning back in his chair and simultaneously fumbling in his pocket for his reading glasses. "Damned if I'll wear bifocals," he mumbled as he slipped them onto the end of his nose and pulled off his other pair. He read the brief report, then put it down and peered over the half-glasses at Leider. "This is pretty strange stuff. An epidemic of cancer? Among homosexual men? I really don't know what to make of it. How can it be?"

Leider just shrugged his shoulders.

"What's so odd here is the presence of multiple infectious disease—pneumocystis pneumonia? Kaposi's sarcoma? Toxoplasmosis?" Branch shook his head incredulously as he spoke.

"Of course, we see immune problems in certain kinds of cases," Leider said, "but not like this."

"Yes, certainly," Branch said, not thinking of his words. His mind was distracted, ticking off the scientific possibilities, but he could make no sense of it on the surface. Immunosuppression was a rare condition, usually seen only among the extraordinarily impoverished, or among those rare individuals whose immune systems were haywire from birth—the sorts of people who lived in plastic bubbles to keep the germs out. Immunosuppression could also be medically induced, chiefly for the purpose of keeping organ transplant recipients from rejecting their new organ. But to have spontaneous, unremissable immunosuppression in formerly healthy young men made little medical sense.

"A damn good research question," Leider offered.

Branch leaned back in his chair, taking off his glasses again and tapping them against his chin. He was silent for several moments. The only sounds were those echoing up from the street below, and the seemingly constant distant drone of the hospital public address system, endlessly paging doctors and nurses. Leider watched Branch thinking, saw the shadow cross his face.

"What is it?" Leider asked, leaning forward and hearing the leather creak as he did.

"I'm thinking about the Stone case," Branch said, his shoulders sagging. He sighed faintly, a subtle gesture of disappointment, worry perhaps. "You know, Max, he's shown no improvement since his initial visit. There's nothing evidentially wrong with him. I put him on antibiotics, but nothing changed. Still experiencing the same vague symptoms, coupled with seemingly unrelated infections in just the past month."

"Such as?" Leider asked, his interest piqued.

"That damn staph infection keeps showing up over and over again, twice under the arm, once in the groin. Can you believe that? I mean, I put the lad on cloxycillin for chrissakes, and still a recurrence?"

Leider raised his eyebrows in surprise.

"And he had a yeast infection anally," Branch went on, "that was, as far as we could make out, more or less spontaneous."

Leider frowned, realizing that such a series of problems didn't make sense, except, pehaps, in the context of the CDC report.

"I hate to think that Andy could have this immunity problem," Branch said dourly, "but now that I've seen this report..."

Leider cut in: "The report cautions that we are to be alert for more of the same. Kinder-Mann must have some inkling that these twenty-six will not be the only cases."

Branch shook his head and grimaced. "I guess I better haul the poor guy in for some tests, I don't know what, though."

"Well, the standards, of course," Leider said. "A thorough exam for possible cancerous lesions, possibly a serum electro-immunophoresis, though none of that may show anything."

Branch agreed, "Yes, but what it seems to suggest here is that by the time of detection, it's already too late."

Leider was silent, troubled. He shook his head and folded the report in quarters. "Grim," he said with conviction. "Very grim."

"Gloomy bastard," Branch muttered.

Leider stood to go, opening the heavy wooden door of the office. As he did, there was a rush of noise from the waiting room and phones. It was the end of the day, and Meg was trying to close up her desk and go.

Branch followed Leider out and then stopped beside her desk. "Meg," he said as endearingly as he could. "Before you go, could you call Andrew Stone?"

She fixed him with a mean stare.

"I'd like him to come in tomorrow if he can for an exam and some tests. Cancel someone if you have to; I really must see him as soon as possible."

His tone betrayed deep concern. "What is it?" Meg asked.

"Max just brought a report of an outbreak of Kaposi's sarcoma among young gay men, with evidence of associated cellular immunosuppression."

"Kaposi's sarcoma?" Meg echoed, raising her eyebrows.

"A rare form of cancer, never seen here, never among young men. It's skin cancer of older men, usually Mediterraneans or Africans, in the tropics."

"And you think Andy might have it?"

"I don't know," Branch answered honestly.

"I'll get him in tomorrow morning," Meg said, dialing.

8

The morning was bright, a rare, clear day in midsummer. Andy stood at the bathroom mirror, combing his hair and examining his face. He was looking tired, more tired than ever, he thought. Meg had called the evening before, requesting—rather urgently he nervously detected—that he make every effort to get in to see Dr. Branch first thing in the morning for some tests.

It seemed simple enough; his doctor wanted to do some more work to figure out what was ailing him. So far, they hadn't been able to track anything down, but there remained the fact that Andy was still terribly tired and terribly sick.

David stuck his head into the bathroom. "Hurry up," he said. "We got half an hour. Let's go." David had been worried about Meg's call. After all, Andy's health had worsened considerably as far as he could see, and the lack of answers was beginning to wear on his nerves and patience. He had insisted on accompanying Andy to the hospital.

They left their apartment, opting for a cab at David's suggestion. He was anxious to get there and find out what Branch had in mind for Andy. Twenty minutes later they were midtown, stepping up the front steps of Mt. Zion.

David looked up at the massive building as they walked up the steps. This portion of the building—which contained the lobby—was part of the original brick structure: dark, gritty, foreboding. But to their left as they ascended the steps were the modern high-rise patient wards, a chunk of white concrete, punctuated with long, smoked-glass windows.

To their right extended another wing, part of the older structure, now containing the research and administration facilities. Branch's offices occupied a corner of this wing, on the sixth floor. There were two other massive wings of the hospital to the rear—both containing surgical wards, research labs, and the complex of kitchens, counseling facilities, and emergency department. As they climbed the steps and went through the old glass doors, they could hear ambulance sirens screaming from the rear part of the hospital.

The lobby was jammed at mid-morning, and David was a bit shocked at the bustle of the place. He hadn't been to Branch's office for nearly two years, and in the interim— having spent far too much time pacing the floor of either his apartment or the libraries at NYU—he had forgotten the high level of activity and noise in the big hospital.

They made their way through the lobby, waiting amongst a crowd of people at the elevators. David noticed a young man in white—an orderly, he supposed—was eyeing Andy curiously. Just cruising, David thought.

One of the elevators arrived just then, its burnished aluminum doors sliding wide and depositing a throng of doctors and others into the lobby. David and Andy got on and rode up to the sixth floor. They emerged into a long, fluorescent-lit hallway, smelling sickly sweet with disinfectant and some other unidentifiable odor.

As they made their way along the corridor, David peered through open doors and glass panels at research labs filled with technicians, medical students, and animals—guinea pigs, David reminded himself, reaching for a cigarette and then reading a large No Smoking sign.

The hallway seemed endless. David read the signs on the doors: Nuclear Medicine; Research Division; Epidemiological Laboratory; Center for Tropical Diseases; Infectious Medicine; Immunology. All this on one floor? David asked himself, amazed at the immensity of the place. He wondered why he had never taken notice of all of this before. Perhaps, he answered himself, it was because it hadn't mattered before.

But now—now that Andy was becoming more involved in this hospital culture, this medical nightmare—it all began to affect David as well. The place seemed somehow cold, technological; David didn't like it.

They reached Dr. Branch's suite. It was really more a large research lab, or series of connecting rooms that, taken together, formed a laboratory. Adjoining the lab was his office, where he maintained his clinical practice.

They walked into the waiting room, and Meg greeted them warmly. "Good morning, Andy," she said. "And David! Hello! I'm glad to see you again after so long. When's the last time?"

"Almost two years," David said. "How you been?"

"Can't complain," she said. "But this guy..." She nodded at Andy, who only smiled. "Yes, well," Meg said, suddenly at a loss as she took in Andy's sick visage. She had seen him just two weeks before, when he had come in with another outbreak of staph and herpes, but in those two weeks he had obviously deteriorated, seriously so.

She showed them into one of the two examining rooms, explaining that Dr. Branch had been called away to Dr. Maguire's office for a short meeting, and, in response to David's curious expression, further explained that Dr. Maguire was the chief administrator of the hospital's research division. She left them alone in the examining room, shutting the door behind her as she left.

David walked around the small room, while Andy perched himself on the edge of the examining table, hearing the white paper cover crunch beneath him as he sat. David fidgeted with the equipment, taking the sphygmomanometer down from the wall and wrapping it around his arm. He tried to avoid looking directly at Andy in the medical environment—it brought too much feeling to the surface.

In the last month, Andy had been sick almost continuously, and Dr. Branch had put him on one round of antibiotics after another. It worried David a great deal—more than he was able to handle at times—even, perhaps, more than Andy himself worried. It seemed that Andy was losing more than his health. He was losing his spirit, his will to get back to good health, or even to begin to rally.

David had noticed a subtle acceptance of the illness on Andy's part, as though there were nothing that could be done. And, indeed, it was hard not to fall into that kind of a pattern of thinking. After all, Andy had been failing weekly—daily, even—getting more pale, more tired; no matter how much rest he got, how much good food, how much care and stress-free consideration of himself and his time. It was all useless, or so it seemed; nothing worked to help Andy feel better.

But what had really troubled David lately was that Andy had lost his ambition, or at least had let it slide. His sickness had caused him to cut back to half time with the city, and much of that he tried to do at home. Andy would sit in bed in their tiny bedroom, papers scattered across the bed, doing as much writing and planning as he could, then falling to sleep. He'd go down to City Hall and put in a few hours at his office, but without his constant sur-veillance of the progress of the gay rights ordinance, it had begun to lose ground.

Apparently, in Andy's absence, Mitch had been able to divert attention away from promotion of the gay rights ordinance by recruiting staff members to work on his pet projects. Andy couldn't be there much anymore, and his illness left him tired when he was there; he kept fighting, but he was losing to Mitch and to his own absence from the issue.

He had tried to get Marianne—a young woman on the staff—to take over for him , but she was ill-suited for the task; she lacked an understanding of the issues involved. Sure, there were the gay leaders and promoters, but with-out the internal support that Andy had been generating, the ordinance could easily go down.

David felt that this great disappointment to Andy was one of the primary factors robbing him of his spirit. But David couldn't open the subject for discussion, because there was no answer to the problem. David had nothing to offer; besides, he was too hung up in his own work, trying to make ends meet now that Andy's income had been re-duced by fifty percent. Thank god they had health insur-ance for all Andy's problems.

Well, David resolved hopefully, perhaps Dr. Branch has got an answer now; perhaps something has come up to answer the puzzle of Andy's failing health. He hoped so. The illness was not only affecting Andy; David witnessed his own anxiety as strongly, just as he was at that moment in the examining room, awaiting the doctor. The illness had come between them, completely dampening their physical relationship. And now, lately, their emotional bond was souring as Andy's spirit diminished and David stood by, helpless, almost out of reach. What could he offer to Andy?

Their sex life had been good until the hepatitis scare, but now, through Andy's fatigue and the uncertainties of what the affliction was, that seemed to be finished. But if their emotional life was weakening, then David found it difficult, if not impossible, to draw on any reserves to support Andy, much less to support their relationship. After all, David concluded miserably, relationships—and love—need nurturing. But what they had instead was a gradual debilitation, a constant erosion of all that they had worked for.

David put the blood-pressure cuff back on the wall just as Dr. Branch walked in, interrupting David's depressing flow of thought.

"Good morning, fellows," he said. And then, addressing himself to David, "It's been a long time since we've seen each other." He reached out and shook David's hand. "Of course, Andy's kept me filled in on you."

"I suppose," David said. His nerves were jumpy; he didn't want small talk. Instead he retreated to a corner of the small room, leaned his back against the wall and door frame.

Dr. Branch sat on a rolling stool and took his glasses off, fishing around in the pocket of his white lab coat for his reading glasses. He found them and slipped them on the end of his nose, peering at Andy and then into his medical chart. There seemed to be an air of tension or mystery in the room, as though the doctor were unsure of himself, didn't know where to begin.

He looked over his half-glasses at Andy. "How are you feeling?" he asked.

"The same," Andy said flatly, the first words he had spoken since the doctor came in. The doctor set the chart aside and stood to examine Andy, running his hands along the underside of Andy's jaw and down along the sides of his neck.

"Glands are still swollen," Branch said, taking the stethoscope, opening Andy's shirt and placing it against his chest.

Andy laughed—tickled by the cold metal of the stethoscope. "Any signs of life?" he asked, still laughing and then lapsing into a fit of coughing.

"Some," Branch said wryly. "Tell me, seriously, how have you been since you were last here?"

"Well," Andy started, "not so good. The staph went away with the drugs again, but I've had some diarrhea, kind of like the flu, and this cough. Mostly, I'm so damned tired I can hardly keep my eyes open half the time."

David spoke up, too nervous to remain quietly in the background. "Tell him about the nightmares."

Andy looked irritated, casting a nasty glance in David's direction. "Okay," he said, his palms turned up for a moment as if to indicate surrender. "I've had a lot of nightmares lately, scary stuff. And then I wake up after them drenched in sweat..."

"Cold sweat," David interjected.

Branch frowned. He didn't like the symptomatology at all; everything he was hearing indicated a severely disturbed immune system, and the look of Andy's skin was highly suggestive of a serious internal disorder. Andy was sallow and almost gray in his paleness. "Frankly, Andy, I'd like to do some more tests on you, some very specific tests this time. And I'd lke to give you a complete exam now as well."

David didn't wait. "What's wrong? What is it?" he said rapidly, wishing he could light a cigarette. He was anxious to find out what Branch was driving at.

Dr. Branch composed himself, sat down again on the small rolling stool. He pulled the half-glasses off his nose and chewed on the end of them without thinking. "Yesterday we got the weekly report from the Center for Disease Control in Atlanta. Dr. Kinder-Mann at UC San Francisco has reported that there is an outbreak of some rare diseases among young gay men, mostly in New York, some in California."

David stepped beside Andy, almost protectively. Andy seemed to be less disturbed than David, though he was concentrating fully on the doctor's words. "What kind of diseases?" David asked.

Branch shook his head, indicating patience and calm. "Now please don't get all worked up about it and for god's sake don't jump to any conclusions." He took a deep breath. "But I want to be honest with you."

"We know very little at this point," he went on. "And my main concern with Andy is to check very carefully, make sure that none of this is involved in the case."

Andy remained taciturn but attentive, sitting perfectly still on the edge of the examining table, betraying no emotion about the situation. Finally, after a rather protracted pause, he repeated David's question. "What diseases?"

Branch fumbled in his pocket for his other pair of glasses, a nervous gesture. "Well," he began, "I want you to understand that we are going to rule these things out. But primarily, there is an outbreak among gay men of a very rare form of cancer known as Kaposi's sarcoma . . ."

Andy's shoulders fell and there was a sharp intake of breath from David. The word "cancer" had shot through them like a burning knife. Almost in an instant they slipped into a sort of numbness, listening to the doctor's explanation, feeling—for the moment, at least—very little.

"We refer to Kaposi's sarcoma by its initials—KS," he went on. "Apparently the disease is resultant from some sort of weakness of the patient's immune system, so there are accompanying complications of very unusual illnesses that we refer to as opportunistic infections.

"This means that the body is run down—the immune system is not functioning at one hundred percent—so various infections that would normally be fought off become rather more complicated."

Andy was preoccupied; David was worried. Andy shook his head and said, "Why are you giving me so many details if we're just going to rule it out? You suspect something, don't you? What are some of those unusual illnesses? Anything like what I have?"

Dr. Branch's face was grim; he didn't like to give out such news, or to voice such suspicions, but he knew that he had to be honest, and the strangeness of the medical situation here confounded his traditional experience in dealing with this sort of thing.

"Yes," Branch answered simply. "To be honest with you, the recurrent staph infection and the herpes could indicate that something's awry. And you tell me of a flu you can't shake, and fevers and sudden night sweats. These things make me suspicious—suspicious about your immune system. Obviously, you don't have any of the KS lesions in evidence on your body."

"My god," David said, feeling suddenly ill, all energy and spirit drained from him. Andy remained listless—a fact that troubled David. He jumped right in. "But you said it's very rare, right?"

"Yes..." Branch said.

"So the odds are in our favor?"

"Yes, of course," Branch said, detecting that David's anxiety might be out of control. "And let me emphasize that I want to run some tests and examine Andy thoroughly, chiefly some blood panels, hopefully to rule it out. I want to be as precautionary as possible; I don't mean to alarm you; please don't be alarmed."

David was slightly calmed by the doctor's assurances, but deeper inside he had a chill.

"Sounds like I've got it," Andy said plainly.

"Don't," David warned. "The doctor will rule it out. I'm sure."

Dr. Branch smiled, trying to appear as reassuring and confident as he could. The situation in the examining room was explosive at the moment; he had been ill prepared for David's obvious anxiety level. "Would you excuse us now?" he asked David. "I want to examine Andy and draw some blood. Make yourself comfortable out there; it'll only be a few minutes."

David hesitated, looking at Andy. Andy shrugged his shoulders and told David to go on; he'd be out in a minute. David left the examining room and went to the waiting room, noticing the numbers of patients backed up, waiting. Meg smiled at him and assured him that it wouldn't be long.

But David could not relax. He sat down, looked at a couple of magazines, but he couldn't read them. He couldn't think about anything but his lover, his friend, the man he lived with. He couldn't imagine how their life together could be so disrupted by illness.

And now this, he thought, realizing even as he did that he was laying it on thick with the worry and anxiety. But he couldn't help it; what kind of freaky story had the doctor just told them? Gay men in New York contracting bizarre cancers? Strange diseases? It didn't add up, didn't make any sense to him at all. What was going on? And why hadn't they heard anything about it before?

David tried to put it together, realizing that the reason they hadn't heard about it before was because it was just happening, just then. The doctor said he'd only had the report from the CDC the day before. But he had also said that only a few cases were reported—that seemed good. What was it? An unusual set of complications of diseases because of something wrong with the immune system? How could that be? What would cause their immunity to freak out?

As he sat and pondered the few details—knowing that his lover was being examined for just the same thing—David felt the panic spring up inside him, setting his nerves on edge.

He looked over at Meg, who sat typing with the dictaphone headset over her ears. He looked at the other patients in the waiting room, a middle-aged fat lady with a large growth on her neck, an old man looking very sick, half-dead, a young girl with her mother, neither looking very ill at all.

The typing grated on David's nerves, setting his irritability up high. The more he thought about it, the more he felt a strong conviction that Andy was in real trouble. He kept trying to console himself with thoughts of "the odds" being in Andy's favor, but it didn't help. And what the fuck was taking so long? He looked at the clock. It had only been five minutes.

He alternated between hope and panic. One moment he felt calm, realizing that the CDC story was just too far-fetched to affect Andy. But the next moment the panic seized him, sent him into a wild fit of uncertainty.

He looked up at the clock again. Now, it had been ten minutes. Then the door opened. Dr. Branch came out, bent to speak to Meg. She looked up, removed the headset, nodded her head, and reached for the phone. Dr. Branch disappeared into the examining room again.

What the hell is going on? David asked himself. He went to Meg and asked her what was taking so long, what was that all about? She was startled. "Oh, David," she said, "the doctor just wants a lab tech here to draw the blood and, uh...like that. It'll be just a few more minutes."

David sat down again, a little more relaxed. In a moment a lab tech arrived, a young blonde woman carrying a tray and looking very serious. She went into the examining room, emerging a few minutes later with Dr. Branch.

The doctor came over and asked David to come into his office. David followed him in and waited. He watched the doctor move around behind the big wooden desk and sit down. Dr. Branch motioned for David to sit as well, so he did, sinking into the big leather armchair at the side of the desk.

Dr. Branch passed his hand across his face and forehead, rubbing his eyes and looking quite weary. "Andy's resting for a short while," Branch said. "I had to give him something to calm him down."

David sat up straight. "What is it? What's wrong?"

Dr. Branch leaned back, still rubbing his eyes, as though he didn't want to look directly at David. "Well," he said, finally taking his hand away from his face, "while I was examining Andy I found a lesion on the roof of his mouth. We had to biopsy it. Most likely, it's KS."

*

And then the waiting began, that dreadful waiting when the stakes are so high that one tries in the beginning to think of anything else. But there is something powerfully persistent in the grim reality of the expectancy: life hangs in the balance. Andy had been taken home by David; both were benign and placid, Andy because of the drug, David because of the shock. David hadn't even the slightest idea how to approach the subject, and Andy, stupefied by the drug, remained mute.

Andy was silent, but not unfeeling. For this reason he shut David out, because he could not, at that moment, open his mouth to express what he was so intensely feeling. He had known something was wrong, and as Dr. Branch had explained the curious outbreak of cancer and immunodepression, Andy had experienced an alarming sense of doom. But to find and biopsy a possible KS lesion . . . well, it was too much to take all at once.

All of a sudden it seemed as though the tide had turned for Andy. Now that he feared the worst—this freaky cancer—his health problems of the past few weeks seemed inconsequential. Hepatitis, staph, yeast, fatigue—what were these beside cancer? How could he, in just a matter of minutes, have crossed some border from being a normal human being with some undefined medical problems to being a man possibly stricken with a bizarre form of cancer that was attacking gay men? How could he have been turned from life to death in the space of a morning?

David watched Andy closely as they rode home in the taxi. He knew that he must be thinking about death, or the possibility of it. Cancer—and the diseases as Dr. Branch had described them—was such a terrible thing. David felt numb. His only interest was to get Andy home and into bed, to let the shock pass and to get to a point where the waiting might be at least a bit less unbearable.

*

That evening, as David and Andy were preparing a light dinner, Andy remained quiet. For him, this was a very private matter. He might have expected to cry and shudder and turn to David for consolation of some sort, but instead he was taciturn, contained. Again and again he looked down at his body, held his hands out and examined them as though to detect some outward sign of his body's deterioration, but there was none.

They ate, and the food made Andy brighter. They spoke finally about the morning, David asking only how Andy felt about it, Andy answering that he would rather not discuss it. There was no bitterness in his voice; he was simply unprepared to talk.

They were finishing dinner when the doorbell rang. David got up and went down, knowing it must be Jim and Rita on one of their surprise drop-ins. He laughed when he saw the two of them waiting outside the building. "Hi, honey!" Rita called out. "Can we barge in?"

"Sure," David said, hoping that their visit would cheer Andy. "But it's a bit rough around here right now."

"What's rough?" Jim asked as they followed David up the stairs and into the apartment. They found Andy already settled in the couch, smiling. David left Jim's question unanswered as Rita launched into a lengthy diatribe about Andy's looks, finishing with a jest: "What you need is more sugar in your diet, that's it!" But when she saw the hollow look in Andy's eyes, saw his shoulders drop at the joke, she knew she had misspoken. "Okay," she said quietly, "I goofed again. What's wrong? Something's serious around here, isn't it?"

Andy shook his head and looked to David for support. David began to tell them of the outbreak of Kaposi's sarcoma and Andy's part in the problem. The room grew tense and somber as he explained their day.

"Oh, shit," Rita said, shaking her head. "What can I say?" She looked at Jim, but he was not himself; he looked to her as though he might leap up at any moment and dash from the room. "Well," she said to Andy, "if there's anything at all you need or want, I'm here."

"Thanks," he said, the first word he had spoken. "But for now, we just wait."

"Yes, I see," she said. "Well, I don't know ..." For once, even Rita was at a loss. "Hey, how about the ordinance? What's cookin' with that?" She had tried to be upbeat, but she immediately realized she had made another mistake. Andy wore an expression of utter pain; he was crestfallen. "Oh, shit, honey," Rita started. "I guess that's a bad question right now, huh?"

Andy nodded. "It's okay," he said. "I'm just really fucked up about it all; I can't bear to let it go down again, but ..." He was clearly anguished.

"Okay, okay," Rita said. "So it's tough, I see that. You just keep fighting, okay?" She paused to assess the room. She concluded she should go, if only to get Jim out of there; his "bad vibes" were being cast all over the place. "I guess we'll be letting you get some rest," she said. "But I want to hear from you the minute you know, okay? This is tough stuff, and you shouldn't have to bear it alone you two." She stood and smiled, gathering herself together to go. Jim turned to Andy and said something about feeling better soon, then stepped to the door and watied for Rita. She tried to conceal her expression of irritation over Jim's behavior as she crossed over to Andy and gave him a hug. "You take care of yourself," she commanded.

"Okay," Andy said. And then they were gone.

*

Later, as they were fixing to go to bed, Andy and David reached an accord based on the brief experience with Rita and Jim. They would simply not discuss the problem with their friends, except, of course, with Rita.

"Did you notice?" Andy asked, "that when Rita came to give me a hug, Jim made a straight line for the door, as far away from me as he could get?"

"I noticed," David said. He laid his hand across Andy's as they sat on the edge of the bed. And then, for the first time in weeks, he felt Andy's fingers close around his in a way that suggested only one thing. "We'll have to be careful," he whispered to David. David sat stiff; he was horny, lord knew, but considering everything, he couldn't, just couldn't do it. He didn't know how to get out of it without making Andy feel more isolated than ever. And so he went through with it, for Andy's sake, not his own. But as he yielded to the feelings, Andy's hand began to stroke the fear and misgiving from him. It was a rare moment, and for some reason, David knew it might very well be their last expression like that. Andy had withdrawn so completely until that moment, and it was likely to happen again. But then Andy's hands forced David to abandon thinking, and he lay back, once again giving himself to his lover, so much like the past, but really so different. Everything had changed.

*

Later, in bed, Andy spoke: "I need my family, David."

Oh, shit, David thought to himself. "What are you going to tell them?"

"I don't know," Andy answered. "But I've got to talk to

them, somehow. I'm afraid, though. I can't call them up, that's out of the question."

"Why at all, Andy?" David asked, passion in his voice. "Why? It's bound to bring nothing but more pain. Just avoid it."

Andy shook his head. "I can't do that. I'm so alone in this that I have to tell them, or let them know somehow."

"Then call Elizabeth," David said. "Tell her what's going on, and have her tell them. I won't stand to have you call them; I just won't let it happen. But..." David began, then paused. There was a long silence. "I told *my* mother about it," David said quietly, hesitant.

"When?"

"This afternoon, when you were sleeping."

"What did she say?" Andy asked.

"Nothing," David answered. "Just that she wanted me to call when we knew for sure. I think you should wait to call Elizabeth until you know the test results."

Andy was silent. Then: "Okay, I'll wait." Their hands met again, and soon they were both asleep.

*

In the middle of the night, Andy woke suddenly, frantically. He sat bolt upright on the edge of the bed. He was covered with sweat; he was hot, feverish. He turned and saw that David was fast asleep. He clutched at his stomach as he sat on the edge of the bed; he wanted to throw up. He started to tremble, then got hold of himself. He had felt like this before, the sweating, the nausea. It would pass, if he could just get out of that stuffy room. He walked into the short hall and into the front room. He noticed David's clothes scattered across the couch, saw that the front window was pushed wide open. Just getting out of the bedroom made him feel better. He was terrified of David seeing him like this, sick to his stomach, scared.

He walked around the small room, behind the couch, across the hearth, past the window, then back all over again. So much was on his mind, so fucking much! The damn biopsy, Jim and Rita, telling Elizabeth, sex with David, his life, the ordinance. Why, all of a sudden, did it

have to cascade down over him like a storm of worry? He
sat on the ottoman in front of the armchair. He pulled his
knees up to his chest and wrapped his arms around them.
He felt cozy, protected in himself.

Now, Andy, just what the fuck are you going to do about
this? he demanded of himself. He rocked side to side
very gently, tried to caress himself into calmness. He could
feel a cool breeze blowing through the window, could hear
the sound of distant traffic, horns honking somewhere,
muffled. He sat still, listening to the night sounds through
the window: a dog barked, far away; someone ran down
the sidewalk; cars drove by; and underneath it all, that
low roar of Manhattan.

He felt more calm. But there were still strong feelings
of anxiety pushing their way through. He scratched his
ankles and put his feet down, leaning his elbows on his
knees. He stared down at the carpet and let the feelings
come clear; disappointment and worry about the ordinance not passing without his input; uncertainty about
David; and above all—he had to face it—terror at the
prospect of his own possible death. Strange, he told himself; he might have expected to break down and sob about
it, but he felt almost numb.

After a few minutes, he began to feel drowsy again. He
lay down on the couch and curled up in a ball; the fetal
position, he said to himself. He had an image of Jim crossing the room to get to the door as fast as possible; he
thought of Rita's hug, so good and warm; he remembered
the look on David's face that night when Andy had brought
him to orgasm. What was that expression? Release? Fear?
Revulsion? Surprise? Maybe a little bit of all that?

Andy popped a pillow under his head and wet his lips.
He was glad the bad moments had passed. He drifted off,
but almost as soon as he did, he began to sweat, tossing on
the couch as his mind played out image after image from
that same damn nightmare. Dark silhouettes moved aimlessly along a hallway lit by burning candles. Again there
were the clumps of men and women standing outside the
doors to tiny rooms off the hall, but he couldn't see inside.
He milled about with the silhouettes, trying to make out

faces, features, but they remained as shadows. Then, quite suddenly, he was aware of being followed; it was a sensation that made his flesh crawl. He turned and looked behind him, but he could make out nothing; yet he knew that he was being followed. He started to run down the dark hall, bumping into the crowds of people; he kept running, fast, until he was gasping for air. And then he saw it—an open door to one of the small rooms. He ran into the room and tried to slam the door, but then, just as he had the sensation that whatever was pursuing him was about to enter the room, the scene went dark.

*

The next morning was one of those mornings when Andy opened his eyes, looked around the room, and then pulled the covers over his head. Sometime in the night, he had returned to bed. Now, it was already stifling hot, and one glance at the clock told him it would be a bad day for heat: it was ten-thirty in the morning and already sweltering. David wasn't in the room; Andy wondered where he was. He couldn't hear him in the other rooms. The street noise irritated him as he lay there, trying to sort out his reluctance to get up; he smashed the pillow over his head to block it out. He squeezed his eyes tight and moved his body under the sheet, felt his thighs pressing against the mattress, his dick squashed beneath his belly. He lay there like that for a few minutes, until finally, the early morning nerves let go and he was able to open his eyes and remember that oh, yes! it was Saturday morning, David would be at his exercise class.

It was the last weekend in July. So far the summer had brought with it nothing but unhappiness and bad news. Andy told himself that he shouldn't let it get him down, but for chrissakes, how else should he feel? He got out of bed and stepped into the shower, then put on a worn-out pair of jeans and a loose black T-shirt. He made a cup of coffee and sat down with the newspaper, which David must have brought in earlier. Nothing in it interested him this morning. He pushed it aside and fixed himself a bowl of granola. When that was done, he walked into the living room and looked out the window.

Yeah, it was a scorcher. Everyone was out in shorts, bare-chested or tank tops, tennis shoes. It would be a long, hot day. Andy started to browse through their bookshelves, searching for something good to read that might take his mind off his troubles. He passed over Virginia Woolf and John Updike—too much trouble. He took down the heavy volume of John Cheever stories, but couldn't work up an interest. He took down the copy of *The Brothers Karamazov*, with the bookmark stuck in at page 128. Andy smiled; it had been on page 128 for two years now. He opened it up and read a sentence or two, then put it back, realizing that even if he weren't dying young, he'd probably never get all the way through. He looked at the book David had just started reading—*Atlas Shrugged*, but the thought of Ayn Rand's overextended narrative deterred him.

Finally, he saw the book he had intended to read for some time, *A Reckoning* by May Sarton. He knew it had to do with death, and, just maybe, it might have something in it he could use. Preparing himself for a good Saturday depression, he sank down into the armchair with the book and started to read. At one point, he was stuck on three short sentences: "Dying—no one talked about it. We are not prepared. We come to it in absolute ignorance."

He stopped reading. He wasn't dying, at least not yet. They had merely performed a biopsy and made a vague conjecture. But then he started reading again. He was torn between two modes: denial and preparation. He had to keep reading, had to see what it might be like. But at the same time, he wanted to forget it, to brush it aside. He had, in the past over minor things, felt this way. But the grim reality of this Saturday morning was settling in on him; he couldn't ignore this one.

PART TWO

9 *Late July 1981* • *NewYork City*

Dr. Branch sat at his desk in the late afternoon and stared at the slip of paper in his hand. ANDREW STONE: TEST POSITIVE: KAPOSI'S SARCOMA. He dropped the small piece of paper onto his desk. He felt sick and angry. He stood and walked to the windows, looked down into the hospital entry. The trees there were looking dry and dismal; it would soon be August.

The heat of summer had been merciless. Long ago they had expected some sort of break in the incessant heat wave, but now they had given up. The entire city baked like an oven. Manhattan was grimy and grotesquely hot. Branch wiped the sweat off his forehead with a handkerchief and shook his head; the handkerchief was gray where he had wiped it.

Dammit, he said to himself, as he leaned against the window casing and stared blankly out. He had known about Andy ever since he first read the CDC report, but he had hoped he was wrong. But now, as he stared out into the broiling heat, he realized that his hunch had been right. There it was, in black and white, on the little slip of paper from the pathology lab.

But what the hell is going on? he asked himself, over and over again. Everyone who had heard of this wild new epidemic seemed in the dark. He was himself one of the nation's leading researchers in infectious diseases, but he could think of nothing, nor did he know where to look.

He had spoken with the CDC, had read up on immuno-suppression; but the trouble was, immunology was an infant science. Nobody knew anything. And suddenly there was an outbreak of KS and other opportunistic infections among gay men.

He had phoned around, tried to find out who was working on it. Other than Kinder-Mann in San Francisco, nobody was researching the question. He really couldn't do the work himself; his lab was tied up with his own research, even though that was going nowhere without a grant. Maybe, just maybe, he thought to himself, he could begin research on the problem.

Perhaps he, too, might have remained vaguely disinterested had he merely heard about the KS outbreak without being involved by Andy's contraction of the disease. But that—coupled with his life-long association with Andy—made him itchy to get into the research.

It made him slightly angry that when he had phoned around, very little was known. He was almost furious—this because of his personal involvement—that nothing was being done to discover what was happening. Other researchers—if they had even heard of it—remained impassive, unmovable in their own research concerns. Certainly there was talk. There was always talk when something unusual like this surfaced, but talk was cheap, and research cost money, a great deal of money.

No one seemed to care—really care—if a handful of gay men were suffering at the hands of an unknown infection that wore them down and made their immune systems worthless, leaving them susceptible and defenseless to this freak cancer. Even Branch understood this, somewhat. The cases were isolated; the victims were not government leaders or members of the chamber of commerce. Were it not for his personal caring for Andy and David, he too might only blink, nod, and say how interesting.

But what could he do? He had just lost out on that grant to further his own research, so he couldn't divert any of his own research money into the question. He knew that he should call Kinder-Mann, but their rift was too deep, their scissure too great for him to pick up the phone. Even in this moment of worry and excitement, it was twenty-five years of silence that prevailed. He could not call Kinder-Mann. He would have to initiate this on his own.

He looked away from the window and wiped his forehead again. His shirtsleeves were rolled up, his shoes were off, his tie was thrown over the coat rack. The heat had forced a complete abandonment of decorum. He walked back to his desk and sipped from the glass of water he always kept there.

He sat heavily in his desk chair. He knew that if he wanted to do anything with the KS problem, he would have to go through Dr. Maguire, the chief administrator. He didn't relish the prospect. He sat thinking for a few moments, sizing up the problem as he might present it to Maguire.

He wondered just how much would be involved in discovering the roots of this problem. Truly, he told himself, if this is an epidemic of cancer—and if it shows any signs of spreading—scientists should be jumping on it left and right; it was possible that it could hold the key to the mystery of cancer.

"Walt," Meg said over the intercom, interrupting his train of thought. "Will there be anything else before I go for the day?"

Branch sat up and answered, pressing down on the button that activated his end of the machine. "Yes, please," he said. "Would you get me an appointment to see Art Maguire this afternoon?"

"It's nearly five o'clock," Meg reminded him. "But I'll try."

A few moments later Meg buzzed him. "Walt," she said, "Dr. Maguire's secretary said to come up in fifteen minutes. He'll see you then."

"Thanks, Meg," Branch said. "And one last thing. Please get Andrew Stone to come in tomorrow. Cancel somebody if you have to. I've got to see him, and it's got to be in person. And," he added, "be discreet. That biopsy was positive."

"Oh, no," Meg gasped. "All right, I'll get him in tomorrow afternoon. There's a big gap in your schedule then. Don't worry."

*

Fifteen minutes later, Walt Branch was pacing the floor outside Arthur Maguire's office. He was impatient, damned impatient. He had considered the problem and come to the realization that it was potentially very serious and merited good research funding. But he knew that Maguire would be a tough one to swing to his side for support.

His relationship with Maguire dated back to med school. Maguire had been ahead of Branch by two years, so there was little competition between them, but Maguire had always held an edge over Branch. Branch had—at one time—felt friendship for Maguire, but things had happened to destroy that friendship. Now they were only tolerant of one another.

Maguire's office door opened just then, and Maguire stood in the doorframe and looked out. "Okay, Walt," he said rather gruffly. "You've got ten minutes. Come in." He followed Maguire into his office. Maguire sat on the edge of his desk, as if to indicate a short meeting.

Branch studied him for a moment to read Maguire's mood. He thought Maguire looked exceptionally tired and preoccupied with administrative worries. But even on a good day, Branch thought to himself, Maguire doesn't look so good. In the past twenty-five years, Art Maguire had aged well beyond his years, in large part due to an increasing problem with his weight. Now rather grotesquely obese, Maguire had, in his youth, always been rather large. But what had once been the weight of a big frame and hefty musculature was now the weight of rolls of fat slumping over his belt and bulging in three or four chins.

The man is more than porcine, Branch thought as he took in Maguire's deep frown and trembling chins; he resembles a rhinoceros—and with much the same personality. Branch had to resist a smile. His dislike for Maguire extended back quite a while. Branch knew a great deal

[72]

about him, too much really. Most of it extended back to medical school, and that being the case, Branch knew it was unfair to continue to judge Maguire on that basis. But so far as he could see—and so far as he experienced on a regular basis—Maguire had not changed one jot since those days in med school, so long ago. Maguire was still cold and calculating, thinking only of his own fat hide, nurturing his own desires and hatreds. But he was a great medical administrator, no doubt about it; he had what it took.

Secrecy was, perhaps, Maguire's greatest talent. Such a talent, Branch thought, owed a great deal to having a motive for secrecy. And that he does, Branch reminded himself, remembering there were one or two things about Maguire he could have done without, knowing all these years. But it was in understanding the secret motives that Branch understood Maguire's complex nature—the reasons and abilities at secrecy, the expertise with which he lied and manipulated others to both shield and promote himself.

Branch thought that of all the people he knew—particularly those of his profession—Dr. Arthur Maguire was perhaps the most curiously and complexly motivated. There was a drive within Maguire that exceeded the average human ambition. And it carried with it a threatening, almost dangerous mode of conduct—full of deceit, lies, manipulation. Not a very complimentary picture, all told, Branch realized, feeling only slightly guilty that he should tear the man apart in his mind just moments prior to requesting assistance.

"I'm surprised I could get in to see you so soon," Branch said, breaking his reverie about Maguire. But the instant he asked the question, he realized that his negative thoughts had forced him to form a remark that carried with it an implication of hostility. Off to a flying start, Branch chided himself.

"Oh?" Maguire said, smiling as though he were puzzled. He punctuated every remark with an automatic smile, a habitual and ingratiating curling of the lips that dropped just as soon as it was formed, encouraging his chins to tremble in unison. Years of politics had taught him to maintain a seemingly pleasant demeanor, but now the habit was so disingenuous as to be almost vicious.

"Well, then, Dr. Maguire, let's make this brief and to the point," Branch said, nodding and smiling disingenuously himself. "I'll get right to the point; I want research funds made available to me for this Kaposi's sarcoma epidemic."

Maguire's face went white, his chins taut. "Absolutely not," he said abruptly.

"What? Why so firm?" Branch had expected some resistance, had expected to argue, persuade. But he was ill prepared for such a strong and complete denial.

Maguire's color had returned; he was shaking his head back and forth, appearing very vexed, and saying: "We just haven't got the money for it, for this sort of thing..."

"But..." Branch started, but Maguire rushed on.

"This is the wrong time of year, and you know as well as I that you just can't find instant funds. Don't be naïve all of a sudden, doctor; these things have got to be proposed, studied by the committee, evaluated, etcetera. You know that," he concluded, his hands stretched out, the palms turned up. He wore that fixed smile and concerned frown; the posture was nearly ecclesiastic.

"But," Branch began again, "this *is* something of an emergency, and you could activate emergency funds, find benefactors in a matter of hours."

"Can't be done." Maguire was shaking his head vigorously again and fumbling on the desk for a cigarette. "It's impossible. And besides, they're already working on it in Atlanta. And Sloan Kettering has someone on it. Of course there's Dr. Kinder-Mann in San Francisco; it's his baby, anyway. Why are we discussing this so?" Again he held his hands up, as if to bestow or receive a blessing.

Now Branch was vexed. "Atlanta is simply monitoring the problem now, and the work at Sloan will be good, I'm sure. But for heaven's sake, Dr. Maguire, for Mt. Zion *not* to do something is mighty hard to accept. Of course I understand procedures and all that; I was hoping you could help speed things up while I prepare a formal proposal for approval, more or less as a technicality to having already initiated the research..."

"Sorry, Branch," Maguire interrupted him, expelling a cloud of smoke as he spoke. He flicked the ashes all over himself and the floor. "You know I'd like to help. You know I'd do everything in my power to assist you if it was at all possible. But this is not in the cards right now for Mt. Zion. You realize, of course, what sorts of research all this would require? Why, it could cost millions!" Maguire feigned shock at the figure.

Branch was shaking his head, disgruntled. Maguire went on: "Now why don't you begin to look in on it in your spare time, draw up a formal proposal, let me bring it before the committee after the first of the year..." Again the ashes all over the place.

Branch interrupted him: "The first of the year is far too late. Don't be unreasonable, Art. Someone very close to me has contracted KS, a patient and friend, and I have every intention of working on this problem at Mt. Zion, with adequate research funding."

Maguire was shocked at the slight outburst. He straightened on his desk, his face registering disgust and contempt for Branch. "Calm down, Walter; this is no way to behave about it. Now I see your urgency and involvement; I'll talk to a few board members, see what I can do. But I hope you'll have a talk with yourself about your position in all this before formulating your proposal and research plan. Personal considerations are not good." Maguire crushed out his cigarette and slouched again.

"Sorry," Branch said, examining Maguire's words in his mind. The administrator had just offered to speak to board members, but was that enough? Was it a political ploy? Branch was up against a wall. "But it does seem very frustrating to me to be so helpless about it, particularly because of my personal involvement."

"I sympathize with you," Maguire said perfunctorily. "But honestly, this is an extremely sensitive issue already, and I'm not sure Mt. Zion needs to get mixed up in it. You've got to remember the kinds of problems we have. We're facing major cutbacks in funding of every research topic. And with something this politically loaded — what with the homosexual element and all — well, it's all delicate and avoidable." Maguire's hands were in the air again, this time with a shrug of the shoulders.

"I understand that," Branch said, "but still..."

"This will pass quickly anyway," Maguire said, an odd edge in his voice.

Branch could not believe his ears. "But do you know the significant numbers? More are reported each week. This could really be big."

Maguire was scowling, but his mind was somewhere else; he wasn't paying close attention to Branch's words. He looked up, almost as though distracted, and murmured: "Yes, vanguard research..."

Branch wasn't sure what Maguire meant, so he kept still for a moment, waiting for Maguire to go on. But the man said nothing; he just sat there, his fat belly heaving in and out as he breathed heavily and stared blankly at the floor. Finally, after only a few moments, Maguire's eyes became clearly focused on Branch, who shifted in his chair under the scrutiny. "Let me get back to you on this," Maguire said softly. "But I'd warn you to keep quiet about it, at least for the moment; don't want to mess up possible avenues..."

Branch nodded, captivated by Maguire's sudden change of mood. Branch thought the use of the word "warn" a bit curious, but he questioned it only for a split second before forgetting it. Branch still felt frustrated, but he was pleased that somehow he had broken through Maguire's earlier rigidity. He was ready to leave, to let the matter be until Maguire got back to him, but he remained seated, sensing that Maguire had something more to say.

Maguire leaned back and crossed his arms across his stomach, then said: "Have you considered asking your wife for the funds?"

Branch bristled at the suggestion. "How dare you," he whispered, lost between his shock at Maguire's question — at Maguire's nerve — and his wish to leave on good terms, with a promise of some help. "That's not the course I had hoped to take," he said coldly, standing to go.

Maguire shrugged his shoulders, as if to dismiss the whole thing. He smiled, perked up and extended his hand. Branch shook it and tried to smile, tried to shuck off his annoyance.

"I'll get back to you," Maguire nodded. "Sorry about that..."

Branch was uncertain what Maguire was expressing, but he didn't question it. The man was too politic to warrant very serious consideration in such matters as apologies. Branch said nothing else. He was torn between anger and hope and hurt. The hope came from Maguire's promise to talk with the board members; the anger came from the futility of the situation and Maguire's callous remark in reference to his wife's fortune. And it hurt because the fact remained: his wife had more than enough to fund his research.

*

Branch headed straight for Max Leider's office. It was a long walk from Maguire's executive offices on the fourteenth floor of the rear wing to Leider's office and labs on the seventh floor of the old wing, the same wing where Branch's lab was located. When he got there, he found Leider hunched over a sheaf of papers in his lab, making notations with a pencil. His red hair and bald pate were the first things Branch saw when he walked in. Leider looked up, surveying Branch's crestfallen face.

"No money?" Leider asked. "And no help or encouragement I'll bet."

"Right on target," Branch said, sinking into a wooden chair beside Leider. "He was really tough—nearly absolute in his refusal. He's worried about the politics of asking for more money right now when the topic is so sensitive, as he put it. Can you believe that? He did soften up a bit, though, and said he'd talk to the board about some possibilities."

"Well, that's something," Leider said. "You know how I feel about these things, but when it comes to funding, the committee is really worried about public relations these days. I mean, look, you've got the federal government trying to cut back on everything except their own limousines; and then you've got these stinking rich power-mongers here. The last thing they want their thousands . . . wait, make that millions . . . of deductible money going for is research into something that they would consider as the natural result of . . . how do I put it . . . of a reckless, deviant lifestyle."

Branch shook his head and rubbed his forehead. "Come on, Max, you know that's not true. This thing can't discriminate as to sexual preference. How could it? It doesn't make the least bit of sense. It's got to be a coincidence at this moment, and as such, it's liable to spread to others at any time."

"That's probably right," Leider said, worried. "That's damn probable, I fear."

"Well, if that old curmudgeon won't budge, I've got a trick or two to pull, but I'd need Carolyn's help. And she's so damned moody, don't know how she'd react. You know, Maguire suggested I ask her for the money?"

"Would she give it?"

"No, of course not. It's *her* money, and believe me, she needs it, all of it. But she does have something else we could use to get Dr. Arthur Maguire to sing a different tune."

"What *are* you talking about?" Leider asked; he detested coyness.

"Nothing, Max, nothing," Branch said. "If Carolyn decides, I'll tell you then."

Leider shrugged his shoulders. He didn't care what Branch was up to, and he had to go. Branch stood there for a moment, after Leider had walked away. There was a sly smile curling his lips.

10

Twenty-four hours later, Andy was leaving Mt. Zion in a strange and distressed mood. Branch had given him the results of the biopsy and explained the ensuing treatment for the cancer. Andy had expected the news, so he felt no sense of denial, but he had been unprepared for the overpowering fear and loneliness he suddenly felt. He felt a terrible isolation, as though he were frighteningly and absolutely alone. Never in his life had he felt such real terror, such horror that his body was diseased and that he would, most likely, die. Though Branch had given him an injection of intravenous diazepam to calm his anxiety, he had experienced a growing sense of terror so piercing it approached numbness. He had, with his strong sense of pride and dignity, collected himself sufficiently to convince Dr. Branch he was able to walk home. But in the few moments following his exit from Branch's office—as he made his way through the sterile white halls of the hospital, with that sickening smell, dammit, he cursed—he had wanted to run screaming from that monstrosity of a building, to escape that harsh fluorescent light and noise.

The noise—clatter, voices, loudspeaker, laughter, feet scuffling, phones ringing—nearly caused him to strike out at someone. But then he was there, in the lobby, the outside just beyond the doors. Crossing that lobby seemed a tremendous effort. He wanted to shove the people aside, to shout some obscenity at their indifference to his isolation. He felt so very alone.

But then he was there, outside, and he no longer felt trapped. The fear lessened as he began to walk along the busy streets—a late afternoon in Manhattan. The noise here didn't bother him, the clatter of cars and taxis, the crowds, the hustle. Really, he wavered between loneliness and anger; he couldn't understand how his body had betrayed him, how his sexuality had somehow led to this horrible verdict.

Walking down the avenue, he looked up, high, to see the sky, but it meant nothing. He saw the rows of shops, the long lines of cabs, the few small trees jutting up out of the sidewalk here and there, punctuating the garbage with weak flutters of greenery. It all meant nothing, didn't register, really. He couldn't properly focus on anything, nothing other than his feelings.

Aside from the fear and loneliness, there was that creeping anger, a fury rising from somewhere deep. It was only half-formed, though, a momentary cringe of violent irritability that blended into revulsion, then the bland numbness of fear.

He was afraid to die. Even though he had known that the biopsy would prove positive, he had not yet received the death sentence—as he now thought of it—until the words were out of Dr. Branch's mouth. Now he knew; now it was certain. So, "I am to have my own death," Andy said aloud as he walked along, quoting a line from May Sarton. Now the moment was here, and the prospect of having his own death, no matter how well or poorly he might face it, terrified and infuriated him.

He had to sit down; he had to spend a moment to take stock. It was true what they say about one's life flashing before one's eyes, he thought, finding a dusty old bench and sitting down. The late afternoon sun slanted down across him, making him sweat. He sat, and remembered. Everything seemed to spill out of some deep reservoir, everything that had meaning. It made a jumble in his mind, though—the memory of his grandmother's death, of his parents' coldness, of church, of the week in Yosemite. He realized that in the next few weeks—or would it be months?—he would have to sort it out.

Of course Dr. Branch had given him hope, telling him that since it was all really one big question mark, there was no telling how it would turn out. He had told Andy that KS need not be fatal—there was treatment, and sometimes remission—but Andy doubted it in his case. The doctor, then, had refused to give an estimate of Andy's "time left," but Andy had his own sense that it wasn't very long. How long could his body hold up under these circumstances? That's what it came down to, wasn't it? How long his body could hold up? He had been failing for weeks, and there was, he was certain, simply not enough reserve left to fight a virulent cancer. His weight was precipitously low, his fatigue level high, his various infections many. It couldn't last long.

But how he envied life all of a sudden! He saw the

people hurrying around him, he saw a child in his mother's arms, and, trying not to be too sentimental (but why worry about that now?) he felt a great rush of envy and joy. Yes, in the past few weeks he had begun already to see it, to understand that he should have done more, that he ought to have just lived it out, fully, with gusto as they say. Because now, in this dry moment of clinical reality, he knew there wouldn't be enough time to do much about all the missed things—that ballet he had wished to see, the house he had planned to build with David in the country sometime when they were old.

How it all seemed both important and trivial now. He *should* have done it all, but then again, why? For what? Here it all was, ending in an ugly disease, a bleak, short future of chemotherapy and sickness. Even if he were to survive somehow, what would be left of him? What would be left of David? And of their relationship?

And then, as he absent-mindedly stepped into the street and was narrowly missed by a speeding limousine, he felt his sorrow turn to denial. It can't be! To end like this? The equation did him wrong, he felt; it wasn't fair. He *had* worked hard; he *had* been good to himself, to David. He *had* lived it out; he hadn't been one of those to duck under the covers and waste the day. He had been out there, in the thick of it. And so the denial turned again to bland acceptance. After all, he thought, it all ends sometime, so why not now? Why not be aware that my time is come, my number is up? Why not face it with dignity? With a fight?

Oh, but he felt an edge of anger, of betrayal, but still the persistent fact: he would die. The sense of betrayal disturbed him the most. He felt he had been betrayed beyond his control too many times. First, it had been his sexuality, different from others. Though he had learned fast enough to accept that, it had been the crux of the matter for his parents' betrayal of him. And now the cancer.

The passing thought of his family brought into focus another issue. Something else to examine, he told himself. Who would he have to tell? Surely David knows already; I'll have to face him soon. Aside from David and a few co-workers, who was there? Rita, of course. And his family. God, he was torn. Earlier he had felt the need to let them know. Now he wasn't sure. He knew he would tell his little sister Elizabeth. But he would ask her not to tell the folks. He'd rather they didn't know. Perhaps he would change his mind; he still felt a strong urge to reconcile, but maybe it was like David said; too late.

He and David had few other friends. It would be easy enough to tell them. But how would they react? With fear and horror? Would they drop him as if he were a leper? Or would they rally to support him? It was all very difficult to consider, and he was feeling weary; it was something more he would have to decide.

He walked along, noticing a man and woman fighting in the street, shouting at each other. The woman was pounding the man's chest with her clenched fists. To Andy, it seemed almost comical; it seemed like nothing beside the fact of his illness. It's funny, he thought, feeling for the first time that afternoon lucid and rather practical, it's funny that this thing should suddenly alter my entire world. And with that thought came a flash of freedom, as though a great burden had been lifted from his shoulders. He was free to do as he pleased; he was dying! No more social graces, no more worries about "what will they think"!

A gentle excitement flushed through him at the prospect. And the first urge he had was to hug David, to hold him close and tell him just how deeply he had taken him, how fully he had loved him. I can't postpone anything, he realized, the light exhilaration still coursing through him. I can declare my love, my deep feelings, my anger.

But as soon as the exhilaration had come, it was gone, and Andy was filled again with that angry denial. How could he face chemotherapy? How could he go on with living, as Branch had told him, continuing to work when he could? Branch had told him to fight, but how? How to explain to the people at work? What was he to say? "Hi, I'm dying because I'm gay?" He shook his head. He would not think about it now.

He neared their building, and he felt nervous. He would have to face David now, whom he had refused to allow to accompany him. Andy had foreseen that he would need the time alone, and now it was done. He would have to tell David the truth, the outline of what was left for them. God, how? he asked. He couldn't bring such sorrow to David.

But there was no way out. It would work, somehow. He grew anxious as he mounted the stairs.

*

"Andy!" David jumped up when Andy walked in. He looked at Andy's face and knew at once that there was bad news. He crushed out a cigarette and crossed the room. Without waiting to hear, he put his arms around Andy and hugged him close. They held each other for several minutes, the tears streaming down their faces, unwilling to let go. It was a brief moment of strengthening, when David held Andy tight and let him know that he cared, that he was there, that he would be there in the future. Neither of them had suspected how this moment would be approached, but now it was here, and they were ready for it.

Finally, they sat down. The late afternoon and early evening light cast a Titian richness across the room, enveloping them in a warmth that seemed soothing, necessary. As they began to talk, Andy examined the room, letting his eyes rest on the etching of a spot in the Hudson River Valley; it was an unusually pacific print, the rich greenery tumbling down a hillside to the river below. Andy let his eyes take in the entire room. He looked at the stereo system in the corner, at the soft white rug, the warm, creamy-colored sofa and chair.

One window was open, letting a rare summer breeze rustle the gossamer curtains. "For the next several weeks," Andy began, "I have to go to Mt. Zion for weekly chemotherapy, probably cobalt treatment as well. But it begins the day after tomorrow, the chemotherapy." Andy was speaking almost from rote, repeating the doctor's words. His attention was focused on David's reactions to the whole thing.

David was oddly still, despite his trembling hands. Andy

could tell that he wanted to light a cigarette, and so he offered one to David. David took the cigarette and inhaled deeply, letting the smoke exhale through his nostrils. "What is it?" David asked.

"I don't know," Andy answered, unsure of David's question; he assumed he meant the chemotherapy. "Dr. Branch said that there was a variety of drugs they could use. What they do is spend the morning filling you with it, intravenously. Then afterward, I'll feel sick and tired, nauseous, stuff like that..." Andy's voice trailed off at the prospect.

David wore an expression that was a cross between horror, revulsion and concern. He seemed to be struggling to accept the facts. Andy wondered if he might not just walk out, call the relationship quits and get out while the getting seemed good. But no, David seemed to be hanging on, to something. "What happens then?" David asked.

Andy was finding the conversation more difficult. He related the facts to David, even though he was desperate to voice his fear and terror at the prospect of dying. "Either I get better," Andy answered, "or we keep it up. There will be a respite period, just to gauge my response to the therapy. Or, of course, I might get worse and die." So there it is, Andy said to himself; the worst moment is out.

David was shocked at the bluntness of the statement, but another part of him had already prepared to hear it. "You'll be better," David said. "I'm sure of that." He puffed on his cigarette, not believing a word of it, but hoping it might come true. He had watched Andy waste away, rapidly, suddenly. He knew the end was inevitable.

But then it made him angry. "What the fuck is it?" he exploded, slamming his fist. "Didn't Dr. Branch tell you anything?"

"Nothing," Andy said. "They don't know why or how. He's been in touch with the CDC in Atlanta, but they don't know what's going on. There are more than a hundred cases already. So I'm not alone."

"Some consolation," David said. "A hundred, though?"

David was surprised. "I had no idea. Why isn't somebody doing something? Isn't this some sort of public health emergency or something?"

"What's to do?" Andy said, shrugging his shoulders and feeling sick to his stomach. He hated the fact that there were no answers much more than David could. "Anyway, Dr. Branch said that he wanted to start researching it himself, but that funding was a big problem. He said only a few people are working on it, but that it's already generating a lot of interest. You know, they don't even know what to call it yet."

David frowned. "I thought it was Kaposi's sarcoma."

"The cancer is KS," Andy said, "But the immune problem is something else. Dr. Branch said that the doctor in San Francisco who discovered the epidemic is calling it Gay Related Immune Deficiency Syndrome—GRIDS for short. But that's all they know, and nobody is looking beyond that."

David was lighting another cigarette and shaking his head. "That's impossible," he said. "Hard to believe. You can't have a hundred people with an epidemic and get ignored. It can't be."

"A hundred *fags*," Andy said flatly. He needed to say nothing else. David inhaled and said nothing. He leaned forward on his knees and stared across the room, seeing with repulsion how clear and true Andy's remark was. A hundred fags are expendable, he reasoned, realizing that it would have to be straight people getting sick before anyone would care.

11

Across town, Walt Branch and his wife were dressing for the evening. The weather had cooled slightly, and they were looking forward to another of a long series of summer symphonies. Branch was enthusiastic about the evening; he needed something to take his mind off the day. Not only had Maguire failed to get back to him about his request of the day before, but he had had to tell Andy Stone about the biopsy results. Although Andy had taken the news rather stoically, it had been a tragic moment. Branch wanted to forget it for the next few hours, if he could. He looked across the room at his wife.

Carolyn Whittier Branch sat before her mirror, touching makeup to the two thin lines just in front of either of her ears. At fifty, she looked to be about thirty-seven. She caught her husband's glance in the gilt-edged antique mirror. "You know, dear," she said to him as he adjusted his cumberbund, "I heard that you were stopping your research and are trying for something very strange. Now why didn't you tell me?"

"Carolyn..." Branch began, amazed at the lightning speed at which hospital gossip traveled; it had been less than a day. But he was cut off as she continued.

"...yes, dear, why didn't you say something? I had to feign total knowledge of whatever it is you're up to in front of three of New York's leading ladies. Imagine my surprise when Mrs. Dr. Sakowitz said you must be trying to ruin your career, and then addressed herself to me, saying in the loudest voice imaginable to humankind: "What is your husband doing at Mt. Zion? He should be at UC San Francisco if he wants to study homosexual behavior!'"

"Oh, Carolyn..."

"Why, I nearly dropped dead!" She dropped her hand from her face, laying the makeup brush on the vanity. "Of course, Nora cut in—bless her soul—to point out that the way she was given to understand, you aren't studying that kind of behavior, but rather that you had asked Dr. Maguire for funds to study something to do with possible groundbreaking cancer research. Now, dearest, do tell me what on earth you're up to..."

"Well, it's..." Branch began.

"...You know," Carolyn went on, now drawing a thin black line along her eyelashes, "any diva would give her right hand to have a voice as powerful as that Naomi Sakowitz. After all, what does a diva need with a right hand anyway?..."

"Please Carolyn!" Branch cut in, almost shouting, "Will you never come up for air?"

She laughed, genuinely amused at herself. She finished applying the mascara and began to brush a light powder across her face. "Please, darling, don't make me lose my composure. It'll ruin my makeup; this is very delicate." She glanced at him in the mirror. He had given up and was sitting on the edge of the bed, looking across at the windows that framed Central Park, several levels below. He shook his head and looked back at her; he loved her dearly, but he had never reconciled himself to her incessant ramblings, much of which were contrived for the effect.

He shook his head and said, "Would you please stop referring to doctors' wives as 'Mrs. *Dr.* so-and-so.' It's very unbecoming."

She fastened a string of pearls around her neck. "It's merely a point of reference, darling. Now, please tell me what you're up to over at that awful hospital before we get to the symphony. I'd like to appear at least vaguely knowledgeable should the subject come up, god forbid. But if I know Naomi, she'll be shouting it from the front steps of Lincoln Center. But what is this about groundbreaking cancer research? You could certainly use something like that in your career right now, couldn't you darling?" She stopped talking so that she might begin applying a red lipstick.

Branch saw his opportunity. "Well, Carolyn, I'm glad you brought it up. How foolish of me to forget to mention it to you earlier." He was conciliatory. "I've been very concerned about a recent epidemic..."

"Epidemic?" Carolyn said incredulously, her lipstick falling. "Epidemic of what? Can I catch it?"

"Not unless you're a gay man, it appears."

"Well, that I am *not!*" she asserted. Then, reaching again for her powder, she said; "What an unseemly remark, dear. What *are* you talking about?"

Branch crossed the room and sat in a velvet chair. "A very rare form of cancer called Kaposi's sarcoma is attacking gay men who are, for some unknown reason, immuno-depressed."

"Depressed, darling?" she cut in. "Of course they're depressed. It's all that disco music..."

"Please, Carolyn!" Branch couldn't deal with her sudden levity. "It means their immune systems are not working correctly, but we don't know why."

She shuddered. "I know what it means," she said coldly. "It was just a little joke. You're so serious, darling. So sincere."

"Well, Andy Stone is one of the victims," he said simply.

"Oh, my dear God," Carolyn said, her hands falling and resting on the vanity. "How very dreadful, how awful." She was genuinely distressed. "I'm so sorry." She suddenly dropped the façade of breathless socialite and revealed her plain concern. Her hands remained motionless on the marble top of the vanity. "I had no idea," she barely whispered. "How did it happen? What will happen to him?"

"We don't know," Branch said. "The whole thing is some sudden freaky thing, something like Legionnaires' disease. Andy's quite sick."

There was a long moment when neither of them spoke. Branch, momentarily disturbed by his emotions about Andy, walked to the windows and looked down and across into Central Park. Carolyn was quiet, though she had begun once again to gently powder her face.

"I feel rather sick all of a sudden," she said. "The symphony might be a trial."

"No, we must go," he said. "I've felt sick about it all day; I need the symphony to take my mind off the whole thing."

"How disturbing to think that Andy..." Carolyn didn't finish the sentence. "I see now what Naomi was talking about. Surely your research is very important, then, isn't it?" She turned away from the mirror to look directly at her husband.

Branch turned away from the windows and looked at her from across the room. "There's no money," he said simply. "I talked to Art Maguire about it at once, but he refused to help, said there wasn't enough money to fund any research into it at Mt. Zion."

"Why?" she gasped, raising her thin eyebrows.

"Why?" Branch echoed her. "You tell me." He let the remark hang between them, watched as recognition crossed her face.

"Ah, yes," she said. "Of course; I know what that's about. Such a prig." She turned back to the mirror and resumed powdering her face. "But of course he won't deny you any of that big federal grant he's got in the works. So at least you'll have some of that."

Branch was incredulous. "What are you talking about?"

Carolyn shook her head. "Oh, dear, I can't believe it. According to Naomi *and* Nora, Dr. Maguire's been commuting to Washington frequently and has just about wrapped up a huge federal grant for research at Mt. Zion. In the millions, even. Surely you knew?"

Branch was silent. Leave it to the doctors' wives, he thought, realizing how much they always seemed to know. It was a separate network of gossip and the passing of important information.

"No, I hadn't heard," he answered, his head down.

"Yes, several million from what I hear..." she said, her voice almost a whisper. She sensed the pain her husband was feeling. It had been difficult for him these past few years, she knew. And now, to be coldly cut out of the picture—even in the preliminary stages of something— must hurt terribly. She looked down at the scatter of cosmetics and beauty implements on the vanity and wondered what had gone wrong with Walter's career. Part of it was age—he wasn't holding up as well as, say, Max Leider; Walter wasn't keeping up with the new research. And he had never pushed himself that extra step. About this she felt anger, frustration, and pity. Surely she was one of the most prominent of the doctors' wives' social set; certainly Walter had achieved a great deal. But there was something lackluster about the whole thing; their marriage, his career, even her money.

She smiled at the thought of her money. It was the six-million-dollar trust she had inherited when her parents passed away seventeen years ago. It had been odd suddenly to be the beneficiary of such a sum, even though she had always known it was due. She had been raised Carolyn Whittier, of the Atlantic City Whittiers. Not much of a family, really, but oh, they had money! And oh, they had lived! Carolyn had that Atlantic City spirit, something almost vulgar in its reveling in life. During college she had turned her back on the family and entered nursing school; hence her involvement in medicine. Then, slowly, she and Walter had risen—first in the world of medicine, and then, in the world of society with the acquisition of her fortune.

Now she appeared to have it all—prestige, wealth, even her beauty had remained (thanks to a bit of help here and there). And now, she had to witness a subtle and saddening decline in her husband's career. Well, she concluded, not if I can help it. She would see to it that Art Maguire would share the riches when they came rolling in; after all, she had yet to play her trump card when it came to Dr. Arthur Maguire.

*

Later, when the evening was over and they lay in bed, Carolyn brushed her lips against his ear. "Darling, it was wonderful tonight at the symphony. We should stay in town during the summer more often. Summer arts are much better than I remembered."

Branch stirred, turned to her and put his arms around her, feeling the smooth skin of her bare back. "Except for the heat," he said, then: "Art Maguire has it in for me, I know."

This was unexpected, but Carolyn answered: "He doesn't have it in for you, dear; he has it in for everybody, you know that." She kissed him gently, ran her hands down his chest and stomach, between his legs.

He shifted on the bed. "I deserve some of that money, you know, and Art is not going to give it to me." He was quiet for a moment, enjoying the pleasant sensations her playful hand was creating.

At the same time, they both said: "Unless..."

Carolyn kissed him again, running her lips along his cheek and then kissing him fully. Their tongues met and played, probing the softness of their mouths, teasing. She pulled away slightly. "If he doesn't come through, dear," she said softly, "I'll do something I've always wanted to do."

Branch smiled in the dark. He hadn't had to suggest a thing. "I'll go in and have a little talk with Art," she went on. "Remind him of our long lost youth. That should do the trick."

"It would," Branch said, chuckling. He ran his hand over her body, touching her breasts, feeling her nipples go taut. They kissed and rolled on the bed, the warm night air blowing gently across them from the open window. For a moment, Branch thought of Andy and David, of what sorrow lay in their life together. But then he felt the insistent pressure created by Carolyn's fingers, and then she was offering herself fully, pulling him beneath her as she lay atop him and brought him in tight. He put everything out of his mind at that moment; it was the release he desperately needed.

*

On the other side of town, Andy and David lay beside each other in bed, not talking. Andy had decided to tell Elizabeth about his illness, about the diagnosis, about the whole thing. He and David had argued over this, for David assumed that Andy was merely inviting more trouble into a situation that was steeped in suffering already. And so they didn't speak; their silence was not angry, though. They had just reached an accord.

Earlier, Andy had wanted to make love again, but this time, David had refused him, trying to mask his fear with excuses of disquiet and worry. Andy had not argued about it; he seemed somehow to understand; he had, in fact, anticipated that moment when David would cease to find Andy attractive in his illness. Somehow, it made them seem closer.

The closeness was due, they both knew, to the fact of the cancer. Now that the cancer was certain, now that the first mystery was undone, they were brought more intimately together than they had been during the uncertain weeks.

Though the time was dark, at least they now had something against which to fight. In the dark, David lay there, near sleep, realizing that there was now a definition of Andy's condition, something to which they could pit their fight, their strength and struggle. He was almost content in that last moment before sleep, satisfied that come morning, they could begin that fight, possibly to save Andy's life.

Andy didn't notice that David had drifted into sleep. He felt very close to David, for suddenly he seemed very precious, very much to be appreciated. Andy lay uneasily, as he saw that David had fallen asleep; he was glad it was over. He realized that now the diagnosis was given, he had something to which to concede his health, his life probably. There was in it—though he remained filled with confusion—a slight blessing; the unknown would soon cease to instill fear.

But at that moment, just as he thought he might not fear, he was filled with confusion and uncertainty. He disengaged his arms from David and sat up. Knowing that it would be a long time before he could sleep, he let himself out of the bedroom and made his way along the dark hall to the front room. The night was pleasant, but not cool, and he opened the window wide and sat on the sill, looking down into the street.

He knew he had some sorting out to do. He was too bright to surrender himself to panic. Anyway, the time for panic was past; it seemed to him that the panic of unknowing had given way to the confused feelings—was it almost longing that he felt?—of a terminal diagnosis. There were persistent questions playing themselves in his mind over and over; why me? why now? how? But this pervasive, somewhat fearful curiosity (a sense perhaps of betrayal?) alternated with resignation to the knowledge that it was over.

Andy knew that there had been times in his life when it seemed so tragic, all of it: living, breathing, being on earth. He knew that everyone felt like that at times, and he had always rebounded from those depressions with a feeling that life is a passage of sorts. Short or long, hard or easy, he felt that life was just a passage from one thing (place? time? past life?; he didn't know) to another. He felt that way now: transient.

He stared into the street, then checked the clock. In the dim light he saw it was early, not yet midnight. No wonder, then, he thought, there are still so many people out. He felt a little mixed up, but reasonable. What bothered him, what confused him, was his fear. He sat there and tried to isolate the fear, discover its nature. And, rather suddenly, he did: he was afraid not of death, only of dying, of the long and maybe painful experience he now knew he must endure.

The thought raised him immeasurably; it was a relief. He felt his shoulders drop their tension, his lungs breathe deeply. He nearly smiled at his discovery. It was the process he would have to confront.

But just as he felt some relief, just as he stood and turned to go back to the bedroom, he felt another, sharper perplexity: it was the entanglement of his sexuality with his disease. But no, he would not think about that now. That would have to wait.

12

Clear across the country, Dr. Alfred Kinder-Mann looked up from his desk to see the sun set on the Pacific Ocean. He watched as the brilliant rays cast a warm glow across the Golden Gate Bridge. But the scenery didn't register completely in his mind. He was troubled, troubled by two things that nagged at the back of his mind.

They were losing their patients too fast. The young men with Kaposi's sarcoma were not responding well to any attempts at treatment. Mostly, they were using chemotherapy, weekly injections of vincrystine or vinblastine, sometimes coupled with cobalt therapy. But so far there was very little positive response. The young men rapidly withered away and died at a shocking rate. There was, in addition to the Kaposi's sarcoma, another, perhaps more deadly opportunistic infection affecting these men. *Pneumocystis* pneumonia, a parasitic lung infection, was claiming the sick young men with appalling frequency. Sometimes Kinder-Mann had seen young men with the cancer who seemed to be responding to chemotherapy suddenly contract the pneumonia and be dead within days. It was shocking and frustrating.

But there was something else that troubled him, even more deeply. It was there in the data he was collecting, that he had laid out on his desk and spent the day examining. Mostly, it was an incredible mess of statistics—clinical, epidemiological—as amassed by the CDC in Atlanta. Kinder-Mann didn't like what he saw: the disease syndrome, whatever it was, was spreading, and spreading fast. The onset of the clinical cases reported was far too sudden and the sharp upswing in numbers was far too great. This problem—this medical curiosity—did not fit any known models of epidemiology. This plague is a freak, he thought to himself as he leaned over the material on his desk. It doesn't add up to anything that makes sense.

Kinder-Mann leaned back and stretched, realizing that it was already twilight and that he was dead tired. He ran his hand through his brown hair, graying at the temples. He yawned and stood up, stretching his arms high above his head. It was time to call it a night, he decided, though he had an urge to remain at his desk, poring over the statistics and medical records he had acquired.

He had begun to study—on an individual basis—each case as it was reported to the CDC. He had received some copies of victims' medical records; others he still awaited. He knew that, together with the CDC, these people had to be studied, examined, compared, their medical histories carefully scrutinized to discover the common link that would point to the cause.

But in the meantime, the number of cancer victims was increasing at an oddly rapid pace. Certainly on a vast basis it was nothing, perhaps a hundred cases. But in terms of epidemiology, it was already approaching a disaster. One hundred cases of a rare cancer or other strange immune disorders constituted a health emergency, as far as Kinder-Mann was concerned.

But he had to get home, he told himself. The night was falling and he was tired. He was hungry, too, and he knew that he couldn't do his best research in a physically depleted condition. So he gathered his things and slipped his jacket on, locked the office and headed for the plaza which led to the elevator to the parking garage.

As he descended in the elevator, he remembered that he had an appointment the next morning with two officials from the National Institutes of Health in Washington. Or rather, they had an appointment with him. Apparently they were beginning to track this thing as well, and the two men had called earlier in the week to arrange a meeting with Kinder-Mann. After all, he was still the most visible of the few medical researchers already working on the syndrome, having discovered the epidemic in the first place.

The elevator doors slid open and Kinder-Mann crossed the lobby, looking through the glass walls and seeing a friend of his approaching. They saw each other, and his friend—a lawyer in the gay community—waved to him. Kinder-Mann detected a dark expression on Scott's face. They met outside the building.

"What's up?" Kinder-Mann asked, the preliminary greetings over and the dark mood still in evidence.

Scott spoke softly, "I just had a call from Warren in L.A. I thought I'd come and tell you myself, because I know he won't call you."

"What is it?" Kinder-Mann said.

"He has KS."

Kinder-Mann felt as though he had been sliced open with a scalpel. "My god..." was all that he could say. The young man, Warren, had been Kinder-Mann's lover for many years during the seventies. Scott put his arm across Kinder-Mann's shoulders and helped him walk to his car. The shock was, to Kinder-Mann's thinking, almost unbearable. All at once he felt angry, horrified, and above all else, incredibly driven to further the research. Now that the epidemic had hit close to home, Kinder-Mann knew that nothing would stop him. In the fading twilight, Scott drove Kinder-Mann home.

*

The next morning was again foggy and grim, typical summer weather in San Francisco. Kinder-Mann had not slept well; he had worried about the bad news of the evening before. He had tried, unsuccessfully, to call his friend and former lover. Finally, in the middle of the night, he had resolved two things. First, he would discover the root of the epidemic if it took the rest of his life. And second, he would pressure the government officials for research money.

Now, in the dim light of early morning, Kinder-Mann felt groggy and a bit grumpy. He carried his resolve of the night before, but the shock and pain of it still lingered. And, he thought irritably, he was not looking forward to the interview with government officials from Washington. It had been his experience that most civil servants were somewhat less interesting than a Baptist sermon. Usually drab anyway, Washington officials tended towards a certain bureaucratic tedium, the result, undoubtedly, of serving in a city rife with political claptrap, in a profession complicated by Byzantine machinations and undue avarice. The combination was venomous, noxious, and altogether wearisome.

Somehow he managed to pull himself together and prepare a presentable package to the world. He studied his face in the mirror just prior to leaving, fully expecting to witness the ravages of the night etched there, but, as always, he looked excellent, the gift, he knew, of his good looks.

When he arrived at his office he found the two men from Washington already there. Bright and early, Kinder-Mann thought to himself, inwardly laughing at the ability of government officials to face the early morning hours. He introduced himself to them and led them into his office.

Both men were older; one was bald and short, the other

gray and of medium height. They were truly unremarkable, Kinder-Mann said to himself, as he tried to remember which was Robert and which was Howard. He couldn't remember, but he decided it didn't matter anyway.

"We simply wanted to discuss the epidemic in general," the gray-haired gentleman was saying, while the bald one nodded in agreement. "You've worked closely with the CDC, and we at the NIH are, for the moment, just monitoring the situation."

"Yes," the bald one said, still nodding, "as Howard says, we're interviewing the researchers working on this so that we have a full picture for the Secretary..."

"The who?" Kinder-Mann cut in. At least I can tell them apart, he thought to himself, since the bald one called the other one by name.

"The head of the whole Department," Howard answered, cutting in. "We're actually preparing a report for the department, along with the CDC."

"With funding in mind?" Kinder-Mann asked, hopeful.

"Not at the moment, I'm sorry to say," Robert answered. "Of course, the CDC is adequate at the moment, and we'll continue to monitor this as it progresses..."

"If it progresses," Howard cut in again.

"Oh, it will," Kinder-Mann said. He was beginning to like these two gentlemen. They seemed sincere and honest, not as he had expected. "But we will require a great deal of money, I can assure you of that," Kinder-Mann went on. "From just the few facts I was looking over last night, the epidemiological pattern is already quite alarming, enough to warrant a great deal of research. What about some funding from NIH? Will we have to go through the usual application procedures? You know they can take up to two years to get through..." Kinder-Mann was pursuing the question full steam; he knew the syndrome was serious and would take a while to resolve.

"Well," Howard began, "we've encountered the same question already, and all we can say is that what is there, is there, mostly at CDC. NIH will screen applications as always, of course, but the word is—and I tell you this from the higher-ups and in confidence—that we're more or less waiting to see what happens."

"That's already evident," Kinder-Mann said, irritated. "But you do have researchers on it?"

"Yes, of course," Howard answered. "But as you know, your work is the forefront. You and the CDC. That's why we want to get some sense from you where this is going, what sorts of questions you're looking into."

Kinder-Mann found this rather odd all of a sudden. His work was reported to the CDC; they were working on the same questions. It hardly warranted a special meeting and discussion. Irritated, he answered: "I'm examining a number of things, as you must know already. I just spoke with Liz Cronin at CDC this week."

"It was Liz that recommended we speak with you directly," Robert said.

"Oh," Kinder-Mann said, shrugging his shoulders. He realized it would do no harm to polish the apple with fellows from NIH. After all, it would take grants to continue his work. "Well, of course we're looking at several things. I've got medical records of a lot of the patients involved so far, and we're looking for epidemiological data as well as... well, anything, really. Since treatment for the immune problem keeps failing, our real task is to stop it. Which means finding the cause."

"A needle in a haystack is how Liz put it," Howard said.

"Exactly," Kinder-Mann said. "Look, we've got so many possibilities. It might be something in the environment of these people—for example, gay men use a lot of nitrite inhalants for sex. Or maybe it's specific sexual practices, like fist-fucking or something. It could be multi-factoral as well—a combination of disease history, poor health, certain medication histories, etcetera—that brings on the debilitated condition that eventually may lead to Kaposi's sarcoma. I just don't know right now."

Robert spoke up. "But what exactly are you doing right now?"

"My main assistant, Jack Slater, and I are preparing a study of the nitrite inhalants, but I already think that's way off base. From examining the few medical records I've gotten so far, I think we're looking at a specific infectious agent, a virus probably. Of course my reasoning is based on the fact of the few cases reported from the Haitian immigrants who haven't had any contact with the gay men or anything associated with them."

"Pretty much what Liz told us," Howard said, "but she didn't mention your report. Can you be sure you get a copy to us? We can include it in our report."

"Well, it will be some time before it's ready, but sure I will," Kinder-Mann agreed. He thought for a moment as he watched them sitting there, so placid, and decided that he needed to push some more.

"We *are* going to need a lot of money," he said to them. They both nodded in agreement. "I mean," he went on, "the sorts of tests and experiments we're already doing are extremely costly. And the treatments we're proposing—interferon, traditional chemotherapy, plasmophoresis—well, they cost a fortune, as you well must know. Can you do anything in your report to encourage more rapid funding?"

They both nodded again. "We'll certainly try," Howard said. "But it will undoubtedly take a while."

"But that's what I mean," Kinder-Mann said. "Can't you influence them back there to get the money-giving process quickened? We need money now, and we'll need a lot more very soon."

"We'll do our best," Howard reassured him. "After all, it really can't be long before grants are made, given the severity of the epidemic as you describe it and as CDC is recording it."

"Exactly," Kinder-Mann said, leaving it at that. They stood and shook hands and Kinder-Mann showed them out of his office. After they had gone, he stood at the windows and looked out at the ocean and the Golden Gate. He had a terribly uneasy feeling once again. This whole thing was taking a frightening turn. Not only was he dealing with a freak epidemic that defied all medical knowledge, his life was being disrupted by officials and by someone close having been struck by the disease. It didn't sit well with Kinder-Mann. As far as he felt at that moment, it was getting out of control.

13

In New York, Andy had spent an hour on the phone with his little sister. It had been a difficult conversation, more so than he had anticipated. At first she had been shocked, then, barely concealing her revulsion at the particulars, had grown unexpectedly cold and distant.

She had promised, at Andy's insistence, not to tell his parents or the other sisters about his illness or about the KS epidemic in general. But Andy wondered if she would keep her promise. He wondered if he really wanted her to.

After the call he had gone downtown to the office, hoping to put her response out of his mind by immersing himself in work. But he had ended up having to tell his supervisor the whole thing (why had he not realized he would have to sooner?), and so the workday became a wash, a useless puttering as he tried to maintain a veneer that would—within a very short period of time—fool no one as the news spread in City Hall.

To save his emotional life from total wreckage, he had finally abandoned himself to the reality that things were tough that day and had gone home and put himself to bed.

That afternoon, David, too, had called his family to tell the results of the biopsy. He had spoken to his mother, who had thanked him for telling her, but who then refused to discuss it further, denying his insistence with rejoinders about "social diseases" and promiscuous homosexuals. David realized it wasn't hatred; it was simple ignorance. And so together they put their heads under the covers, neither of them able to cheer the other. But it became a slow, quiet form of strengthening for them. Together they buried their heads and slept; together they held hands and said nothing; together they began the difficult task of facing it.

*

That night, in Philadelphia, Elizabeth Stone was telling her parents about her brother's biopsy and KS. "They don't know why it's happening, but gay men are getting this disease, and Andy's got it, too," she said.

Andy's father was shaking his head, his face a deeply vexed red. His fists clenched the arms of the recliner in which he sat. He was breathing heavily, unable to contain the information that Elizabeth was giving them.

Andy's mother sat there, seemingly mute. She had never fully adjusted to Andy's "problem," but to have it linked up somehow to this ghastly news was more than she could comprehend. Her stomach churned inside her — a mixture of nausea about the subject and a stronger horror, that of losing a child. "But Beth," she started, "Isn't there an operation for the cancer? Something to treat it?"

Elizabeth shook her head. "It's some kind of blood cancer or skin thing; I'm not sure. But it's not like a tumor or something they can cut out."

Andy's father exploded. "No more! I won't hear another word. I'll tell you what *should* have been cut out a long time ago!" He was trembling, on the verge of apoplexy.

"Please, honey, calm down," Andy's mother said. Elizabeth sat there, observing her father and wondering at his extreme reaction. She feared the worst: that he would somehow contact Andy and thus reveal that she had, already, broken the confidence.

"No, no more! That's the end of it," he commanded, picking up the remote control and flicking on the television. He pressed a button and the volume came up loud. Further conversation would have been impossible.

*

That night, in Brooklyn, Ruth Markman was telling David's father about the biopsy and Andy's ĸs. "Poor, poor David," she was saying. "To be involved in that kind of a situation and now this, too."

David's father shook his head. He wiped a tear from the corner of his eye. "It's awful, Ruth," he said, "the things that go on with all of that. So much suffering, so many problems. I never told you this — I never told David either, or anyone for that matter — but Harold was like that, too."

"Your brother?" she asked.

David's father nodded. "It runs in families, I'm sure. Harold was lost at sea in the merchant marines . . ."

"I know," she cut in.

"But I'm sure he threw himself overboard," he concluded. "That's why I've always been so worried about David. Now this." He shook his head and looked down at the floor.

Ruth Markman clasped her hands and muttered a prayer. Together they sat in silence, a single lamp casting a dull light around the living room of their cramped house.

14   *August 1981 • New York City*

Dr. Branch was thinking about the hospital morgue again. The heat was deadly. He had begun to feel sorry for himself, sorry that he had not, after all, taken a long summer vacation on some cool island off the coast of Maine. He looked at the clock on his desk and shook his head at the reading: 7:30 A.M. The day had barely begun, yet the place was already a furnace. Obviously, the so-called air conditioning was, once again, malfunctioning. And to be housed in these old bricks! he moaned to himself, wishing for the millionth time that summer that his offices were in the new wing, the wing where the air conditioning always worked.

But that wing contained the patient wards, and, he acceded, the patients required fresh, cool air, more than he. But as he wiped his brow with his handkerchief, he flashed on the chill morgue, seven stories below, in the basement. He even considered how cool and refreshing it would be to be lying on a long steel drawer, pushed into the dark of the morgue's vaults. He took an index card and scribbled his name across it, then fastened a rubber band to the card. He laid it on the edge of his desk and smiled; he would laugh whenever he saw it and thought of attaching it to his big toe, then heading for the morgue.

He had to be in the rear wing at eight o'clock, to be with Andy for his first treatment with chemotherapy. It was not a task he anticipated with much relish; it was bound to be painful—for him psychologically and for Andy physically.

This situation was one of the more difficult cases for Branch, as far as personal-patient involvement went. Having known Andy since he was delivered, so to speak, in that uptown restaurant, Branch found it painful to consider that he was now treating Andy for something that had a high probability of killing him.

There were few times that he thought the stricture against treating family and close ties was sensible, but this was one of those times. He realized that although it was extremely important for him to be there for Andy's initial treatment, it would be wise for Branch to refer him to an oncologist for the duration of the chemotherapy. Branch just couldn't face it, not on a weekly basis.

He stood up and slipped on his white lab coat, noticing the small tag he had made. True to his hope, it made him smile; perhaps he ought to pocket it and deliver himself to the morgue after Andy's chemotherapy treatment.

He walked into the outer office. Meg was already there, wearing a light cotton blouse and sorting through some files.

"Good morning, Meg," he said, stopping at her desk for a moment. "I'll be in oncology for a little while. Andy Stone's first treatment's this morning."

Meg nodded, a sympathetic look on her face. She understood the difficulty of the situation for all of them.

"Uh, please don't have me paged if there are any calls," he asked as he started to walk out. "I'll be back in half an hour or so."

"Okay," Meg agreed, watching him leave. Branch walked down the wide hall, nodding at medical students and colleagues, all pouring into the labs and offices. Day shift at Mt. Zion, he thought to himself, always too crowded, too busy.

Dr. Branch walked into an elevator and pressed "2." He would have to drop down four floors and then swing past the nurses' station in the new wing; he needed to look in on Margaret Thanberg, a friend of his wife who was confined to the hospital for breast cancer. The elevator stopped at the second floor, and Branch got out, turning to his right and making his way along another busy hall. Then, turning down another bright hallway to his left, he felt the first faint breezes. Air conditioning! he whispered to himself, realizing that the new wings were always perfect. He walked towards the patient ward, enjoying the cool air.

The nurses' station was a bustle of frantic activity as the graveyard shift gave way to the day personnel. The nurses were gathered in a circle, reporting their patient's conditions to the new shift. Branch stepped up to the station, hunted for Mrs. Thanberg's chart, and bumped smack into Dr. Irving Krantz, friend of Art Maguire and formerly chief of staff.

"Hello, there," Krantz said to Branch, already bristling with snobbery. Krantz was one of the most successful of Manhattan's surgeons, slick, costly, and powerful. He despised anything new, young, or different. At sixty, the man was tall, silver-haired, polished and altogether too spiffy for Branch's tastes. Word was that Krantz spent more time with his stockbroker than his patients.

"Good morning," Branch replied. "How are you, Irving?"

"Never better," the doctor replied, not looking up from the chart in which he was making voluminous notations. "What's up with you?"

"The usual," Branch replied, unable to locate Mrs. Thanberg's chart. He just stood there, waiting for a nurse to help.

"What're you doing down here?" Krantz asked, referring to Branch's presence in a patient ward.

"Oh, personal," Branch answered. "I'm on my way to oncology and thought I'd stop by to visit a friend of Carolyn's, Marge Thanberg."

"Ah, yes, Margie," Krantz said, finally looking at Branch for the first time. "She's doing very well. We got all the cancer and I'm sending her home first thing next week."

"Glad to hear it," Branch responded, wondering how anyone could tolerate this man.

Krantz turned toward Branch and leaned his elbow on the nurses' station, bending forward to speak more softly to Branch. Branch drew back momentarily; he trusted this man about as much as he would a scorpion.

Krantz spoke in low tones. "I heard you were trying for funds for this queer cancer thing."

Branch said nothing. He assumed Krantz had more to say.

"My advice to you is to go for it," Krantz went on. "I think this could be a really big thing; really big. And you need something like that."

Branch shook his head at the insult. How ridiculous this man is, he told himself, trying hard not to get snarled up in the games Krantz played. Finally, Branch answered: "That so?"

Krantz leaned back, a smug look on his face. "Come on, Walt, this is going to be a big deal, bigger than Legionnaires' or toxic shock. Fags are big news nowadays, and dead ones are even better news. Think what coverage this will get."

Branch was shaking his head, unbelieving, but Krantz went on.

"I mean, look; the day the CDC issued that report, the wires picked it up. That story appeared in the *New York Times,* the *L.A. Times,* everywhere there is a major paper. And I understand Fred Kinder-Mann is going hog-wild with research out there in California. Jump on it while it's hot, man."

Branch was still shaking his head. The unbridled avarice of this man irked him. But... there was a little voice inside him that knew Krantz was right. And he wanted— desperately—to work on the problem. In a matter of moments Branch decided that Krantz could be a good card to play.

Suddenly he was nodding his agreement. "You know, you're right. I spoke with Art about funds, but he was adamantly set against it. Cited UC San Francisco and Sloan-Kettering as being too far ahead of us."

Krantz was nodding now. "Right, I heard. I don't understand that either. I think you ought to go back and try again. Point out to him the media coverage this little outbreak has already had. And I know that others are picking up on the report. This month CDC will issue a follow-up report on it. And the *Times* may follow it up on that report as well."

Branch was playing the game. "Think you could drop a hint or two to Maguire?"

Krantz smiled broadly, but it was a conspiratorial grin. "Already done," Krantz said. "I spoke with him last night. Even put in for the funds myself."

Why the little prick! Branch said to himself. Standing here encouraging me to do something at which I've already been thwarted.

"What the hell do you mean by this?" Branch said mildly, irritated at Krantz's bizarre ploys.

Krantz smiled more fully. "There's room on board for everyone, Walt," he said. "Look, if this thing keeps developing, as I predict it will, we could have a whole new industry springing up overnight! Think of it!"

Branch didn't like to. Andy must be waiting by now. But Krantz was right. If what was circulating in the rumor mills was true, then Kinder-Mann was already eagerly pursuing a variety of research projects, and—word had it— several more cases of the rare cancer and pneumonia had already been reported to the CDC in the last month.

Branch was too irritated with Krantz now to keep up the game. "I'm sorry, Irving," he said. "But I've got to go treat a KS patient this very minute. A friend of mine, a young man, not even thirty yet. He's waiting in oncology for his first chemotherapy. I find it hard to share your enthusiasm."

Krantz nodded. "I see," he said, "the dedication is profound. Sorry about your friend." Krantz seemed genuinely embarrassed, but perhaps it was another ploy. "But..." Krantz said dully, "the wages of sin..." With that he turned and walked away. Branch had expected something like that; it would have been out of character for Irving Krantz to be truly embarrassed by his own carrying-on.

Branch glanced at his watch and realized he was already several minutes late. Mrs. Thanberg would have to wait. He hurried away to the stairwell, hoping to take the quickest route to the oncology department in the rear wing.

Irritation over Krantz's thoughtless remarks followed him as he hurried down the crowded halls.

Sure, Krantz was right. The outbreak of cancer and pneumonia was pretty amazing stuff from a research point of view, and it warranted attention. And it would probably get it. But to disregard so callously the suffering of the handful of men who had already contracted the diseases—in some self-gratifying hopes of personal accomplishment—was to disregard human dignity and medical ideals altogether.

But who was he fooling? Branch chided himself. Had he not, in his eagerness, literally begged Maguire to fund his research? Had he not, in some plain way of hope for his career, already dreamed of the glory to be gained by researching an epidemic of cancer? Krantz was right, and there was going to be a mad scramble to apply for grants, to jump into the fray. Where was he to fit into this scenario?

*

Andy had arrived at Mt. Zion precisely at eight o'clock. It was not something he was looking forward to. Not only was he scared beyond his wits, but the intense heat of an unrelenting August aggravated him greatly. He had found his way to the oncology department, and a pert young nurse had taken him to a small room and told him to lie down on the table and relax until Dr. Branch arrived.

Relax! Andy almost laughed at the suggestion. He lay down on the small table and stretched out, tried to position the tiny pillow comfortably under his head. He stared up at the white ceiling, one of those ceilings composed of square tiles punctuated with small holes. He tried to count the number of holes per square, but gave up when he got dizzy trying to focus his eyes. A long fluorescent tube hung from the ceiling, covered with a white plastic shade. The room was cool, at least. For the moment he could forget the rising temperature outside.

He relaxed his shoulders and closed his eyes, in an attempt to calm himself. He had insisted that David not accompany him: he wanted to do this on his own. For a moment he meditated on the cancer in his body, thinking that perhaps it would go away with the treatments, would vanish and that would be the end of that. But he doubted it. He had become too sick to feel that a cure would be easy, if even possible.

He lay there, waiting for Dr. Branch, slightly hurt that he should be late. But then, he reminded himself, Dr. Branch is very busy and it's very early. But he felt scared, alone, and a little bit abandoned.

He looked around the room. Not much to see, he thought. A set of cupboards, no window, a small stool, a trash bin of burnished aluminum with one of those lids that flipped open. There was a small steel table and several devices—oxygen lines, and so forth—attached to the wall.

Andy was growing uneasy. He was already tired, too; tired from the heat, from the worry. Then the door opened, and Dr. Branch came in. He put his hand on Andy's arm. "Good morning, Andy," he said, patting his forearm and smiling.

"Hi, Dr. Branch," Andy said, feeling even more uneasy. "Let's get this over with."

"Good idea," Branch said, turning to the young technician beside him. He took a syringe and needle from the technician and stood there. "We're going to start you out with 5cc of vincrystine," Branch said. "After about four or five weeks, we'll increase the dosage to 10cc. Now, I already explained to you that you really shouldn't feel anything right now, but this evening you might feel rather sick, so don't be alarmed."

Andy just nodded. The technician handed Branch a small elastic band, which he wrapped around Andy's left biceps, cutting off the circulation momentarily and causing his cephalic vein to stand out. Branch chose the enlarged median cubital vein for venipuncture and plunged the needle into the vein, loosening the elastic band as he did so. He depressed the plunger of the syringe, forcing the powerful vincrystine into Andy's bloodstream. Andy lay motionless, having expected something far worse. In a matter of seconds it was over.

Branch withdrew the needle and placed a cotton ball on

the puncture wound, then bent Andy's arm up to hold it tight. "Just leave it like that for a minute or two," he said to Andy, smiling and looking as reassuring as he could. Branch turned to the technician and said, "Make a note in the chart, will you: bolus injection, 5cc vincrystine, by venipuncture left median cubital vein." The young man wrote on the chart, then left.

"Feeling okay?" Branch asked Andy, who nodded his head. "Then I think you can sit up and get going. But before you go, I want you to meet someone else who's undergoing the same treatments. I arranged for him to come in at eight as well, through his doctor."

Andy frowned. "I don't understand."

"Patrick Ross, a patient of a colleague of mine, Dr. Fitzgerald. Just yesterday I learned that Dr. Fitzgerald had come upon another case very similar to yours, and I asked him to arrange Patrick's chemotherapy at the same time as yours. Won't you meet him?"

Andy was uncertain. "I don't know; I guess so. What's the point, though?"

Branch wasn't sure himself. "I'll be honest, Andy," he said. "I just thought it might be helpful to you to meet someone else who'll be going through the same thing you will."

Andy's eyes were brimming with tears as the reality of the situation sunk in once again, hitting hard as it always seemed to. "I'd like that," Andy finally said, meaning it. "But I'm kind of shy, you know that."

"Nonsense," Branch said. "Let's go." Branch and Andy walked out of the small room into a larger waiting area and hallway. Sitting in an orange plastic chair was a youngish-looking man with a light brown beard. Next to him, engaging in a quiet conversation, was Dr. Fitzgerald. Branch walked over to Dr. Fitzgerald to introduce Andy to Patrick Ross. Andy shook his hand and smiled. He had expected to feel some apprehension, but he felt a vague relief, something like coming home after a long trip. Andy sat beside Patrick and made small talk while the doctors conferred in the hallway. In a moment, Dr. Branch came back and interrupted them.

"I'm glad you two met," he said to them both. "Andy, I'd like you to come up to my office with me, if you can. I'd like to discuss the treatment with you."

"Okay," Andy said, and then, addressing himself to Patrick, said: "Why don't you come by on the weekend and meet my lover, too. I really would like to talk to you about this."

"Me too," Patrick said, handing Andy his phone number. They all stood and shook hands. Then Branch led Andy away, down the hall towards the bank of elevators at the end of the hallway. They said nothing as they walked; Branch was thinking about something, Andy could see, and Andy felt like silence anyway.

They got off at the sixth floor and started the long walk towards the front of the hospital, around to the left and into the old wing. As they walked along, there was a noticeable rise in the temperature. Finally, they were in the hall that led to Branch's office and lab. It was already broiling hot.

"Damn heat," Branch said, the first words to break their silence. They walked through Branch's waiting room, which was unusually empty and quiet, and went into the inner office. Branch indicated that Andy should sit in the big leather chair beside his desk, while he hung up his white lab coat and loosened his collar.

Branch sat at his desk and looked hard at Andy. He seems to be okay, Branch noted to himself, pleased that there was no immediate reaction to the vincristine. "You'll begin to feel it this evening," Branch said to Andy, who nodded and made a face.

"I just wanted to talk to you about this thing," Branch said. "The Center for Disease Control in Atlanta has issued an update, and it is becoming more evident that there's real trouble here. This thing is very, very strange: the epidemiological pattern here follows no normal pattern so far, either in time or incidence."

Andy shrugged his shoulders. He already knew that things were weird.

Branch went on: "There has been a suggestion that

there might be a link between repeated venereal infections and an acquired immunosuppression..."

"But..." Andy began to interrupt, but Branch held up his hand.

"I know, but you haven't had repeated venereal infections. So there's an exception to this 'immune-exhaustion' theory. I'd like to report it to the CDC. I'd like to report your medical history to them as well, and then they'll probably want to interview you, here in New York of course — questions about your lifestyle history. Would you object to that?"

Andy shook his head; he didn't mind.

"Good. I'll report your case this afternoon, then. I'd held off, because I didn't want to betray your right to confidentiality. But this is serious enough already to demonstrate that every bit of data that's collectable has got to get to the researchers. And I'm going to keep on trying to win some money to get further into this thing myself."

Andy nodded, impressed with Branch's confidence and determination. Branch noticed Andy's response; he only hoped that he could find a way to get Maguire to lay out some funds very soon.

Andy said he needed to get home and get to bed. Branch agreed it was a good idea and sent him out with the reminder that the reaction to the vincrystine should set in later that day, and not to hesitate to call about it. Andy promised he would if it was too bad.

*

Later that day, just after lunch, Branch had called the CDC and filed a report. Then he had gone over the CDC reports again, his mind a jumble at the incredibly high mortality rate.

At lunch, Branch had run into Irving Krantz again, and for a few minutes Krantz had urged Branch to speak with Maguire. Krantz was extremely crass, with crude references to fags and perverts, but he was damn sincere about the glories to be garnered for Mt. Zion, should a research project be commenced there.

And so, Branch had stormed into Art Maguire's office,

his second such meeting. He had demanded that research funds be made available at once, to which Maguire had responded with his usual rebuttal about the "sensitive" nature of the problem, about the politics of doing research that might alleviate a problem created by "practices of a deviant population."

Branch had blatantly pointed out the nonsense of Maguire's arguments, but to no avail. In the midst of their meeting, Maguire had abruptly called it off and literally ordered Branch out the door. His fat face had been red in his deep vexation. Branch had left, realizing that there would be no persuading Maguire within the usual and accepted methods. If he were to change Maguire's mind, it would have to be in some other way.

*

Branch headed straight for his own office, wishing that anything would happen to cool it down. He might have to leave the hospital early if the heat didn't break. He got off the elevator on his floor and just caught sight of Max Leider disappearing around a corner.

"Max!" he shouted, bringing Leider's head around the corner.

"Walt," Leider said. "I was just stopping in to see you."

"You're back!" Branch said, having missed his friend for a few days.

"Oh, yes, that," Leider said. "I'm getting tired of all this traveling for my research. I've got to slow down."

"What did you want to see me about?" Branch said.

"I wanted to ask if Maguire got back to you on your research request..."

"Sure as hell did," Branch said gruffly. "I'm just coming from a second meeting with the old pig. Won't budge. Not a dime."

"It's the shits, isn't it?" Leider said. "I figured as much."

"What the hell are we going to do here?" Branch asked. "About Maguire? We do need the money, you know. If Mt. Zion holds back, it'll look mighty strange. Besides, it's downright wrong."

Leider shook his head. "Well, you're right, Walt, but

remember, it's not too serious yet. And Mt. Zion has millions of dollars already tied up in ongoing cancer research as it is. Plus the new interferon lab. That's tremendous stuff, and it will encompass any serious developments with this new epidemic; so far, anyway, the KS outbreak is pretty small."

"That's what I know is the reasonable way to look at it," Branch agreed, seeing for a moment the bigger picture as sketched by Leider. "But dammit, I've got a bad feeling about this. Maybe it's my personal involvement with Andy Stone..."

"Yes," Leider cut in, then fell silent again, thinking. "What we need to figure out," he started again, "is what you *can* do, something that doesn't need a great deal of research time and money at the moment, until you can wrangle something out of this grand institution. Don't you have some connection to the media, to the gay press?"

"Yes," Branch answered. "Andy Stone's lover is a journalist."

"Why not get together with them, find out exactly what the gay community thinks of this. Maybe together you can raise a voice to direct attention towards the problem. Form a bond to share and spread information? You've got the stature, he's got the connection to the gay press."

"I'll do that," Branch said, thinking that at the very least he could provide some clear medical information to the gay press.

"But remember," Leider said, "remember that you're a straight doctor representing the straight medical establishment. Always keep that in mind."

Branch thought about that. It was good advice. He also thought about the fact that it was the only advice that Max had to offer. Okay, so Branch would get together with David and get some word out, some useful information. But he wasn't about to give up on Maguire.

15

That night, at home in their apartment, David sat with Andy, who felt alternately fine and miserable. "It's like a battleship rocking in my gut." That's how Andy described the sudden waves of violent nausea, cramps, and migraine that would seize him. Then, after torturing him for a time, it would pass, but only for a short while. Andy was now, of course, in a state of deep anxiety over his existence and the prospect of continued chemotherapy.

"Talk about anything," he had pleaded to David, hoping to turn his fears and pain away from his present suffering. And so they had discussed the appointment of Sandra Day O'Connor to the Supreme Court. When that failed, David read a story from *Time* to Andy—the reportage of Lady Diana's marriage to Prince Charles.

It all seemed at such a remove that Andy did feel better, at least emotionally. But the discomfort that wracked his body could not be allayed; it was the powerful vincrystine attacking him, and, he hoped, his cancer.

Though Andy was visibly wrecked, David suffered as well. On the verge of tears at the sight of Andy so stricken, he summoned all his inner resources to remain strong, loving. But it was almost too hard. Andy had wasted away so much in the last two months, and now this. Had David been less of a man than he was, he would have packed up and walked out. The demand on his strength was nearly unbearable. But he couldn't abandon Andy, no matter what.

Finally, toward the end of the evening, Andy felt slightly better, though completely drained. They lay in bed, and Andy told David about meeting Patrick Ross that morning, about what it had meant to see another gay man with KS.

David listened in silence, unable to comprehend. He was glad that Andy would have someone else to talk with, to rely upon for support these next few weeks of chemotherapy. David knew, unless something changed very soon, that he would become unable to cope with it all. He would not leave Andy, no; but he could feel the tension ebb and flow as Andy murmured about Patrick, and, as he slipped into a semi-sleeping state, his mind felt the real pain, as though it might explode. No, he couldn't stand it; he felt it would—if it all got worse—push him too far after all.

*

Across town, Carolyn Branch languished on the overstuffed velvet sofa, to which she, in her rather austere and overstuffed manner, still referred as "the davenport." Walt Branch, having left the hospital early to escape the heat and spent the afternoon and evening making love to a surprisingly fervid Carolyn, reclined beside her with a stiff drink.

"Walter, dear," she whispered, taking his hand and kissing his fingers, "what is wrong? You've been positively beside yourself this afternoon."

"Oh?" he answered absently. "I guess I needed to get something out of my system."

"What is it?" Carolyn was not one to beat around the bush. Now that they had exhausted their reservoirs of passion, she wanted to know what lay behind her husband's freneticism.

"It's Andy Stone, I guess," he confessed, sensing as he did Carolyn's sigh and sadness.

"I see," she said quietly. "When, by the way, do you suppose that grant will come in?"

"You'll probably know before I do," he said, not disparagingly, simply as an honest appraisal.

"Yes, maybe," she said. "Well, we'll see about the funding then."

"Yes, we will," he agreed. And to end the conversation, he bent down and kissed Carolyn fully.

16

ATLANTA, Aug. 28, (AP)—Two rare diseases have struck more than 100 homosexual men in the United States in recent months, killing almost half of them, and a medical study group has been formed to find out why, the national Centers for Disease Control said today.

The disease control agency reported in June and July that 26 cases of Kaposi's sarcoma, a rare form of skin cancer, and 15 cases of pneumocystis, a form of pneumonia caused by a parasitic organism, had been found in homosexual men since January 1980.

Since the midyear reports, new reports have brought the totals to 53 cases of pneumocystis, 47 of Kaposi's sarcoma, and 7 cases in which patients had both diseases. One additional case was that of a woman who contracted pneumocystis. Of the patients whose sexual preference was known, 94 percent were homosexual men.

The new cases were reported by doctors who diagnosed them after reading the initial report, said Dr. Harold Jaffe, a member of the study group.

Kaposi's sarcoma is a rare disease that characteristically strikes elderly men and is seldom fatal. But the majority of homosexual patients were young men and 17 percent of those who were stricken have died so far. The disease agency says that of every three million Americans, two persons could be expected to get that form of cancer.

Almost 60 percent of the pneumocystis patients died. In some cases, pneumocystis preceded the cancer. The two diseases sometimes occurred separately and sometimes in combination. The disease center has no statistics on the incidence of pneumocystis in the general population, but said that its occurrence was extremely unusual, although it has become slightly more common among cancer patients whose immunities are suppressed by medication.

Nobody knows why homosexual men get the disease, Dr. Jaffe said. There may be a link to some previous infection, or the victims may have a problem with their immune systems. The diseases may be linked to their sexual lifestyle, drug use or some other environmental cause, although no evidence of those connections has been found.

The study group of 20 experts from the disease control center's cancer, viral, parasitic and venereal disease branches is trying to determine if the problem is limited to homosexual men and, if so, why they seem to be catching the diseases at unusually high rates, Dr. Jaffe said.

17

That night, Jim and Rita stopped by David and Andy's apartment for a few minutes to see how Andy was doing and to talk about the article in the *New York Times*. Andy had been somewhat shaken by the article, even though he had heard the details prior to its publication from Dr. Branch. But to see it in print in the *Times* was another matter. He and David sat on the couch opposite the armchairs in which Jim and Rita settled themselves. It was still hot, the dog days, and the windows of the apartment were open wide.

"I can't believe my mother," Jim was saying as they talked about the report in the paper. "She calls me up this afternoon, from Bangor, saying 'Did you see the piece about gay cancer, Jimmy?' Then she proceeded to read the whole thing to me over the phone, despite my reassurances to her that I had already seen it."

"Oh, god," Rita moaned. "Your mother is such a nutcase." She shook her head and smiled.

Andy looked amused. "I wonder if my folks saw it," he said. "But then, they don't much read the *Times*."

"Neither do mine," David said. "What else did your mother say, Jim?"

Jim was shaking his head, indicating his amusement with his mother's behavior. "She warned me not to eat in any restaurants that had gay waiters!"

"Oh, no!" Rita shrieked. "You'll have to go to Wyoming then for dinner!"

He fixed her with a helpless expression. "Cowboys, Rita, cowboys. I'm afraid the country is rife with faggotry."

She shook her head. "You wish, honey." There was a slight lull in the conversation. David lit a cigarette and sat back. Rita took a good look at Andy and felt her heart skip a beat. His hair was thinning out a bit, no doubt from the chemotherapy. His cheeks were hollow and there were deep, dark circles around his eyes. It was the eyes that troubled Rita most; though Andy was attentive, his eyes betrayed that glazed, preoccupied look of the terminally ill, all of which was heightened by the shadows.

"Oh, honey," she said, seriously, looking at Andy. "How is it?"

He nodded, not speaking for a moment. "I'm doing okay, really I am. The treatments make me sicker than the disease, though. I mean, look at me. I wasn't this bad off until they started in with the injections."

She nodded. "But they're necessary, huh? I mean, you don't have any choices, do you?"

He shook his head and raised his eyebrows. "No, not according to Dr. Branch. The disease is serious enough that anything less just wouldn't do it."

"Shit," she said with such conviction that the expletive became a word of encouragement. She slammed her fist down on the arm of the chair. Visibly anguished, she began to speak in harsh political jargon: "I can't bear to see this happen to my gay brothers." Jim stared at her in astonishment at her passion. "To think that there is a killer out there, striking gay men down because of their promiscuity or whatever it is...it isn't fair! There's no good reason that any of us should have to suffer anything like this! No fucking reason at all."

"I don't know about that," Andy said. "Maybe all that bathhouse life just isn't healthy, and this is simply the result."

"I don't know," she said. "I get so angry and hurt about this topic. You know how political I am. I've never satisfied myself about how to reckon with you guys' promiscuity. I mean the piggish take-what-you-want thing is so macho, so intrinsically male." She held up her hand when she saw the three men bristle at the remark. "Wait, now hold on and hear me out. I understand the liberation of it, the opposition to standard moral strictures, the freedom of male sexuality in an atmosphere completely un-dictated by females—straight women, that is—and their love-and-marriage routine that just says fuck the men and their sex needs. But the part that screws it up is that you guys don't do it with any respect, not any different than straight men would do it. Just take what you want, forget that the other man—or men—has feelings, is a warm human being who needs to be nurtured and responded to, and . . ."

She stopped at her own digression and looked at the three men, all of them looking alternately like reprimanded boys and defensive men. "I'm sorry," she said, directly to Andy. "To turn your problems into my soapbox again. I hope that doesn't happen with everybody else."

"I know what you mean," Jim said. "When you went into such an impassioned speech just now, it occurred to me that if the epidemic persists, everyone from every imaginable political and religious persuasion will have to make their own passionate comment on it."

Andy was silent, as was David. Rita addressed Andy: "Honey, I hope you don't become a topic of debate around town."

"So do I!" he said, somewhat half-humoredly.

She went on. "God, it could be touchy, couldn't it? Imagine this—anybody could take this and use it as evidence to slander gays and their lifestyle, forgetting, of course, about lesbians. Let me think for a minute . . ." She paused and closed her eyes, bringing her hand up to her forehead as she thought something through. The men were silent, knowing her posture signaled an imminent comment that was, quite probably, going to be right on target. "And," she started, still keeping her eyes veiled, "there will be a role for dykes to play here . . . and it will be easy to confuse it with us trying to jump on the bandwagon of your problems, which will happen, believe me . . . when the real role for lesbians in matters of gay health problems is . . ." She stopped to focus her thought. "Is...is to remind that lesbians have health problems as well, needs for lesbian-oriented care, and...wait, that's off-beam again..." She stopped short of her point.

David spoke up. "And to help pull all gay people together to adopt a new approach to health care for gay people?"

She shook her head. "No, no, not health care—although that's important, yes. The focus should be to adopt new attitudes towards each other, attitudes that respect each other's souls and bodies. That's it!" She held her hands up triumphantly.

Andy nodded, but said nothing. He resented, slightly, that his serious problem was the brunt of all Rita's preaching again. She read this in his face. "Oh, no," she moaned. "I'm still doing it. How awful." She shook her head and then said, "I'm sorry, Andy."

He smiled. "It's okay, Rita."

"Remember, honey," she said. "I love you."

"Thanks!" Andy said. He needed the support. She turned to Jim and said, "Let's go and let them rest, huh?" They got up to go. Rita went and hugged Andy, but, for the second time, Jim went straight for the door. It was apparent he did not want to be near Andy, no matter what his concern. It was a small thing, really, but Andy noticed it. And he would not dismiss it.

18   *October 1981 • New York City*

In celebration of the end of summer and its merciless heat, David and Andy had spent the afternoon walking in Central Park, enjoying the vivid fall colors, the cool bite of the autumn air. Autumn was Andy's favored season, a time when he always felt a surge of energy, reveling in the strangely warm days, the crisp nights.

And now, this fall, he again felt that surge of extra energy, despite the drain of the cancer and the chemotherapy. Their walk had to be punctuated by frequent rest stops, when Andy would sit quiet and catch his breath.

He was very thin now, very pale. It was difficult to recognize that this was the same young man who, just months before, had been strong, muscular, exercising with weights regularly at the gym, avidly pursuing his job at City Hall. The chemotherapy had taken its toll in the few weeks since it had begun. How he dreaded that weekly visit to the hospital, the mundanity of being shown to the same room by the same technician, asked to lie down and wait. The drug that poured into his veins was powerful, destroying not only the cancer, but always chipping away at what was left of his stamina.

He hadn't been able to talk with Patrick as he had hoped, because within a week of commencing chemotherapy, the young man had taken a serious turn for the worse and been hospitalized in isolation. Knowing that Patrick had done so badly did not reassure Andy about his own progress. He remained scared and doubtful.

And so they walked together in the park, trying to create a small moment of privacy in the medical horror that their lives had become. They had walked aimlessly, had listened to two violinists, had picked out the few elms and maples here and there, now vivid in autumnal splendor, had remembered their first walk in the park, four years earlier, when they had met after the gay parade.

They didn't talk too much as they walked. There was, at times, more distance in their relationship. Some of that distance was a result of the physical withdrawal from the relationship that Andy had accomplished. Dr. Branch had warned them to observe precautions as though Andy had infectious hepatitis, which didn't rule out everything, but as Andy grew weaker and more involved in his illness, his sexual inclination was dimmed. This had been hard on David especially, for he remained vibrant and sexual, while Andy, at his own admission, had lost all interest in the activity which he held responsible for his disease. The tension had not been so much between them over this—surely David could not blame Andy—but rather became a growing problem for David, who felt at times overwhelmed with sexual frustration.

But in that tension, and in that ending, there had emerged a new strength, something neither of them had really bothered to contemplate. Because it was the cancer itself — and its ensuing imposition on their lives — that had, in another way, forced them together, closer in loving support, more so than before. Andy had learned to be dependent; and David had had to confront his life, see that he had let himself become too wrapped up in their relationship, letting his career and other interests slide. Though now, when he should have been considering the future, he felt more and more drawn into the world of illness, its rhythms and concessions.

Andy had not decided fully to fight the cancer, and this indifference to life had drawn David down further, in a sense of protection, of helping Andy to make the transition. It was something unspoken, this acceptance of impending death and its accommodation, but it was a deep current, running strong.

They both knew that the prognosis was not good. The chemotherapy had really shown no results; in fact, two more lesions had appeared since the treatment had begun, and both Andy and David knew that the probability of remission was slim. They admitted this reality in their own ways — Andy remaining listless, David protective and brewing beneath the surface. It was as if the cancer had deepened their bond, while still chipping away at it.

They left the park when the evening began to close in on them. They walked home, a long walk that tired Andy a great deal, but which he insisted they continue. They maintained a silence as they went; they had talked it all out, it seemed, already. But for the first time, Andy noticed that other young men were cruising David, turning their heads to get a second look at David's compact, muscular body, his flashing brown eyes, the quick, sexy movements as he walked, always nervous. And in that, Andy felt an assurance that David would be all right once he was gone. Andy turned to catch a glimpse of the two of them reflected in a storefront glass. David was still strong, sexy, but he himself was a bad sight, so thin, so very exhausted. There was nothing he could do; the illness wore itself on his face. But yes, David will attract someone else, Andy told himself.

David, too, noticed the young men glancing in his direction, but he, unlike Andy, took no reassurance from the fact. For it had begun to work its way into his thoughts that he, too, might be infected with the disease that would eventually take Andy. And how could he knowingly attempt to connect himself with another man under those circumstances? Even more, who would wish to risk the chance of connecting with David, once they knew that David's lover of four years had contracted the deadly gay plague and eventually died from it? It would turn David into a monk, really, because there were no options for him once Andy was gone. The fury of the hopelessness in the situation soured in David's mind, turned his fears and anxieties in on himself; he was becoming more and more distressed by the events of the disease. Somehow, something had to come to the surface, had to expose the mystery and the "I don't knows" and all the goddamn suffering.

When they finally got home, Andy fell to the couch and breathed deeply, grateful for the beauty of the day, disappointed at his body's inability to cope with it. David put some music on the stereo, a Schubert quartet. He sat beside Andy on the cream-colored couch, sinking deep into the cushions. He pulled the brass lamp alongside, picking up his book to read. Ever since Andy's diagnosis two months before, he had been reading Ayn Rand's *Atlas Shrugged*, savoring the protracted unfolding of the story.

But he couldn't read. He turned his head and glanced at Andy, now with his eyes closed and breathing deeply, asleep. He realized that Andy wasn't doing well at all; he had taken particular note of Andy's pace of late, a subtle, almost undetectable letting-go of haste, as though the race were done. It was there in the stack of unread paperwork beside Andy (he hardly worked at all now); it was there in his indifference. It was something David did not fully understand.

But was it a good thing? Was it perhaps some sign of recovery after all? A letting-go of stress? Or was it the other, the darker reality, an abandonment of the fight, a fuller concession to cancer, to inevitable death? David knew, of course, that it was the latter, for Andy himself referred more frequently now to the end, to his death, but they had not discussed it, not yet. David greeted such comments with silence, because, honestly, he didn't know how to reach Andy with the real questions about it. It was too much to talk about, too painful to face that Andy was giving up, that the disease was winning the battle.

And while David shouted in his mind a refusal to believe, his refusal resolved always in two contradictory feelings: acceptance and suspicion. He would realize that yes, it's true, Andy will die; and he would grow suspicious of the disease, of medicine, of the fact that no one offered any answers.

But no, he told himself, putting the book back down, he would think of it later, after dinner. Now it was time to cook.

*

Later, after dinner, he and Andy lay in bed again. Andy had needed to get to bed early, and David had decided to join him. He sensed that Andy wanted to talk, and he hoped that it would be the moment to open up those questions and unresolved fears he knew they both kept silently locked away.

Then he felt Andy caress his neck, very gently. "What's the matter?" Andy asked.

So here it is, David thought, the moment to talk, to really talk. But David didn't answer. He knew he must go gently—not so much for Andy's sake as for his own.

"I'm afraid," David finally said, simply, unable to continue.

"Of what?" Andy asked quietly.

There were tears in David's eyes. He broke away and sat up in bed, leaning his back against the headboard, ran his fingers over the edge of the sheet. "That I'm going to lose you." He began to cry, realizing that he had just joined Andy in finally admitting their helplessness.

Andy sat up beside him, put his hand on David's leg. He

said nothing. Finally, he spoke: "We need to talk about it. I have things to say."

David sighed. They were on dangerous ground now. The subject was open, wide open. David began to talk, turning to clinical realities; he was evading the issue. "But we still don't even know what's wrong, not really," he said. "What did Dr. Branch tell you? There are already a hundred cases across the country, and half of them are dead? That's too bizarre. I just can't believe that's happening to us."

"But you read the thing in the *New York Native*, didn't you? I know you saw that stuff in the papers; it's real, very real. It just doesn't make much sense right now."

"Jesus," David whispered. "What the fuck is it? How did it happen?"

Andy shook his head, reached over to the bedside table for a glass of water. "That's what we're all asking ourselves. I've asked Dr. Branch, but nobody knows why or how. Especially the why and how of the gay connection. That's why I had hoped to talk to Patrick, to find out just for my own peace of mind how he thought he got it; but it's already too late for that..." Andy broke off for a moment, and David could sense his pain and isolation; it had troubled Andy deeply that Patrick had worsened so rapidly. Finally, Andy went on: "Dr. Branch says it's highly unusual for any disease to confine itself to any one social grouping. Ethnic groups, yes, but not like this."

"Maybe it's a coincidence?" David said, not believing his own words.

"No..." Andy said, his voice failing. He sat silent for several minutes. "But I can't help but wonder if it's something we did. I mean, what if I weren't gay? There are all those happy heterosexual family units all across America; they've never even heard of this thing. It's like a punishment, that's how I feel sometimes. Like God has waved his hand and said that we must pay."

David was shocked. "Pay for what?" he said angrily. "That's ridiculous!" he exclaimed. "This is a matter of germs, poisons, chemicals, cancer, the real science stuff, not the middle ages. Not God exacting revenge. Really!"

"Don't mock me, David, please," Andy pleaded. "I'm just thinking out loud, just let me talk. I don't know if I really feel all these things or not, but it all seems so dark, like it's just the beginning of something awful. Being gay is so hard, and you should see the way I feel at the hospital. Everybody is nice and all, but they know what's going on; it's like they look at me and think 'There's one of them.' It's hard to understand until you've felt it, but it's like an exaggeration of all the stigma we've always felt for being gay.

"It's always been so hard, and now this doesn't make it easier. It's the final blow, really. Nobody will let you be yourself, and now that I'm sick, its a double whammy. You know how they treat me when I do go into the office? I've had to come *all* the way out because of this, and the admission that goes along with it—that I have gay sex, that it's made me sick somehow . . . it's like they always said. And they treat me like a leper, like I'm leaving germs all over the place.

"I keep coming back to that feeling that it's so hard to be gay, to be yourself. Everywhere you look there's a constant reminder that we don't fit—billboards, magazines, TV. Nothing speaks to us; nothing speaks *for* us. We're shut off somehow, locked into our charming little ghettoes, dancing in our fabulous discos, but nobody sees us. Nobody sees us! They just want us to be invisible, gone, just like the blacks thirty, forty years ago.

"But now they have to see us, and they have to see us as sick. You know Mitch at the office? He won't even look at me now that I'm sick. He won't come near me. It's worse than if he had hated me for being gay, worse than it was in school when everyone shunned me because I was gay. It's much worse, because he's staying away from me because I am gay *and* because I have gay cancer.

"I can't help but wonder if it isn't somehow to their advantage. You know, fags getting sick with AIDS and cancer, dying, spreading disease. It plays right into their hands, lets them stigmatize us for real, with good, hardcore scientific evidence that we are sick, dangerous. And when we're gone? When I'm gone? . . ." His voice trailed off.

"They'll be happy," David finished the sentence, feeling dark and grim. Andy was depressing him—he had no idea he had grown so morbid—but he also knew that everything Andy had said, he had already thought.

*

Later, as Andy lay sleeping, David reconstructed their conversation. Something Andy had said had lodged in his mind and was providing strength. It nagged at him for more consideration, but he couldn't quite pinpoint it. And then he remembered. "Nobody sees us," Andy had said. "They just want us to be invisible..." That had been aching in the back of David's mind for the rest of the evening.

And as he lay there in the dark, listening to the soft breathing of his lover, David Markman decided that it was about time to do something to change that. He felt the pent-up tension and insanity flow out as he realized a goal; he would write about the medical crisis, would let those people know that something was going on in gay America, something serious, something deadly. At least I can play on their darkest wish to make them see us, he thought, force them to confront the reality of their hateful instincts. He knew he was overreacting, overestimating the prejudice perhaps, but he also knew that it was the force that compelled him to write. He had felt, lately, that he might burst if something didn't change, and now he saw that he could help change it by blowing it up, publicly. He quickly fell to sleep, his mind at peace once again with the vision of a goal.

*

The next morning, David told Andy what he had decided to do. He would start writing, interviewing, calling—uncovering whatever information he could about the crisis and getting it into print. He wanted to find out what had been done, and use his reportage to urge that more be done.

"It won't be easy," Andy said. "Although I see how dead fags will make good copy."

"Christ, Andy, cheer up," David said, his enthusiasm

[127]

for his pet project casting energy all around him. But Andy would not be cheered. He was due at the hospital that morning for more chemotherapy, the last of the present treatment before he would undergo a brief respite. If he failed to respond—as was the case so far—the next step would combine chemotherapy with cobalt, not a pleasant prospect.

But Andy was distracted, preoccupied; David could sense it. "What's wrong?" he asked Andy, "What's got you so quiet?"

Andy looked up at David. "It's Patrick Ross," he said. "Something in the back of my mind keeps tugging at me, and it has to do with Patrick."

"The guy you never got to talk to?"

"Yes," Andy answered. "I think he's dying; I feel it somehow."

David looked askance at Andy. What's this? he asked himself.

"I'm going to try to get in to see him this morning, I think," Andy said.

"Will they let you?"

"Yes, I think so," Andy said, sounding mysterious. He wasn't sure himself why he was so absorbed with Patrick, a young man he didn't even know, whom he had met only once. But something was there, something that compelled him to visit the young man.

19

Andy made his weekly sojourn to Mt. Zion, but before going to the oncology department for the injection, he stopped at the twelfth floor of the new patient wing, to see Patrick Ross. At the nurses' station he had only to say that Dr. Walter Branch had sent him to get the okay to visit the young man, but the nurse in charge specified that Patrick was in isolation, and, therefore, Andy would have to wear a gown, mask, gloves and cap—primarily to protect Patrick from further invading organisms that Andy might bring in.

Just as he was about to go in, the nurse took him aside to stress that he shouldn't stay long, that Patrick was in critical condition. "And," she went on, "you are aware that he is blind?"

This fact struck Andy hard. "No," he gasped.

"The worst of it struck his nervous system," she explained tactfully. "He's fine otherwise, he just can't see you."

Andy nodded, took a deep breath, and went in. Patrick lay in the hospital bed, his head turned toward the window. He sensed that someone was in the room. "Who's that?" he asked weakly.

"It's me, Andy Stone," Andy said, "the guy you met a few weeks ago at chemotherapy. Remember?"

"Yes, yes, I do," Patrick said, turning his face in the direction of Andy's voice. Andy walked up to the bedside and touched Patrick's hand. Patrick smiled. "I'm glad you came. My family's been here, but still it gets lonely. And I wanted to tell you something."

"Yes?" Andy asked, wondering at the remark. After all, they didn't know each other. How could Patrick want to tell him something?

"Yes," Patrick said, his voice almost a whisper. "I wanted to tell you how this happened."

"Oh . . ." Andy said. It was what he had hoped to discuss with Patrick before the young man had taken so ill, but had never had the chance. "That's what I wanted to ask you, too," Andy said.

"Good, then you know, too?" Patrick asked, his tone slightly conspiratorial.

"Know?" Andy said. "I don't know. Nobody knows. Do they?"

Patrick nodded his head feebly. "Yes, I know. I overheard it in the hall; I'm sure of it. And when I asked the nurses and doctors about it, they all acted as though I were dreaming. So I know it's true."

"I see," Andy said, a tear forming at the edge of his eye for this stranger lying before him. He could tell now that this shell of a man was just a whisper of the one he had met only weeks before, and the senseless babble was disheartening; Andy didn't like to consider that he, too, might end in madness.

"Yes, yes," Patrick mumbled on. "It's the government, you know. They did it. To get rid of the homosexuals. I'm sure of it now. They got some kind of virus from the Pentagon, something wild, vicious. Yes, yes, they got something from their germ warfare bank and you see, then they let it go in the bathhouses or something like that, don't you see? And then, of course, it spread, slowly, but getting more and more of us, until finally, you see, they can round us all up as public health hazards or something like that? It's perfectly reasonable what I'm telling you..." His hand reached out for Andy, but not seeing, it grabbed at thin air. Andy reached for his hand and held it in his own.

"Please, Patrick," Andy said gently, wishing that there was something he could do. He had never heard a wilder tale, the ramblings of a mind gone bad. "Please stop talking and rest." Andy realized that they could not have carried on a decent conversation after all. Patrick was too ill, too far gone.

"But you must let them know," Patrick protested, his voice cracking. Speaking seemed to be a great effort for him. "You've got to let them know that they can't get away with this...it won't work. They got me, but you can stop it all by letting the cat out of the bag..." He broke into a fit of coughing that virtually shook his body from head to toe.

Andy sat on the edge of the bed and held onto Patrick's hand. The coughing subsided, but Patrick didn't speak. Andy tried to talk to him further, but he was too far, in a state somewhere between sleep, madness and death. For a long time Andy just sat there and stared at Patrick, sick with the image of a bright young man dying in such misery and wildness. It had a profound effect on Andy at that moment, and Andy felt that he had, somehow, not tried hard enough; he had conceded to the cancer too soon.

And as he sat there, holding Patrick's thin, weak hand in his own, Andy decided that he would either beat this thing or go with dignity. After all, he told himself, remembering that day two months earlier, "I am to have my own death."

Finally, when Patrick had slipped into sleep, Andy let go his hand, let it fall gently on the sheet, and then left.

20

Branch, anxious to execute Leider's suggestion about teaming with David on press coverage, had arranged to meet David and Andy that night. He had seen Andy that morning, when he'd been in for his chemotherapy treatment—and he had noticed that Andy seemed very troubled, preoccupied, though he had declined to discuss it. And so, Branch knew that the evening might hold more than a brief meeting with David about the AIDS crisis. He was prepared to talk.

They met at David and Andy's apartment for dinner. Andy asked to hear the Hindemith *Ludus Tonalis* after dinner, and so they gathered in the living room to listen and talk. It had been some time since Dr. Branch had been to their place. Once, about three years earlier, he had stopped in on a Sunday afternoon at Andy's request, as they were giving an open house. He was impressed with the improvements they had made.

Andy was in unusually good spirits, though a bit weak and tired. He had managed to eat only a small portion at dinner, but now, settled in the sofa, he was relaxed, ready to talk. There was—both Branch and David could detect— some subtle change in Andy's attitude. He seemed less desperate, less hopeless; there was a hint of something stiffer in his posture, and his face no longer hid an expression of fear.

It was his dignity they witnessed, the resolute and abrupt decision on his part that morning that he would face the cancer and his death with dignity, with strength. It wasn't that the fear and anxiety were gone; it was that he perceived it as solely his burden, that he would shoulder as he could. He would not end it in madness and confusion.

The conversation was plain, Andy reflecting rather abstractly on his condition and the state of the medical crisis in general. Finally, out of curiosity, Branch decided to push it with a question about work, about how Andy's co-workers had dealt with it all.

"Well, it's been tough on me," he answered, "But now I'm more or less resigned from the position—an extended leave of absence they call it." There was a bitter tone of irony in his voice. "But before—at the onset of the cancer and the treatment—I had to come completely out of the closet, since the *Times* articles and the spot on the evening news. I just couldn't lie about it, and the information was out anyway.

"But still, I'm amazed at how many people hadn't heard of the KS epidemic, or if so, they knew it as 'gay cancer,' something terribly bizarre and beyond themselves. Having me there forced them to confront their ignorance, and their feelings about gays and, of course, about death."

Branch was interested. "What have they said? How do they deal with it? I mean, do they actually sit and talk with you?"

Andy looked down for a moment, his fingers tracing a circle on the fabric of the couch. "Well, no," he said, a little sad. "Most of my friends at work are oddly reticent to bring it up. I suppose it's understandable; I think that's because nobody wants—or knows how—to talk about two things like homosexuality *and* cancer at once. Separately, those topics are loaded, but when you combine them, wow! You've got too much to handle in idle chit-chat. That I understand, but other things..."

"What about your work on the ordinance?" Branch asked, suddenly remembering just what Andy's role downtown had been.

Andy sighed. "Yes, well, that's one of the major sore points of all of this for me. The thing is due before the city council in February, and I'm afraid it will go down in defeat as always."

"But you mentioned other gay workers," Branch said. "Surely they could take over?"

Andy shook his head. "No, not really. I mean, they *can*

take over; and they have. But the thing is, it was my baby this time around, you know? It would be like if you had a proposal in for medical research, and then someone else took it over, you see? The impetus, the whole background and everything just wouldn't be there. And that's what I had going for it."

"February, huh?" Branch said, rubbing his chin.

"Yes," Andy answered. "But I've got a powerful enemy down there, who—in my absence—has been very effectively bottlenecking any progress on the ordinance."

Branch nodded his head, but said nothing.

"He's been quite awful about it all," Andy said.

There was a lull for a moment, then Branch asked what he meant.

"Oh, a guy named Mitch..." Andy paused, as though the subject were too much trouble to pursue.

"Tell him about Mitch," David prompted.

Andy nodded. "Yes, well," he started. "Mitchell is one of the senior administrators. I've always wondered about him, you know, if he's gay or not. He was always very friendly, but withdrawn. Suggestive, sort of."

Branch nodded that he understood.

"As though he wanted to get to know me," Andy went on, "but was afraid. It's not that unusual a situation. Well, two days after I had told a couple of my friends at work about my diagnosis, I ran into Mitch in the hall. I said hello, like always, and stopped to chat, but he just looked at me and walked on. No hello, no goodbye, nothing. Ever since then he's refused even to look at me. He won't even talk to me on the phone; he has another worker call me if there needs to be communication."

"That's awful," Branch said.

"It is," Andy nodded. "But it's not the worst of it. The worst was when I got into the elevator about two weeks ago, one of the last times I went in. It was very subtle, but I noticed that the other people in the elevator moved to the back. At first I thought I was being paranoid, so I did a reality check, you know; I actually turned around and looked, and sure enough, they were all lined up around

[133]

the perimeter, away from me. That made me feel great." His tone was wry.

Branch was shaking his head; he had heard other tales of unkind behavior from patients. "They make you feel dirty, like a leper?" he said.

"Or like I'm carrying the plague!" Andy said. "But it's not all bad, either. There are two other gay men there— Phil and George—they've been very supportive, if a bit reticent. And Catherine, the secretary for our offices, she's been truly wonderful, always there when I wasn't feeling so hot. So really, honestly, I've gotten the whole gamut of human emotions in all of this." Andy was quiet for a second. "But I do worry about Mitch. I don't like to think of him carrying around some burden like that, and then having to see me with cancer, too. Oh, well, maybe he's just straight and unable to cope with it."

"It's not easy for straight people to comprehend," David said. "They can understand disease, and they can understand gays, if they've been around. But I talked with some straight newspeople the other day, and they just don't know what's going on, let alone how to report it."

"I'm afraid this epidemic might not help," Branch said dourly. "After all, the buzzwords that get linked here are gay, cancer, death, epidemic. And the evidence so far points to a connection with promiscuous sexual behavior..."

"I know," David cut in, "But you know what's funny is that ever since Andy's diagnosis—god, how we use that as a time marker—ever since then, I've come to realize that the vast majority of gay men rarely, if ever, went near a bathhouse, not regularly anyway. Andy and I certainly were rowdy enough when we first met, but we gave up most of that nearly two years ago. Given all that fidelity, or monogamy, or whatever you call it since then, it's frightening to think that Andy got it at all."

"Well, like I said," Branch continued, "we don't know, really, if that has anything to do with it. But it is a commonplace among the cases—most of them, among the gay cases that is. There are the exceptions, like the cases from the intravenous drug users; now there's a different line altogether, along with this apparent Haitian conection. But promiscuity looms large, believe me."

David jumped in: "And promiscuity is another of those buzzwords. A lot of people—straight and gay—don't really know how they feel about promiscuity. It has such a negative connotation, but really, what's wrong with it? It's an ethic that oppresses us that tells us it's wrong to sleep around. But that's a big topic, and it doesn't matter anyway. Because, since both Andy and I were not *that* promiscuous for a long time, then how did he get it?"

Andy nodded in agreement with the question.

Branch shook his head. "There are a lot of unexplained mysteries in all this, but I rather imagine perhaps the bug that brings on this condition can lie dormant in the system for that long." He looked away at the window for a moment. He listened to the strange melody of the Hindemith sonata and watched the twilight outside. "I'm following the medical reports closely," he said. "But there's not much. Dr. Kinder-Mann at UC San Francisco is doing most of the work, but there's been no 'smoking gun' so far—you know, a solid clue that would point the way. There's just too much speculation at this point."

Andy looked oddly reflective. "Nobody knows anything, do they?" he asked rhetorically.

"No, I'm afraid not," Branch said, "I assume it's a virus—either a new one or a mutant one, which means, of course, that it's infectious and there should be more cases showing up soon. It also means, thankfully, that the majority of people who contact the virus will most likely develop antibodies and thus be immune. That is *if* it works like any normal virus."

"But we do know," David said, moving the conversation along, "that it's not a normal epidemic. So why aren't more scientists jumping on it?"

"They are," Branch said, "but it takes time to untangle a mystery like this. And you have to understand that when it comes to something like this, even though we would all—presumably—like to band together to find an answer, there will be a great deal of competition among researchers and institutions. So not everyone is going to share all the information."

"Politics..." David said, shaking his head. "If there are over a hundred cases so far, isn't it more important than that?"

Branch was shaking his head in the manner that suggests another's naïveté. "You have to understand two things: one, medicine is an industry. Andy is but one small peg in a larger puzzle of careers, grants, funds, budgets, priorities, committees, and on and on. If this thing gets bigger, so will the industry that springs up around it. It will perpetuate itself into a sort of bland but frantic industry, a new and probably very profitable one. I mean, there's research and medical treatment and books and lectures, psychotherapy, psychiatry, experiments, everything really." He stopped for a moment, but David and Andy said nothing.

"The other thing to bear in mind," Branch went on, "is that people have their careers foremost in their minds. There's an old, old tradition that stipulates that a researcher cannot release his findings to the general public or media *until* they have been formally accepted and prepared for publication in a medical journal. Well, that process can take anywhere from months to years, and anyone who values his career and who hopes to preserve his or her research findings for further serious consideration has got to follow those rules, explicitly, or else risk their reputation altogether. It's just the way it works..."

The music ended just then and David shut the stereo off. The sound of traffic in the street below came through the windows. David turned to face Dr. Branch and Andy, a fury burning in his eyes. "But why?" he said with great anger. "How? It doesn't make any sense to me when you tell me that medical researchers will keep information to themselves for purely selfish and political reasons. I can't believe it! I mean, look what happened when they had Legionnaires' disease or toxic shock syndrome. It was all over the news, and the medical people and government were going crazy with it. But this thing has killed...what is it?...fifty people, and more are sick, and you tell me about an old medical tradition to withhold research find-ings?" David was visibly perturbed.

"Don't be naïve," Andy warned him.

"I'm not being naïve, Not at all. I'm scared to death if you want the truth. I feel suddenly very lost, like a friend has told me of his betrayal... I mean..." David paused to collect his thoughts, then went on. "I mean, if this illness *is* the result of a promiscuous lifestyle, or maybe of some new mutated virus, what are we going to do? People still fill the baths every night of the week; the few articles in the paper and in the gay papers are hardly noticed. I don't think anyone believes much is going on. There's this big gap between what we know—what you're telling us," David addressed Branch, "and between what the rest of the pub-lic, especially gay, seems to know."

"Oh, I'm sure they believe it's true," Branch said. "But most everybody will simply deny it because of the fear it brings on. The fear and denial get compounded when medicine doesn't have any answers to give. It makes the situation appear hopeless."

Andy shook his head, his cynicism taking over. "But isn't that exactly what it is? Hopeless?" There was a long silence. And then Andy spoke again: "Besides, David, it's not true that nobody knows nothing; it's becoming a major subject of conversation, and strange behavior, if you'll re-call what Paul did..."

"Oh, shit," David said. "I had sort of forgotten that..."

"What?" Branch asked.

"This former friend of ours," David said, with great emphasis on the word "former."

Andy explained. "We were invited to our friend's house for dinner about a month ago, right when people were beginning to understand that certain of us in the gay com-munity were victims of KS. Well, Paul served us dinner, but he served me on a paper plate. I didn't mind at first, I understood his concern. But later, I realized how utterly ghastly it was. It was then that I became aware of the leprosy syndrome, as I think of it; you know, like the people all shying away in the elevator like I had leprosy."

Branch was shaking his head, his lips creased in a grim-ace of sympathy and disgust at the ability of humans to inflict unnecessary pain on one another. After a moment, Branch addressed David. "I can't answer you," he said. "I understand your anger at the medical system, but there is, of course, the other side of the coin. Because if every medical researcher—or every crackpot theoretician—loudly vocalized to the media every conclusion about his research, it could bring a lot of pain to the people in-volved. With the standard procedure of waiting for formal publication—when the entire establishment can look and judge and weigh the merits—then premature hope is not given to patients who might later discover that the an-nouncement was premature and maybe worthless. In that sense, it protects everyone involved."

"I hadn't thought of it that way," David said, still stand-ing by the window and stereo. "But why aren't you and others working on it and trying to find out what's wrong at Mt. Zion?"

Branch cringed at the direct question. "Well, there's no-thing to tell, not a goddamn thing." His voice was bitter. "Our chief administrator—for the research division, sort of a chief of staff—says we can't put money into some-thing so sensitive and isolated. He says that the work at UC San Francisco, Atlanta, and the other few places is suffi-cient for the moment."

"Maybe he doesn't know how severe it is?" Andy offered.

"No, that's not it," Branch said. "I discussed it with him, he knew everything about it, but he seemed to downplay its seriousness, said Mt. Zion shouldn't be involved in that sort of problem. He's worried about the association with homosexuality I know; he said as much. I suspect that accounts for his odd behavior."

"What's that?" David's keen journalistic sense was alert. He sensed a story in the making—a major medical admin-istrator actively pursuing a homophobic course in the face of a health crisis.

"Well, I shouldn't say," Branch excused himself, "But he lied to me about a major grant coming from Washing-ton, some of which could have been diverted to me for research on KS. He told me there was nothing like it in the works, but the doctors' wives tell a different story."

David and Andy both frowned; Branch realized he should have said nothing about the internal politics of Mt. Zion or about doctors' wives. But his frustration with his missed grant and his inability to convince Maguire of the need for funding for AIDS research loosened his tongue.

"Why would he lie about something that could help?" David asked.

Branch waved his hand as if to erase the remarks. "No, it's not that. I shouldn't have said. There are many reasons I suppose he could not tell me—most likely to keep me off his back. What worries me and angers me is that he's so uptight about it all; he's so nervous when I tell him about it, and so hostile when I asked for help in winning a grant. It bothers me; no, it gripes me." Branch was blatant in his disregard for his remarks at this point. "It's people like Art Maguire that are holding back the research we need to do, and it's people like me that seem so helpless. He's up to no good, that man, and it makes me mad. He's always been up to no good."

David was mystified. "But how would someone like that get in such a position of power? He can't be that full of hatred or prejudice..." David let his voice trail off; he didn't believe his own doubts. He was, after all, from Brooklyn. But he remained very curious about this Art Maguire, whom Branch was not praising. As a matter of fact, the story Branch was relating was rather unusual, or so it seemed to him, considering the prestigious reputation of Mt. Zion Hospital.

Andy sensed David's suspicions and noted the lull in the conversation. "How about some wine?" he suggested, trying to bring both David and Branch back into the present moment; both had become preoccupied of a sudden.

"Yes, great," Branch answered, drawing himself awake again.

"Sure," David said. "And I'll find another record to listen to."

Andy stood and went to the kitchen in the back. David selected another album, while Dr. Branch reached for one of David's Winstons and lit it. "I hardly ever smoke," he said as he did so, drawing the smoke deep into his lungs. "But sometimes it's just the thing."

"I know," David said, the music starting up and filling the room. He reached for a cigarette himself, lighting up and standing near the window. He nodded to the window and looked at Branch. "Keeps the smoke from stifling Andy," he explained.

Branch nodded. They smoked and waited for Andy to return with the wine.

*

A few minutes later, they were drinking wine and deep in conversation once again. "You know," Branch was saying, "the politics is pretty strange all told. I've never seen anything like it, to tell you the truth."

David and Andy said nothing. Andy sipped his wine and waited for the doctor to go on with his comments. David, having put on some soft jazz and closed the window halfway, wanted to finish the effect; he turned one light off, then adjusted another. The room became warmer, less harsh, more in tune with the balmy autumn air.

Branch was sitting back now, his feet up, the cigarette out. He had a glass of wine in his hand. "One of the strangest stories came straight from Dr. Kinder-Mann himself out at UC San Francisco. For various reasons that I need not go into now, Alfred Kinder-Mann and I don't speak much with each other any more, so I did get the story second-hand from Max Leider." He paused for a moment, realizing that Andy knew Max Leider, but David did not. "A colleague of mine..." Branch explained as an aside to David. "People are acting so strangely about all of this. Apparently—and this was a few weeks ago from what I gather—a group of nurses and orderlies at a hospital there in San Francisco more or less flipped out about one of the more serious KS patients and threatened not to care for him. I understand that the hospital managed to bring them into line, but the whole incident is disturbing, quite telling, really. For health care professionals to refuse to care for a patient because of the nature of the patient's disease...well, it's quite unheard of. I can't imagine what sort of terror they must be feeling."

David was disturbed by the story as well; he was considering what steps he could take to discover if there were a good newspaper story here. Everything they had discussed that evening sounded less like everyday medicine and more like some sort of horror story.

Andy wore an expression of skepticism. "Really, Walter," he said in a rather dry tone, something he rarely used; he also rarely addressed Dr. Branch as Walter, but being a friend all his life, he reserved the right. He fixed Dr. Branch with a doubtful eye; Branch drank his wine and realized that Andy would probably have to reject the story in his own defense, rather than consider the possibility that something of the kind might happen to him at some point.

David said nothing; he wanted to let the talk run its course and see what he could discover. Eventually, after some small talk about Prince Charles and Lady Diana (David now found the topic tired), they returned to the disease, with Branch giving an explanation for the acronym AIDS, as opposed to the original GRIDS.

"Isn't GRIDS more descriptive?" Andy said, really playing devil's advocate; he had heard this story before at Dr. Branch's office.

"At first it seemed that way, yes," Branch answered, "because all the cases were gay men, but as soon as it was evident that others could—and were—getting the disease, then the gay leadership recognized there might be a serious political problem in retaining the name GRIDS."

"It would be inaccurate and damning, I can see that," David said.

"Yes, and so I understand that a couple of people from the American Gay Rights Committee, along with Alfred Kinder-Mann, went to Atlanta and met with the director of the CDC and urged him to drop the GRIDS acronym, while retaining the use of AIDS."

"Pretty smart move," Andy commented, setting his glass of wine down on the coffee table.

"Sure," Branch said. "It was extremely shrewd of the

AGRC to recognize the potentially incriminating political implications of the CDC retaining the acronym that linked such a deadly thing to gay people."

Andy recoiled slightly at the choice of Branch's words: deadly. He had, now that he had located some new source of strength, hoped to avoid the issue. But there it was, and he realized that if he were to face this problem with dignity and resolve, he would have to understand that he was who he was, and the disease was what it was; and others could not be expected to tread lightly at all times for his sake.

The conversation seemed to have stopped momentarily. David stepped to the overstuffed chair and sat down, reaching for another cigarette. Dr. Branch shifted in his seat slightly to prop his feet up on the edge of the coffee table. Finally, he spoke; "Well, David, I wanted to talk to you some more about working on some articles on the epidemic."

"I'd like that," David said. "You know I'm reporting for the *New York Gay Herald*, with a particular emphasis on the KS and AIDS problem. Some of my articles are to be personal essays—about how Andy and I deal with it all. We'll work out some outlines, okay? I'm going out to San Francisco sometime in the next couple months to meet with Alfred Kinder-Mann and see what they're doing at UCSF. While I'm there I'll see how the gay community in the city is affected. Probably not much. It's all been here, so far. Right?" David blew smoke out the corner of his mouth, in the direction of the windows.

"So far," Branch said, "though there is a significant proportion of cases from California, enough to worry the epidemiologists."

"That's true of all of it, though, isn't it?" Andy said. He was leaning back, not drinking. He appeared overly tired and rather weak; apparently the chemotherapy of the morning was beginning to react in his system.

"Yes," Branch intoned. "How are the both of you doing, really?" Branch asked. He was sincerely interested.

It was Andy who answered. "We're okay." There was

emotion in his voice. "Sometimes it can be very depressing, of course, and look at me...it bothers me to look like this, like I stepped out of Dachau yesterday."

"Shut up," David said, jokingly, but with an edge of sincerity. "We're fine. But I do feel very personally attacked. By the cancer. By whatever this AIDS thing is that's fucking us over, royally. It's not fair. Not after all the work we put into our relationship."

Branch was silent. He had no response to this sort of anger; it was justified, and it was one of the toughest things to face in his profession.

"That's true," Andy said. "It hurts me to see David having to cope with my illness; it's become *our* illness."

"Especially now that I'm writing about it," David added, frowning.

"What about your family, Andy? I've thought of them a hundred times. Do you really think they ought not to know?" Branch was deeply concerned; after all, Andy's parents had been his friends long ago.

"Can't do it," Andy said. "I wouldn't be surprised, but I don't care. They were so awful too many times; you know that."

"Yes," Branch said. It was a painful subject for both of them. "But Beth, she'll come around I'm sure."

"I don't know," Andy said. "She *was* interested enough to ask questions about it, specific things. But there was an undertone of horror, almost panic. You have to admit it's damn scary."

Both David and Dr. Branch nodded in agreement. Then David spoke: "It's more than scary or horrible, though," he started. "At least when it comes to families. I told my mother about it last month, well, both my folks. I called her up after we had gotten the diagnosis, and I told her about the epidemic and about Andy. Now she knows about it. She knew about Andy and I; they don't like it, but they're okay. Modern, I guess. But when it came to the KS, my mother was having a really tough time, I could tell; it wasn't easy at all. My mom tried to listen and ask a couple questions, but then she gave up. She acted like I was talking about syphilis. So there's a big thing there about VD, about seeing this epidemic like the clap. You don't talk about it. Nice people don't get it. Fags get it from all their fucking. Not nice. It's a confusing topic." David lit another cigarette.

Branch nodded. "I see how it might appear that way, but it's not necessarily a sexually transmitted disease, not in the sense of what people consider 'VD.' It does appear, however, that the best way to transmit it might be through sexual contact, but that's got to be proven. It could still be some sort of coincidence."

David was shaking his head. "But look at the sick guys already, almost all gay. It has to be something we do."

"Not necessarily, David," Branch said. "Epidemiology recognizes a point—or specific points—of entry for an infection, especially something new like this. Many factors are indeed coincidental, being at the wrong place at the wrong time."

A shadow crossed Andy's face. He was feeling more sick with each minute; his resolve to confront the problem with dignity was failing in the face of the nausea. But he remembered Patrick's unnerving and eccentric ramblings of that morning. Branch's representation of mystery—the wrong place at the wrong time—evoked the remembrance of Patrick's bizarre tale; Andy decided—against his earlier decision to leave the young man's suffering in peace—to relate the freakish paranoia the blind young man had told.

Branch saw the shadow and frown register on Andy's face; it was an expression of illness, disgust, and interest. "What are you thinking?" he asked Andy.

"I saw Patrick Ross this morning."

"Oh," Branch said. David said nothing.

"I didn't know he was blind. And I didn't know he was so...so out of touch." Andy faltered for a moment. "I had decided not to mention it, because it seems like it would strip him of some dignity, but now, well...it doesn't matter much."

"What is it?" David asked, sensing that Andy was troubled by his visit with Patrick.

"He was crazy," Andy said flatly. "He told me that it was a conspiracy, and that everyone was in on it. He said that the government got a virus from their germ warfare weapons and purposely infected gays in an effort to kill them off, and then, when everyone was scared, to round them up."

No one said anything; David was smoking and expressionless. Branch frowned. Andy went on: "I was shocked, really, to hear him go on like that. It wasn't that long ago that I met Patrick at chemotherapy, and I'd hoped to have some good talks with him. Then, when I knew he'd taken so ill, I hesitated; I guess I didn't want to face his condition—my condition, that is. Then, last night, I realized that I *had* to visit him, no matter what, and so I did. And that's what I got. His blindness; his incredible wasting away; and that wild story about a government plot. It was too much..." There were tears at Andy's eyes.

"That's some story," Branch said.

"Yes," David agreed. "And I suppose not altogether unbelievable."

Andy looked at David and then at Dr. Branch. Branch shook his head and said, "This crisis is provoking all kinds of responses from all kinds of people. I honestly can't think of anything so packed with meaning or so powerfully suggestive."

*

Later, after Dr. Branch had gone, David lay beside Andy, wide awake, unable to fall asleep. He reached out and caressed Andy's chest. "Andy?" he said gently.

"Yes," Andy answered.

"Do you feel okay?"

"Yes," Andy said. "The nausea is gone for now." Neither of them spoke for a moment. There was a chill wind stirring the drapes in their bedroom; David got up and shut the window, then crawled back in bed.

"I worry about you," Andy said.

"That's backwards," David said. "I'm supposed to worry about you."

"But when I'm gone, I worry about you finding somebody else," Andy started, but David tried to cut him off.

Andy went on. "I mean, who will want to love you now that you've been exposed to all this? It'll scare them."

"Shut up," David said, scared by the thought himself. "Don't get so fucking heavy, okay?"

Andy was silent. Finally, he spoke again. "You know, I didn't mention Jim and Rita tonight to Dr. Branch for a special reason."

"Yeah?" David said; he was falling asleep.

"Because it hurt a lot when Jim refused to touch me those two times. You know, the thing with the paper plate at dinner? That's just obnoxious, but Jim's treatment of me was really hurtful. I didn't want to mention it because neither of them have been over since then. They must be scared of me."

"Shit," David whispered. "Maybe Jim, sure, but Rita's our friend; she loves you. Let's call her tomorrow and make sure she comes by, okay? We can't be weird about it."

"Okay," Andy said. Finally they were both silent. David had come back fully awake again. He lay and listened to Andy's deep breathing that indicated his slumber. He ran the whole evening through his head again, piecing together all the variables and realizing that they made him uncomfortable. He was starting to distrust the health crisis somehow. It had already the flavor of deception, guile: a deliberate disregard, coupled with an acute, though uncalled-for, prudence. He would have to give it some thought.

21   *November 1981 • New York City*

Andy had ended the first round of treatment by vincrystine. The progress of the cancer was impeded; that is, there were no new lesions, but neither was there evidence of remission. The real trouble was the lowered immunity. Andy could not defend himself against the assaults of bacteria and fungi normally present in the world. If it wasn't one thing, it was another. But overall he was remaining steadfast in the medical fight with the disease—stable, as Dr. Branch liked to put it.

Rita had come by once again to call on him at the apartment earlier in the month, bringing with her a batch of freshly home-baked cookies. Andy was so touched by this gesture that he had been speechless, a single tear glistening in the corner of his eye. She explained—though it was difficult for her to do so, they could see—that Jim was simply too flipped out by the disease to face Andy anymore. She put it to them bluntly, though not harshly. She thought that Andy deserved to know.

And, mid-month, Andy had been cheered a second time by a phone call from his sister Elizabeth. It had come on one of those fine autumn days that strike Manhattan in late October and early November, just before the whole thing took the sudden turn for the worse that signaled the inescapable onset of the cold season. It had been a splendid day, the sky a deep blue, the air cool and sweet. Andy and David had, at Andy's determination, gone up on Fifth Avenue to walk. Though the fall colors were done, Andy took pleasure in the remaining brown leaves that scattered themselves across the sidewalk along the Avenue, smashing underfoot with a sound like crumbling paper.

After their walk—which, owing to Andy's weakness, was abruptly short—they had returned to the apartment to find the phone ringing. David had answered it and passed the receiver to Andy, his lips forming silently the name of Andy's little sister, Elizabeth. Andy had taken the call and immediately cried, for she had called to apologize, to make amends for her earlier constraint in responding to his serious circumstances. She had called to voice her love as well as her sorrow, and it was the connection to his family that touched Andy so deeply; he had been so alone, despite David, despite his friend Rita. And although she bore no goodwill from the rest of the family, Andy had been grateful for her humanity, for her outstretched hand. The bright emotion invoked by her call had stayed with him ever since.

And so he kept on. He had learned to breathe deeply, to

hold his shoulders back, to remind himself that he was alive and human, never matter the conditions at any given moment. The value in life was in the appreciation of how precious it all really was. At any time, whether in pain or not, Andy could remind himself that he had it all, truly: he could feel; he could hate; he could love and hope for the best.

PART THREE

22 *December 1981 • Philadelphia*

Andy's mother dropped her magazine on her lap and sighed. She stared at the tiny lights twinkling on the Christmas tree and thought about Andy. The magazine's story about AIDS bothered her; and it bothered her on so many levels that she could barely begin to understand her feelings. She shook her head and turned to look out the window. It was snowing, very quietly, not a bitter storm as they had the week before. She looked back at the Christmas tree, tall and full, occupying quite a bit of floor space in the corner of their suburban Philadelphia home.

Andy's mother sat and stared at the tree, feeling a mixture of pain, worry and revulsion. Certainly she would have to keep the article out of Andy's father's sight. She couldn't bear another of his tirades on the subject. Yet she sympathized with him. She had never understood Andy's problems, had never been able to grasp just what had gone wrong. And now, as she sat alone in the living room the week before Christmas, she was thankful for the brief moment to think about Andy and about his horrible sickness. What could she do? Did she want to do anything? Was it best left alone, as Chuck said?

Edna Stone had not come to this moment of quiet indecision and distress easily. In some sense, she thought, worries and fears about Andy's safety extended back his whole life, all the way back to that night in a restaurant in upper Manhattan when the blizzard forced Andy's delivery in the back room. God how scared she had been!

Would her baby be okay? Would something go wrong there, something that could only be fixed in a hospital, so far away? And to entrust the baby's delivery to a first-year medical student, Walt Branch! That had really been some beginning for Andy! she thought, smiling to herself at the memory.

That had been the start of her worries, and little Andy had been nothing but trouble ever since. He was sickly as a little boy, but then, so was his older sister Amanda. He had, she suddenly remembered, used to fake illness as well, in order to stay home and watch television. Then the trouble in junior high, when he had gotten in with a bunch of rotten kids who started him smoking cigarettes. Thank god he gave that up! But then, just when he should have been excelling in high school, she had found that collection of dirty magazines hidden between his mattress and box springs. That discovery had been the moment when everything changed for the worse.

Such problems! she whispered as she sat and remembered that day. At first she had almost giggled at the discovery, assuming that he had begun to collect some girlie magazines. A strict talk from Chuck would have taken care of that. But when she'd looked closely—at those young men doing exactly what she knew some young men did—she had nearly thrown up. Tears and anguish had filled that day, and she had phoned Andy's father at work to tell him what she had found.

After that, they sent Andy to a psychiatrist, but it was no use; he was lost to them. He grew more distant as the months passed and as he indulged his deviance, and she and Chuck had been unable to control him. Finally, at eighteen, on his very birthday, he had moved out to New York and never come home.

And then Elizabeth had told them about his sickness. And now there it was in a national magazine. What a ghastly, awful thing to happen to my baby, she thought. If only I could change things, she wished hopelessly; but no, nothing would change. He was "like that," and despite all their modernity and love, she and Chuck could not accept his lifestyle. That was that.

And where is he? she wondered, glancing at the clock and realizing that Chuck was later than usual. She guessed it was the snow; it had probably held things up at the construction site Chuck was working. But lord! she had better get supper on. Her involvement in the news article had let her lose track of the hour. She folded the magazine and slipped it in the wastebasket. She went into the kitchen, put on her white apron, and started to fix dinner.

*

Thoughts of Andy's illness plagued Chuck Stone as he made his way home that night, driving the truck carefully along the streets of Philadelphia. It was snowing gently, and he was late for dinner. He hoped that Edna wouldn't be too mad. He hoped that Beth would be there for dinner and not out with her friends again. His troubled thoughts about Andy needed distraction. He needed to see Beth—young, pretty and healthy—sitting at the dinner table to assure him that all was well, after all, in the Stone family. That business with Andy would have to be put completely out of his mind.

But he couldn't get it out of his mind. It had been nearly ten years since Andy had moved out. The first few years had been rocky, tough going, because Edna had been so intent on trying to patch things up. But he had prevailed, finally ordering Andy out of their lives for good that weekend of Grandma Stone's funeral. He hadn't spoken with Andy since then, and that suited him just fine. He could do without having a fag son around.

Still, he was plagued by memories of it all. He had never forgotten that it was 1969—in May, on a fair, warm spring day—when Edna called him up at work and told him about the dirty magazines in Andy's room. And then the two years of psychiatry, such an expense for nothing! It had even pushed Andy further into his perversion. Chuck had blessed the day Andy moved out and left for New York. It was his greatest disappointment in life that his son—his only son—was a queer. For all it meant, he may as well have had four daughters.

And now, now that he was used to the idea that it was

over with, that Andy was out of their family and fully disowned, the subject had come up with this disgusting illness Beth had told them about. He wasn't surprised; he knew the sorts of vile things that queers did—fucking strangers in alleys, sucking every cock that comes along, in bus stations, public parks, anywhere they could satisfy their groping lusts for men's flesh. And there was worse, he knew. Fucking assholes and fingers up the butt and lord knows what else—it was no wonder Andy was sick. The whole subject made him nauseous.

He knew that Edna still had some soft spot in her heart for Andy; it was woman's weakness. But he would never give in, not now. Andy had made his bed and would have to lie in it. And that was that.

He pulled up in the driveway of the house and shut off the truck's engine. For a short moment he sat in silence and looked at the house. He could see the little colored lights on the Christmas tree through the front room window. He just sat and stared at the house for a minute, then took a deep breath and went in.

"You're home!" Edna said as she finished setting the table in the kitchen.

"Hi, Dad!" Elizabeth called out from the other room.

He was glad she was home. "Hello, there," he said, kissing his wife and then hanging his coat up in the small alcove by the back door. "We had a bit of trouble with a piece of equipment late this afternoon," he explained. "It wasn't bad enough to call home about. I knew it wouldn't be too late."

He went and sat in the living room to read the paper and talk to Beth. Edna waved him away, content to have a few more minutes alone to finish fixing dinner. She knew that she would probably bring the subject of Andy's illness up at dinner, and she wanted to be sure she had her opening sentence right. She hoped to convince Chuck to let her go to New York to see Andy, remote though that might be as a possibility. She had to at least bring it up.

*

[154]

Dinner was tense. The evidence that something was being avoided was everywhere—in the vague silence, in the meaningless small talk, in the way Beth pushed her food around and never really ate. Edna chattered on and on about the least significant things; she didn't know if she had the nerve to bring the subject up. Beth didn't know what was going on, but she had a pretty good guess it was something to do with Andy. Chuck didn't care why Edna was carrying on so, then lapsing into an uneasy silence every now and again; if he thought for a minute, he'd know what she was up to. And *that* he didn't want to hear.

Finally, the tension broke. Edna put her fork down on her plate with a clatter, brought the napkin to her lips for a moment, then said: "Chuck, there's something in this week's *Time* magazine about that new epidemic." Her voice sounded casual.

Without hesitation, Chuck stuck a piece of pork chop in his mouth and kept on chewing. "Oh?" he mumbled through his full mouth.

Beth hid her face behind her wine glass, taking a long, endless sip.

Edna was grateful that Chuck hadn't responded in fury, as he was wont to do with reference to the subject. She hoped it would stay that way; if she could talk with him calmly for even a few minutes, perhaps she could make him see that a visit to New York would do no harm. "Apparently it's worse than they thought it might be," she said, scrutinizing her husband for any sign of anger. There was none. He put another mouthful of food in his mouth and kept chewing. Beth was still sipping from her wine glass. Edna was glad that Beth was there as a buffer; Chuck wouldn't make too big a scene in front of Beth. She went on, carefully: "You know, with Christmas and all coming up, I wondered if perhaps I might..."

"No!" he suddenly said, firmly, sharply, cutting her off.

Edna sat still, her mouth still open to form the next words. The tone of his voice had betrayed the rage hiding beneath the surface. She stared at her husband in wonder at his ability to conceal emotion; he sat chewing, stuffing one forkful after another into his mouth.

"But Chuck…" she started again, only to be cut off once more.

"That's the end of it!" he commanded.

There was a tense silence around the table. Edna looked back and forth at Chuck and Beth. Beth was stirring, something mean in the corner of her eye. Chuck kept eating, almost menacing in his oblivious control. Edna knew that there was nothing she could do at that point. She had broached the subject, and when Chuck said "that was that," well…he generally meant it. She had learned long ago never to cross him when he made such emphatic pronouncements. Women's lib notwithstanding, she had accepted it. After all, she told herself, there is more to a marriage than love and family. There was something larger at work, and she deferred to her husband for that reason. And she realized that this did not mean she had to abandon the subject altogether; she knew that if she felt strongly enough about it, there would be a way for her to sneak to New York, perhaps on the excuse of a shopping spree.

She wet her lips with the wine and glanced at Beth once more. Oh, my goodness, Edna moaned to herself, seeing in Beth's face and posture that some sort of confrontation was imminent. Perhaps I should never have brought it up.

Beth slammed her fork down on her plate and glared at her father. She was tired of his macho priggishness; she had been tired of it for some time, but now that she saw his intractability over her own dying brother, she wouldn't take it for another minute.

"Father," she said in a stern tone, "what is it with you, anyway? Huh? I mean look at you, you're as wound up as a coil and there you sit, silent, eating like it was the end of groceries or something. How dare you ignore Andy's problem like that! I talked to Andy, twice already, and he is very, very sick. How can you just sit there and not care?" Beth couldn't go on; her voice trembled with anger and fear. She had never spoken against her father. He sat and glared back at her; he could not tolerate her outburst.

"Listen, young lady, this is between your mother and I. You will not talk to your father like that, and if…"

"Dammit!" she interrupted him, her face burning red. "We're talking about my brother, too, and he's dying. Don't you care?"

"Andy died a long time ago," he said angrily.

"Cut the shit," Beth said. "That's so stupid and trite it makes me sick. Where'd you get a line like that? John Wayne? Attila the Hun?"

He started to get up, to walk away, but Beth insisted that he stay where he was. "All I want from you is an answer," Beth said, her voice pleading and on the verge of tears. "One honest answer about why you can't resolve this thing with Andy. Can't you even be reasonable about it?"

He stared coldly at her. "There's nothing to be reasonable about," he answered, his voice strangely controlled. "It's black and white, it's that simple."

Beth breathed deeply; she had broken through. He had stopped his defense and was letting the anger fall. She had engaged him in conversation, had gotten at least the start of an answer from him. Now she knew she would have to tread lightly and cautiously if she were to maintain the discussion without raising his hackles again. "But what's that simple?" she asked, vaguely. She knew better than to attack him with questions that would put him on the defensive. She had to lead him along. "Surely you're no stupid man, you're my daddy; there's got to be a reasonable answer here. Mom can't sit here and cry her eyes out while her baby dies and she can't even call him on the phone? What's the problem? Where's the resistance coming from?"

He frowned and stared at Beth. Oh, no, she thought, too much at once. I blew it.

And she had. "No," he was shaking his head. "No, it *is* that simple. Andy is not my son anymore, no matter what's happening." He stood and left the room.

And so abruptly, Beth said to herself, disappointed that the moment for a breakthrough had come and gone. She was frustrated and cold, unhappy with herself for forging a confrontation that would probably never be resolved. But why? she asked herself. Why can't he just relax and see that Andy is what he is, and that he's in trouble? Oh, she could think of answers—the only son, machismo, old-fashioned notions of propriety. But none of that held up in life-and-death matters like this. Why did he have such a tough time just facing it?

Edna felt empty as she watched her husband leave the room. She watched Beth's face register disappointment and frustration, watched and wondered what the rest of the evening would be like, having to sit and watch television with Chuck in such a riled-up mood. Damn! she thought to herself. It's best to leave this thing alone, no doubt about that. And besides, Chuck was right; Andy had failed them miserably.

She stood and started to clear the table. Beth looked at her mother, a pleading expression in her eyes. "Mom?" she whispered.

Her mother shook her head. "See, honey?" she said. "See what you've done now?" It was her way of transferring responsibility for the ugly moments onto Beth.

"Oh, mother," Beth protested, clearing away the plates and silverware. "I had to ask him; I can't stand the way he acts about this. I'm glad I'm not around here most of the time. I wouldn't be able to stand it. You know, you've got to go see Andy anyway. Don't listen to Dad on this one."

"I don't know," Edna said, but she began already to lay a plan. A shopping trip, that was the answer. But it would have to be after Christmas. They were busy until then. She would use the big January sales as her excuse; she and Beth would slip off on the train, then see Andy.

They discussed this plan quietly as they did the dishes. Andy's father had the television going rather loudly in the front room. When they were done with the dishes, Edna went to the living room and sat down to watch TV with her husband. Beth went to her room to read. But when Edna saw Chuck sitting so sternly in his chair, not even looking up when she came in, she realized that she would never get away with a "shopping spree" in New York. Her husband would keep her there until it was too late.

*

That night, after Johnny Carson's monologue, Andy's mother and father went to bed. They still had not spoken the whole evening, and now they lay beside each other on the king-sized bed and said nothing. Edna laid her head against the pillow and shut her eyes, thinking about Andy and the news articles. There was nothing, really, in her background that prepared her to understand the situation that Andy was facing; this inadequacy made her uneasy, and as she tossed and turned on the bed, trying to find at least one comfortable position, she realized that a great deal of her problem with Andy and his illness was her ignorance. What did she have to go on? Her answer was sufficient for her; her intuition as a mother. As a mother, she felt strongly the pain of losing a child. Certainly she had felt it long ago, when Andy's homosexuality had been revealed; certainly she had felt it when he had moved out and never really returned home; certainly she was feeling it now. But now it was much, much more acute. It was her baby—the boy she had made and raised—that would be taken before her. She would outlive a child.

But there was something else that troubled her, something deeper that was causing her arms to move here, her legs there, unable to find an easy rest. She didn't want to think of it, not really, because her mind told her that of course it wasn't true. But her feelings were too strong to block: she blamed herself for Andy's illness, because, of course, she blamed herself for what he was.

23 *Christmas Day, 1981*

Andy and David sat with Rita and shrieked in merriment as Rosalind Russell greeted "Gloria Upson" in *Auntie Mame*. The film played on the television while the three exchanged gifts. Three little cornish game hens roasted in the oven; an apple pie sat cooling on the counter; and David and Rita were putting away quite a substantial portion of champagne.

Andy passed on the champagne. Though his spirit was

high with the holiday festivities, his body was weak and pained. The chemotherapy had taken a heavy toll; champagne was now completely out of the question. He sat and laughed with David and Rita, maintaining his high spirits and his determination not to concede to his condition. But there was a maudlin aspect to the merriment of the afternoon, because Andy realized that it would be his last Christmas.

His condition was worse than he let on; he had begun to withhold information from David and Rita. He told himself that it was for their own good, and he knew that it made things easier. But there was no evidence that the KS would remit; it was spreading, and rather fast at that. But not to dwell on that now! he commanded himself, realizing that there was no time left for sentiment or for gloom.

Rita sensed that Andy was putting on a brave front, but since it was Christmas Day, she would not spoil things by bringing up the subject for general discussion. She kept an eye on Andy throughout the afternoon—in case he should start to falter—but as the day wore on, she realized that he was doing a fine job of facing the holiday, quite possibly his last. She had, in these last weeks, come to admire Andy's stoicism in the face of his trials. There was nothing of denial in his approach; he wasn't pretending in some macho fashion that nothing was wrong. No, he was taking each day as it came, some better, most worse. But his smile was always there. She guessed that he must be done with sentiment by now. There was really not enough time left to bother with worries or fretting over the past. It was a tremendous fight he was putting up. And she was proud of his attitude.

David struggled through the afternoon as best he could, grateful for the movie to enliven their spirits. He had never liked Christmas anyway. His Jewish family, of course, never celebrated the holiday, at least not like that—exchanging gifts and carrying on. And today, with Andy so sick and everyone trying so hard not to show any sadness, it seemed the day was dragging. He would be glad to eat, watch some television or listen to records, see Rita out, and then go to bed.

He paid close attention to Andy. He and Rita seemed to be having such a fine time. David almost blamed himself for feeling bad about the day; after all, it was just another holiday. If only people didn't make such a big deal out of it, loading it with all sorts of meaning about family and friends and loved ones. Well, he tried to tell himself that it didn't matter. Just get through the day, he whispered to himself. Get through the day and tomorrow you can get back to work at the paper. And in January, he knew he'd be going to San Francisco to interview Dr. Kinder-Mann. That was something he could look forward to.

*

Across town, Carolyn Branch stood tall and commanding as she distributed gifts to her guests. She wore a simple, elegant beige silk gown and creamy-colored slippers. An elaborate necklace of diamonds, silver and pearls was draped heavily over her bosom. The necklace tinkled as she reached down, picked up the gifts from under the enormous Christmas tree in their salon, and handed them to the others in the room—her husband, Max Leider, and Naomi and Abe Sakowitz.

"Can you believe it?" Walt Branch was saying to Max Leider and Abe Sakowitz. "That we have been here all day and not one single call from the mountain?"

"Don't bring it up!" Naomi Sakowitz commanded as she tore her fingernails into the glistening gold wrapping of her gift. "The minute you do, the phones will start ringing and never stop!"

"She's right," Carolyn agreed, handing the last of the gifts to her husband. "Today, the mere mention of Mt. Zion is forbidden."

They laughed as she said this, concentrating on opening their gifts. She sat down on the end of the divan and regally lit a cigarette. She surveyed the room and waited for her guests to be done. Everything was in perfect order—the tree was huge and gorgeously decorated, the furniture perfectly arranged, the fire roaring in the fireplace. She looked through the long windows at Central Park beneath them, covered in a thin layer of white snow.

The sky above was steel gray, cold and forbidding. But inside, everything was cozy and warm in the company of friends. She looked into the dining room and saw the table, gleaming with silver and crystal. In a few minutes they would go in and eat. It was, she thought to herself with great satisfaction, a lovely Christmas.

*

In San Francisco, Alfred Kinder-Mann and Jack Slater were finishing a short morning of work at their lab in the medical center. They had hoped not to work on Christmas day, but the demands of the crisis forced them to do so. But the morning was over, and as they left the building — noticing that the overcast sky had broken into a warm sunny afternoon — they agreed that they felt better for having put in at least a couple hours of work. For them, the holiday had a dark side; the crisis was deepening so fast that it was difficult to imagine a day spent entirely in cheer and leisure.

They walked to the garage and got into Kinder-Mann's car, then headed over to the Castro. They were meeting friends for afternoon dinner and partying. "Did you ever think it would be this bad?" Jack asked, as Kinder-Mann turned the car off Parnassus Street and headed south.

"No, I really didn't," Kinder-Mann answered. "And I hate to think how much worse it could get."

There was a long silence between them. Finally, Jack said: "Well, that's far too gloomy to talk about now. Let's just forget about it for the rest of the day, okay? I don't think we should ruin everyone else's Christmas party with our worries and sour-pusses."

"Agreed," Kinder-Mann said as he parked the car and got out. It would be tough to be cheery, but he would try.

*

In Philadelphia, Andy's father stood at the head of the dinner table and carved the turkey. It was a crowded family scene: Andy's mother at the other end of the table, Elizabeth between. Andy's other two sisters — and their husbands — were also there. It had been a joyous morning, a clear sky in Philadelphia, bright, crisp sunlight. The family had exchanged gifts and sung Christmas carols, and now they were sitting down to a huge holiday feast.

Nobody wanted to ruin the mood with words about Andy. Although Andy's mother spent a great portion of the day reflecting on him, she said nothing. And his father was silent as well. The others said nothing, but not out of ignorance or spite; they were all quite used to Andy's absence from family gatherings. He had stopped being home for special occasions nearly ten years ago. The fact of his illness was a minor thing at that moment, at that gathering.

But as the afternoon and evening wore on, Andy's mother felt more and more acutely the pain of Andy's absence. At one point, after the dishes were done and the family was sitting about in the living room feeding on chocolates, she stopped by the kitchen window and looked out back. It was dark and quiet. A soft snow was falling, flurries really. She pressed her fingertips against the cold pane of the glass and wondered if Andy had had a good Christmas.

Oh, but then the guilt hit her, that strange confused mix of feelings—sadness at his illness, loneliness at his absence, revulsion at the underlying reason for it. Why was it so difficult? Why had life dumped this particular problem on her? She felt anguish and guilt in that moment; she knew that this was one of the "big things," something she must figure out—and in short order—because not to do so would mean spending the rest of her life in regret, quite possibly shame.

Andy's father refused to discuss it anymore. He had even forbidden her and Elizabeth to mention Andy in the house—a cruel and sad commandment, but one which even she, in her commitment to obedience, refused to follow. No, she would have to discuss it with him again; she would have to resolve these feelings about the whole thing, one way or the other, very soon. If she were to see Andy, she felt it had to be soon. Though Elizabeth had not said anything of late, Edna Stone had a strong intuition that there was very little time left for her son. She would have to risk the subject soon and talk with Chuck.

24 *January 1982* • *San Francisco*

Dr. Alfred Kinder-Mann decided to walk to the medical center that morning. It was one of those warm winter days peculiar to San Francisco, when the sun is bright and the air like spring, a cool breeze moves wisps of white clouds across a sky that seems to have been waxed a shiny light blue. Kinder-Mann felt the air almost sensuous; crazy weather, he said to himself as he walked along—foggy and cold all summer, warm and balmy all winter. He began the steep climb up the hill to the University of California's medical center in Parnassus Heights, noting as he did that the warm sun, coupled with the cool breeze, irritated him; the breeze was too chill to remove one's jacket, but the sun was too warm to keep from sweating. It was a vexing contradiction that he would never become accustomed to.

He nodded to a medical student as his thoughts turned to the frustrating dilemma of the AIDS problem. His anxiety was worsening, the frustration multiplying daily. He had examined the problem in so many ways in his mind, yet he could make no real conclusions, and, owing to a general lack of funding, could make no real studies.

Already the statistics were grim, and his personal involvement even more so. Two of his friends—one of them the former lover—had contracted the disease and died early on, following only a few weeks of intensive chemotherapy and other radical treatments. His whole community was beginning to stir in fear, and yet he—the leading medical researcher in the country, and a gay one at that, he reminded himself—had pursued one course after another, each a dead end.

For a short time he'd suspected he was onto something with nitrite inhalants, suggesting that the "poppers" gay men sniffed for a great orgasm were carcinogenic. He and his chief assistant, Jack Slater, had released their speculations in a paper, but already they doubted its validity. No evidence other than the ubiquitous lab rats, which contracted cancer from just about anything anyway, Kinder-

Mann laughed. And already there were anomalies, exceptions to the epidemiological rules: not all the victims were gay men. He was on shaky ground, and it worried him, for the toll of AIDS patients and victims of KS and pneumocystis was rising daily—not weekly or monthly, but daily.

He reached Parnassus Street and stopped for a minute to catch his breath. Though he maintained his physique through exercise, the steep hill always did him in. He started to walk again, past the student union and the great old clock, its enormous pendulum swaying back and forth. He crossed the small plaza and entered the steel-and-glass edifice, stepped into the elevator, and went to his office.

"Good morning, Jack," he said to his assistant, who was still looking groggy. Slater was young and ambitious, a resident pursuing a doctorate in infectious diseases. Kinder-Mann warned him not to overdo it with AIDS research, but Slater, bright and eager, recognized the potential the crisis held for creating himself a brilliant research career. He would drive himself into the ground over it; it was the biggest opportunity anyone had had in years.

"Morning, Fred," Jack said. "I've been up all night examining these epidemiology stats, but it's all so fucking incomplete. We need more. More of everything."

"Don't I know it!" Kinder-Mann agreed. Despite his efforts and his prestige he had been relatively unsuccessful in securing adequate research funding from the federal government, even though it was already eight months into the crisis, and evidence abounded that something seriously dangerous was going on. "There's no doubt in my mind that we've got a new virus on our hands, with an extremely long incubation period. But on our budget, we can't even begin to look for it."

"Hmmm," Slater hummed; this conversation was their standard opener for the day, all mystery and frustration. Kinder-Mann looked over Slater's shoulder, but he was called away by phone. He had to go across to Moffitt Hospital; one of his KS patients was dying of pneumocystis pneumonia.

*

Later that morning, after Kinder-Mann had attended his patient, he asked Jack to join him for coffee. He had been considering preparing some sort of press release, and he wanted to get his thoughts clear before addressing the gay community on the subject. They sat down with their coffee in a far corner of the cafeteria.

Kinder-Mann got straight to the point. "What's your feeling about the politics of this right now?" he asked Slater. "How do *you* feel the gay community's doing with all this?"

"I think we're doing pretty well," Jack said, turning his coffee cup around and around. "Granted, a lot of people still don't know very much about it all, but there's been enough coverage already in the *B.A.R.* and the *New York Native* to alert most gay people that something's afoot. And those series of articles in the *New York Gay Herald* about the couple in New York—where one of them has KS—has been really good. I think for the most part that a lot of us are starting to realize how grave the crisis really is, that something serious is coming down."

Kinder-Mann nodded and stirred cream into his coffee. "Yes, I rather imagine," he said. He wished that that he had more time to keep up with things outside the medical center. "I hope the gay press keeps a positive coverage. Fear can turn to panic awfully fast, and then we'd have a serious social crisis in the community as well. That's what worries me the most. I want to issue a statement that will both factually report and edify at the same time. I don't want to create a panic, but the facts are frightening enough to do just that."

"One crisis at a time?" Slater said, in agreement. "I agree, but I also think it's a vast underestimation of our community's ability to mobilize in the face of trouble to think everyone will suddenly flip out. I mean, we're a tough bunch of activists; we didn't get this far by flipping out at every crisis. This may be the biggest thing we'll have to face, but we *can* do it, believe me. You know—and I don't mean this to be hard on what you worry about, but . . . it's almost homophobic to think we're too weak to handle it."

Kinder-Mann smiled, "You're right, you know. I justi-
fiably worry, though, because I've already seen it happen
on a personal basis..."

"But Jerry Brewster's been studying just that very thing,
remember," Slater cut in, referring to their mutual friend,
a prominent psychotherapist in the Castro area who had
been working with chronically ill gay men, and, most recently, men with AIDS. He was beginning, as well, to work
with gay men who did *not* have AIDS, but who were terrified enough about it to seek psychological counseling.

"That's right, I knew that," Kinder-Mann said. "I forgot
what he's been doing..."

Slater filled him in. "Brewster's noted that since there
are no real answers yet, it's perfectly normal—even expected—for people to experience some kind of panic and
fear reaction. If they don't, then they're probably blocking
it all out, denying it."

"Right," Kinder-Mann cut in, "and then they accept the
reality and change their lives as healthfully as they can."

"Well, in a nutshell," Slater said. "The important thing
from Brewster's study is that it's okay to flip out a little bit,
because it means you're coming to grips with something
terribly big and scary. A little fear and panic is in order; it
helps to relieve the anxiety and get you past the fear and
into living better."

"I should include something about that in the press statement, I think," Kinder-Mann said thoughtfully. "Brewster
is rather smart, isn't he?"

"Well, he's always right there, right on top of what's
going on in the community, that's for sure. He does good
work."

They were quiet for a moment. Slater got up and bought
a Danish, raspberries and sweet pastry. He returned to the
table and sat down. Kinder-Mann had been thinking and
toying with his coffee cup. "What's happening in New
York?" he asked Jack.

"You knew they just formed the 'Gay Men's Health Crisis'?" Jack answered. "To bring the thing together, fund-
raisers, information, assistance, stuff like that."

"I know about that," Kinder-Mann said. "I was thinking about Walt Branch."

"Oh," Slater said, lighting a cigarette.

"Give it up!" Kinder-Mann chided him, waving the smoke away. "For chrissakes, we work with cancer patients all the time!"

Slater laughed, but crushed out his cigarette. "It won't happen to me."

"Right," Kinder-Mann said. "Tell that to the lung cancer in Room 607."

"Guilt, guilt!" Slater protested. "But what about Walt Branch? I hear Mt. Zion's having terrible political difficulties, that Branch is out in the cold."

"I know, that's what I heard," Kinder-Mann said. "I was talking with Ben Rabim at Memorial Sloan just yesterday, and he said that Mt. Zion hasn't done a thing. I find that amazing, what with Walt and Maxwell Leider. I'd think Max would be on it. Walt, too."

"But Dr. Leider is off on another planet these days, the recombinant work; he's got a dozen contracts with the government and private industry, too. But Walter Branch is..." Slater didn't finish.

"Yes, he is," Kinder-Mann cut him off. "I'd love to know the whole story there. It's such a can of worms back there. I bet I could guess..." Kinder-Mann let his voice trail off; he smiled, slightly, the corner of his mouth lifting only a bit.

Jack noticed the wry lttle grin. "What is it between you two anyway?" he asked, instantly regretting the question when he saw Kinder-Mann's face close in a frown.

"Another can of worms," Kinder-Mann said. "There are many reasons for the rift between us. It's a long story..."

"I've got time," Slater said. He wanted to know why these two men hadn't spoken in years.

"Okay," Kinder-Mann said. "Let's get more coffee first." The two men rose and went to the row of coffee pots, poured their cups full, then returned to their table. "Perhaps the least important is ethical," he began. "To make a long story short, Walt Branch came from a very poor family. He was even in reform school as a kid, you know the scene. He straightened himself around and started working hard—too hard, probably—and you see where he is now. But he always put the business of medicine ahead of the profession itself.

"I'm not naïve, you know that, and I'm not especially venal or socialist. I just work, but you know my basic position—that medicine should be a right not a privilege. Over a period of years we argued violently about this until our friendship had finally been poisoned by it. He even threw a drink on me at an AMA convention one year."

Slater smiled; the drink-throwing struck him as overly dramatic. "But if he was raised poor, you'd think he'd see the real need," Jack offered.

Kinder-Mann sighed. "Unfortunately, it doesn't work that way. Medicine is too efficient a vehicle for achieving great personal wealth and prestige, particularly for someone who has nothing to start out with. Simply put, Walt wants to see that system preserved."

"But not to interfere ethically?"

"Yes," Kinder-Mann said. "He has consistently used his power and prestige to rally against any sort of socialized medicine. And he maintains that standpoint. His position is insufferable."

Slater watched Kinder-Mann closely. The story was interesting, but he didn't buy it as the full history of their rift. Ethics is one thing, friendship another.

"Hmm," Kinder-Mann intoned. "Of course, that's that. It's one of those things..."

"There's more, isn't there?" Slater prompted.

"Yes, personal stuff. Branch began to resent me way back in medical school. But that's a dirty story," Kinder-Mann said.

"Bend my ear," Slater said. "I love dirty stories."

"Okay," Kinder-Mann said, looking both worried and relieved. He was anxious to tell the story, but worried about the gossip; still, Jack was a good friend. Kinder-Mann almost laughed in his pleasure at the memory of his tale; he brushed his hand back along his salt-and-pepper hair. "It was all during the last year of medical school at

Columbia. Art Maguire — Mt. Zion's research administrator — was a T.A. for Professor MacKenzie. He was also dating a gorgeous young lady named Carolyn Whittier, now Mrs. Walter Branch.

"Well, Art Maguire and I had a thing going..."

"What?" Slater was incredulous.

"He's a closet case, always was," Kinder-Mann explained. "He was using Carolyn as a cover, because in those days you couldn't be open about these things without being dismissed from medical school. But in the meantime, Walt was in love with her.

"Since Art and I were very close, I got extra help on everything. I got a key to Professor MacKenzie's lab and personal library, which is something that none of the other students would have known about. And it was a big boost, too. Except that Carolyn found out that Art was using her, so she started using him — as a cover for her affair with Walt. Her parents, being socially strict, would not have allowed her affair with Walt, but they were very accepting of Art, since he comes from old Massachusetts money.

"It all got very complicated the way those things tend to, and Carolyn, being not very discreet really, told Walt everything about Art and me, including the part about the lab and the library and the extra help. When the appointments for residency came around, I got the sterling appointment that both Walt and I were competing for, and I got the heftiest scholarship. Walt got nothing in the bargain but Carolyn.

"He's resented me ever since. I left all that, of course, and came out here to mecca, but Walt is still there, married now to Carolyn — who is amazingly rich since her parents died — and working under Art — who is amazingly in the closet."

"What a complicated story!" Jack said, highly amused.

"You're thinking we were all depraved," Kinder-Mann said, swallowing the last of his refill; it was already cold. "But I'll bet you anything that the reason Art Maguire's stifled Walt Branch's research is because AIDS is a so-called gay disease; I'm sure it suits his lurid secrecy and self-hatred to prevent any research, as much as he can."

"That's really sick," Jack said, making a face.

"Tell me about it," Kinder-Mann said. "It didn't take me long to realize that I was getting suckered into a very difficult and ugly set of political circumstances, so I bailed out as fast as I could."

Slater shook his head. "You know, I wonder how much homophobia is hurting our funding process in all this..."

"Completely!" Kinder-Mann exclaimed. "That's the whole point of it, really. Everyone's afraid of getting involved with this queer disease; it's so stupid. Straight doctors are the worst; they seem as if they couldn't care less at this point. That will change, I'm sure, as the disease spreads."

"You're so confident that it will," Slater observed.

"Oh, yes, no doubt," Kinder-Mann said. "And I can't help but wonder what's going to happen to the gay community as it does. Not in terms of panic and mobilization, but in terms of sex and socializing."

"It's going to have to stop," Slater said abruptly.

"Well, yes, that's the first inclination, of course," Kinder-Mann said, "but really, we don't have a shred of empirical evidence that says stopping sex will stop AIDS. It just appears that the highest risk factor for contracting whatever it is seems to be anyone who has a lot of sex with a lot of different partners."

"But we have the epidemiologic pattern already," Slater said, rather argumentatively. "We have points of entry — New York's gay community and the West Coast's community; we have high-risk populations and we know why: sexual contact is the most efficient means of spreading contagion." Slater was frowning; Kinder-Mann knew all of this.

"Yes, you're right," Kinder-Mann said. "The virus is out there, but I'm not sure how much we can rattle the gay community's sexual lifestyle, until we know more."

Slater was harsh: "We know enough; people have died."

Kinder-Mann nodded. He was torn between not knowing and supposition, between silence and censure. "I know," he said, "but I went out to the Caldron and the Hothouse the other night, just to see what's going on..."

"Just to see?" Slater joked.

"No, really," Kinder-Mann said. "Before the epidemic, sure, but not now. I just went to see if people are being more careful, if it's even probable that they'll stop."

"And?"

"It was just like always. Some of that stuff just isn't good to do with strangers, epidemic or not. But I think it matters a great deal *how* we warn the gay community about the risks involved. This sort of thing is potentially loaded, the perfect target for the Moral Majority types. They could accuse us of spreading disease, of infecting the country with sexual habits that they call bizarre."

"Especially now that it's spread to those other groups, the Haitian refugees and the intravenous drug users," Slater observed. "But we've got to do or say something. We could debate the politics for months, until hundreds more are infected, unless we issue some warnings now."

Kinder-Mann was shaking his head. "No, no, we've got to be careful, very careful, maybe even wait. Should I wait to issue a statement?"

"No!" Slater was emphatic. He could not understand Kinder-Mann's sudden doubt. "There isn't time to wait. What are you going to do? Keep on researching and wait to see what happens? Wait until five hundred people are infected? Then maybe next year, say in 1983, we'll say oops! we should have mentioned that this is dangerous?" Slater was coming down hard. "No, you can't."

Kinder-Mann was silent, thoughtful. "I'm not sure about your scenario," he said. "But I'm sure about my caution. It would be irresponsible to say too much until we know. But then..." Kinder-Mann looked deeply worried. There seemed no resolution to his dilemma, whether or not to speak out and risk being wrong, or, possibly, to risk being correct and thus save lives.

"We better get back to work..." Slater said, standing and walking out. He felt the problem as well, though he felt more dogmatic about it. If there was reason to believe that AIDS was sexually transmitted, they had better damn well warn their friends in the gay community. Anything less would be tantamount to negligence.

25 *January 1982* • *New York City*

How can a man pass each day, knowing that
the man he loves is slowly wasting away? To carry the fear
that it might be next week or next month? To interview
researchers and hear the same thing over and over: we
don't know. How could he plan for the future while his
lover lay at home sick with cancer, sick with medicine? It
seemed to David now that his entire existence was invested
in Andy's illness. Not only was his lover afflicted with KS,
but David spent his days discovering more about the disease, about the epidemic. Was Andy no longer his lover?
Had he begun a lover-relationship with the cancer itself?

And what meaning did this illness make of their past? It
was, in some ways, as if their relationship had been betrayed, though, in one way—David's support of Andy—
it had brought them much closer together than many
couples might ever know.

David was troubled by these things as he made his way
home that day. The whole thing was, at times, almost insufferable. It wasn't right! David protested in his mind.
Their love should not have been crippled by this unknown
science fiction. It was a dark time for David, but it was
darker for Andy. After the brief respite Andy had enjoyed
following the initial chemotherapy treatment, he had rapidly begun to decline. The KS lesions began to proliferate,
and so he had gone back for more intensive chemotherapy
coupled with cobalt. Yet he was worse; the cancer was
spreading. Endoscopies showed the cancer spreading in-
ternally, along the esophagus, in the colon. His digestive
system was a shambles, being destroyed by parasitic infections that antibiotics seemed unable to touch.

The cancer had come to dominate both their lives. David
worried that he was unable to give as much as Andy
needed. How was he to support his lover under such serious circumstances? It wasn't just some abstract health crisis
for them, it was excruciatingly real. David's toughest lesson
with Andy so far was learning when to pull back, when to
allow Andy the space, the silence. It was a delicate matter

of respect; a dying man must go alone at times, no matter how much the silence may afflict his partner.

David had been busy finding out what little there was to find about the crisis, for his job at the paper, and for his hopes for Andy. And David was embittered *and* cheered by what was going on. What impressed him the most was the degree to which the gay community in the largest cities had begun to mobilize, to band together to establish support groups, to gather and release information to the community. Gay people weren't ignoring the health crisis anymore, even though large numbers refused to face the harsher facts.

David was covering the recent founding of a New York group—"The Gay Men's Health Crisis"—which had just formed to raise money for research and provide information to the public. He found such an effort tremendously exciting; something's finally happening! he told himself. But he remained troubled by the lack of advances in the scientific world; the researchers still knew close to nothing, and the whole thing was too sensitive, as they said, for many institutions to deal with.

Of course, David knew that such things took time. And there was more and more medical information circulating. It seemed a matter of government ignorance at this point, something that both shocked and angered David. But he could understand it. Too many people were viewing the AIDS epidemic as a new social disease, VD, something to be swept under the rug and definitely *not* to be discussed over dinner. It was that attitude, coupled with the blatant homophobia of a right-wing administration, that kept research advances at a minimum.

David was looking forward to his trip to San Francisco to interview Dr. Kinder-Mann for the paper. Secretly, he hoped that Kinder-Mann might have some answers or experimental treatment that could help Andy, but he doubted it. He wasn't sure what Kinder-Mann would be able to tell him, but David wanted to find out all that he knew, see for himself what was going on in San Francisco. New York had been the hardest hit so far in the epidemic, but San Francisco wasn't far behind. David wondered how many more cities would feel the impact of the disease before something was discovered to stop its deadly path.

How many blows can we take? David asked himself, repeating Andy's question about the gay community from way back. It had been such a long struggle to be able to declare simply that they were gay, and then to establish real, loving relationships. That had taken decades of hard work, and then, beyond that, they had had to fight the hard political and moral fight for civil rights, for the simple human right to feel and express love. That fight was still being waged, but now it would be more difficult. There would be the incredible distraction of the health crisis—economic and social. And there would be the increased paranoia on the part of the heterosexual community to deny gay rights, to wrongly perceive gays as sick, infected.

These would be potent forces to combat, but David had confidence that it could be done. After all, they had come this far. He was sure that gay folks would band together to fight this thing. In fact, he reminded himself, thinking of the Gay Men's Health Crisis project, they already were. How he hoped that the darkness of the moment wouldn't erode the vision of the future that all gay people had worked for. We've got to keep it together, he declared to himself, climbing the steps to the apartment. We've got to stay strong and see this thing through.

But when he opened the door and saw Andy there resting, saw the thin pallor and horrible devastation of the cancer, David was filled with a sense of violent fear, an irritable mood that threatened to break all his good sense and logical conclusions. It was at that moment—that passing microsecond of near insanity—that the paranoia began to form, an irrational passion that seemed to seduce David into hysteria. It was a long moment of terror; Andy lay resting, his eyes closed. He couldn't see David standing there, his back pressed against the wall, his neck and shoulders tight with enormous and sudden tension. The sensation was that of falling and being frozen in place, all at once, unlike any anxiety he had ever felt. And though he knew—could predict with all his wits—that within a minute he would cross the room and take Andy into his arms to greet him, the present moment seized him and showed him the depths of his fear and loss. There was in that moment a great selfishness, something David had denied in his focus on Andy's sickness. But now, his mind grasped the fear and made a panic of it. How the hell was he to go on, not knowing if he had AIDS or would get it? Had he somehow given the virus to Andy? Or had Andy given it to him, and now, at this very moment as his heart beat and his cheeks flushed, the virus was incubating, ticking away in his system like a time-bomb, working its devastation on him as well? Or was he now immune and thus safe? Or could he pass it to someone new? He felt a palpable terror at the sudden onset of reality, for he had only once before considered a remaining life of solitude—no one willing to take him, or he himself unwilling to risk the chance. The prospect made chaos of all he knew; in that moment his world, his entire cognitive framework turned to dust. He could nearly feel the particles of that destruction settling around him, for it seemed that there was nothing more appealing at that moment than death itself. He looked at Andy, now stirring and opening his eyes, and felt a great wave of jealousy that it was *his* turn, *his* dignity that was facing death. David wanted it then, wanted to go with Andy. But then Andy smiled, yawned, and beckoned to David. The moment was past; the fear distilled to bland expectancy. David went to the couch and hugged his lover.

26 *January 1982* • *Philadelphia*

It was a cold Saturday morning. Edna Stone got out of bed, glanced at Chuck—still sound asleep—and pulled on her heavy terrycloth bathrobe. She found her wool slippers and quietly left the bedroom. She went into the kitchen and fussed over the coffee-making machine. She opened the front door, retrieved the paper, and returned to the kitchen. The smell of the coffee already filled the room as the machine made its gurgling dripping sounds.

She sat down at the kitchen table and spread the newspaper before her, but she couldn't read. She sat and stared out the back windows. The weather was awful, just awful, she thought. The snow lay crusty and sooty on the ground, the sky was a dull slate gray. A cold wind blew, occasionally battering the house and windows with a sudden blast. It was the type of day she would have preferred to stay in bed, curled up with a book.

But after a night of tossing and turning, worrying about how to approach the subject of Andy with Chuck, she had finally given in and got up. She poured herself a cup of coffee and sat down at the table again. She reached into an open package of cookies and took one, nibbling on it and sipping her coffee as she planned her scheme. She would tell Chuck that morning that she and Elizabeth were going up to New York for the January sales. They'd take the train at the end of the month, and once there, they'd call on Andy.

With this simple plan in mind, she at least was able to read a bit of the paper. But over and over again her mind returned to her apprehensions. Chuck would not like it, possibly he'd forbid them to go. And if that happened, she didn't know what she'd do. Chuck held such power over them all; if he told her not to go and not to call... well, that was what she'd have to do. She really couldn't cross him. She never had.

She shook her head at her own confusion. Part of her wanted to defy him, to simply state that what she wanted to do, she would do. But another part of her recognized that Chuck was the provider, the one to whom she owed her allegiance and her obedience. This had been their promise to one another so long ago, and she had stuck with it ever since.

And, also, she felt that perhaps he was right, on one level at least. It *was* Andy's doing that he was now in such a ghastly predicament. He *had* brought it on himself after all, with all that gay living in New York. Lord knows they had tried to help him back then when they'd first found

[177]

out. Did that effort discharge her responsibility to Andy? Should she, as Chuck recommended, forget about him and let him die in peace? In the loneliness that he himself had chosen by adopting a life of perversion?

But oh, that argument held less weight with her now. She was no fool, no stupid housewife. She watched the news, she read the papers and the magazines. She knew what kind of world they lived in. Andy was hardly alone in his deviance; there were tens of millions of like-minded young men—and women, she supposed—in America, and nobody really knew how it happened. Was it a perversion? Had she and Chuck done something wrong in raising Andy? Was it that he had had no brothers, but only sisters?

She rolled her eyes and took another sip of her coffee. All those excuses seemed so foolish. Because she knew, when she remembered, that Andy had been different from the very beginning. There was really no special moment or event that she could point to and say, there, that's why Andy turned out that way. She could see his difference in the whole pattern of his childhood, and so she wondered—as she had heard on a talk show—if it wasn't just that some people were born like that. If that was so, then she and Chuck were wrong to shut him out as they were doing.

But the shutting-out was not all their fault. After all, Andy had stepped out at eighteen and very stubbornly refused to return. He had shut them out as much as they had shut him out. It was too complicated! she suddenly protested. And did it matter? If he was dying, as she felt he was, did any of it matter? Shouldn't they just put their differences aside and reconcile before it was too late? Before he carried their separation and pain to his grave?

*

It was nearly noon when Chuck Stone finally got out of bed. He had been lollygagging about, rather uncharacteristically he thought, in an effort to avoid seeing Edna. He had a suspicion that she was about to spring something on him, most likely something about Andy. And he was both unprepared and unwilling to deal with it. He wished that the whole thing were over with. If Andy was dying of some creepy disease, then let him die and get this prickly subject out of their lives. He was damned tired of hearing Edna and Beth whisper in the kitchen. He was tired of their inability to recognize the larger moral issue at stake and put Andy out of their lives.

He knew he was right. There were good reasons for men not to behave like Andy did. Plenty of good reasons, he knew, that helped keep things together and helped keep the human race alive. If every man gave in to every sexual whim, no matter how perverted, there would been nothing but chaos in the country. And so he knew he was right. When Andy had refused to get cured, and had furthermore insisted on moving to New York City and practicing his deviance, then Chuck had no choice but to disown him and consider him dead. What else was there to do with a son who refused to be a son? Who refused to be a man? He already had three daughters, and Andy had been the only boy, the only one to pass on the family name and continue his existence in another family.

They were right, he thought, about the family. If it weren't for the family, where would they be now? Everybody couldn't just step out and do as they pleased. There had to be discipline and structure to keep things going. He was irritated that Edna and Beth couldn't see this, but then, women often refused to look at things coldly and factually.

He tried to put these thoughts out of his mind as he stepped into the shower. He'd dress and have lunch and go down to the office. There was no way he would stick around the house all afternoon and watch Edna mope, and, quite possibly, bring up some conversation about the whole thing.

*

Edna had prepared a nice lunch of hot roast beef sandwiches and coffee when Chuck came into the kitchen. He sat down at the table to eat, and they chatted about the weather, about the news. Chuck asked if Beth would be home from college for the weekend, and Edna told him that no, she'd be away for the rest of the month.

Finally, he told her that he'd be going down to the office that afternoon.

"Oh, then, Chuck?" she started, and he thought, oh, shit, here it comes. "I just wanted to ask you if Beth and I could run up to New York for the January sales next weekend? I'll take the train up and meet her there, or she can come down here and we'll drive up. I hate to miss the..."

"No," he said, cutting her off. He was shaking his head firmly. "I will not have you running up there to see him, and that's all I'm going to say about it. Drop it, Edna."

She sat stunned at the immediacy of his answer, though she was not surprised. She watched him throw his napkin down on the table in anger as he shoved his chair back and stood up. He turned and left, She heard the front door open and slam shut, then heard the roar of the truck's engine as he started it up. She sat there, her hand toying with her coffee cup. She was annoyed and disgusted. She agreed with him about some of it, but her overwhelming sense was that she had to see Andy, at least once. She decided in that sudden moment of anger and humiliation at his response, to simply ignore him this one time. She would buy a ticket for New York during the week and simply go. And he wouldn't stop her, not on this one.

27 *Late January 1982 • San Francisco*

When David got off the plane at San Francisco International, it was storming badly, one of those howling tropical storms that batters the peninsula on which San Francisco is perched. The rain poured down in sheets as David's shuttle turned onto the freeway for the short drive to the city. The shuttle bus swayed with every blast of wind. David saw Candlestick Park, and then, as they rounded a low hill, he could see the skyline of San Francisco, gray, cold, blurred through the driving rain. He had never enjoyed San Francisco; the few times he had visited the city, it had either been storming like this, or been cold and foggy. Once, though—and it was odd that he should remember it now—he had spent a week in the city when the weather performed the miracle it's famous for: warm spring-like days, when the sky is a delicious Florentine blue, as though it had been waxed shiny; then, as the afternoon closed in, the great white mass of fog had appeared above Twin Peaks, boiling and tumbling down the mountain like the Dead Sea at Moses' parting, creating a perfect evening of chill coziness.

It wasn't like that now, David thought as he got off the shuttle in downtown San Francisco and hailed a cab to take him to the University of California Medical Center. He climbed into the cab and leaned back, brushing water from his hair. He looked out the window of the cab, watched the rain come pouring down as the taxi turned onto Fell Street and headed through the gray city. His mind wasn't clear. Images of Andy kept bothering him; they'd hovered around the edges of his thoughts the whole trip. The flight had been something of a trial, actually, as he had to constantly fight the worry that something bad was happening to Andy. No, Andy had said go, go see Dr. Kinder-Mann, find out what's happening, what can be done. And so David had left Manhattan as planned, left on a crisp January morning that was caked with ice and soot.

Now here he was, riding through rain-drenched San Francisco, with worries about Andy still uppermost in his feelings. He was anxious to meet Alfred Kinder-Mann, to find out what he was discovering about AIDS. But he knew that there had been no breakthrough; he could feel it in his bones, as his grandfather used to say. David had an idea the epidemic was going to be around a long, long time. Branch had warned him just the day before not to get his hopes up; this trip, after all, had personal implications for David far beyond his journalistic interests, a fact of which David would have to beware.

The cab pulled up in front of the sleek glass and steel edifice of the medical center on Parnassus Street. David was impressed by the futuristic design of the center, perched high aside a hill, overlooking the park, Golden Gate Bridge, and downtown San Francisco. After the crowded urbanity of Mt. Zion in Manhattan, this institution seemed oddly insular, removed, as it was, from the busy city.

David looked up at the glass building, then walked around its glass-encased first floor lobby to the northeastern terrace. He remained under the grand awning of the building and took in the magnificent view, curiously filtered through the sheets of rain. It all seemed strangely placid, even with the wild storm. The sleek medical center, its position on the hill, the tremendous natural beauty of the setting — all of it seemed incongruous with David's purpose. Yet he knew that in the building above him, part of the medical horror of AIDS was unfolding.

He turned and walked around to the front of the building. A great blast of cold wind drove heavy droplets of rain against David's face, and he quickly dodged through the sliding glass doors into the protection of the lobby. It was warm and quiet; through the glass walls he could see the great view again, but the quiet coziness of the building's interior cut him off. He made his way to the directory, found Kinder-Mann's office number, and made his way to the elevators.

He found Kinder-Mann's office and was shown in by a young man wearing jeans and a simple shirt. David noted, looking down at his own open topcoat, muffler, and wool slacks, that things were much more relaxed. It was a matter of a few minutes until Dr. Kinder-Mann walked in, smiling and extending his hand.

"Good to meet you," he said to David. "I've seen some of your pieces in the *Herald*. I don't read as much as I'd like to, though, but I've been pleased to see that you're keeping it level-headed."

"Thank you," David said, truly appreciating the comment. He was already highly impressed with Kinder-Mann. There was an air of bright confidence around him, and he seemed more youthful than his fifty years. Somehow, David had thought of Kinder-Mann as being a younger man, although he knew that he and Branch had been in medical school together. David liked the tall, handsome man.

Kinder-Mann indicated that David should sit on a couch beside a tall bookcase. He did, and Kinder-Mann sat down in a chair beside the couch. It was a tidy, modern office. The desk was covered with papers and volumes, and an open door in one wall revealed a large study, or, David assumed, perhaps a lab.

"We're working awfully hard here," Kinder-Mann began. "Night and day, literally."

"I heard," David said. "What are you doing? What have you found?"

"Quite basically..." he began, but David cut him off.

"Just a minute, doctor," David said, fumbling with his small tape recorder. "Let me get this thing going; I quite nearly forgot."

"Sure," Kinder-Mann said, watching as David set up the small machine. Kinder-Mann smiled as David fumbled with the thing, unable to get the mechanisms to function. "Isn't it always?" he said in sympathy.

David shook his head and banged the tape recorder. It started going at once. Kinder-Mann smiled and asked David if he wouldn't like to take his coat off first and get a cup of coffee. David nodded and laughed. In his haste, he had urgently rushed in and started right off.

He stood and took his coat off, shaking the rain onto the rug. He laid it over the edge of a chair, then put his muffler on top of it. Kinder-Mann had stepped out of the office for a moment and was returning now with a cup of coffee for David and one for himself. They settled down again, ready to talk. David got the tape recorder going again and nodded at Kinder-Mann.

"Well, basically," Kinder-Mann started, "in the last month I've been looking at two things—the nature of AIDS itself and its patterns. That is, its epidemiological manifestations. Of course, one leads to the other. I'm sure it's a virus, possibly a new one, something we've not seen before.

"A month ago, I was intent on finding that virus, but of

course, finding a virus is like looking for a needle in a haystack, if you'll pardon the colloquialism."

"Why is that?" David asked. "I mean, one thing that has troubled me is why don't you just sit down and look into your microscopes and find it? Can't you take blood or whatever from people with the disease and see the virus in there?"

Kinder-Mann smiled, a broad, almost tragic smile. "It's not quite that easy, you see. There are, quite literally, millions of viruses, and they're much, much smaller than bacteria, for example. A virus is about the size of a strand of DNA, with a protective shell. Finding them requires enormous time and cost, electron microscopy, stuff like that. It can take years simply to isolate one virus, let alone do anything about it."

"But what about the Hepatitis B virus?" David asked. "They found that and made a vaccine."

"Yes, that's right, and it took many, many years. First, the virus has got to be screened, isolated, identified, etcetera. It's really an enormous task.

"Now, the reason I'm delving into the epidemiology is because until we've enough money to hunt the virus, our next step is to retrace the outbreak of the disease, to find out what are the interconnections here, how are the victims related, if indeed they are. You see, don't you, that it's that deliberate pattern that intrigues me so. Because if I can backtrack enough, then perhaps I can find the common link that could lead me to something that would help identify the virus—maybe a specific place or context. If that happened, then we could go looking for the virus there, just as they found the Legionnaires' infectious agent in that hotel."

"I understand," David said, "and I want to know more about that common link idea, but another question just popped into my head. What, exactly, is the nature of AIDS? You said that was one of the things you're working on. What goes wrong to make the patients so vulnerable to KS and those other diseases?"

"Okay," Kinder-Mann said. "We're studying what goes

wrong in the body once an individual has contracted whatever it is that causes AIDS. I'll try to put it as simply as I can."

"Please do," David said, getting out his notebook and pen as well as checking on the tape recorder.

"First, let me explain the basic nature of the human immune system. It's composed of two main faculties, which we refer to as T cells and B cells. The T cells produce T helpers, which together with the B cells manufacture antibodies that fight off anything foreign—such as disease, viruses, cancers, and so on. There are also T suppressors, that monitor the production of antibodies. And there are T killers, which attack and ward off certain invading organisms."

"Like Raquel Welch in *Fantastic Voyage*," David joked.

Kinder-Mann laughed. "Yes, exactly, like Raquel Welch. Now, for some reason, when an individual has AIDS, there are not enough T helper cells to produce antibodies. And that, in turn, weakens the individual's immunity such that any number of bizarre, opportunistic infections may attack and overcome the individual."

"Like KS, and pneumocystis pneumonia," David said.

"You got it," Kinder-Mann said. "Now what we are trying to find—what *everyone* is trying to find, that is—is what accounts for that lack of T helpers. And this was where we started. I think there is a specific infectious agent—a virus, or perhaps a constellation of viruses—which destroys the T helpers. We need to find it. That's why I'm backtracking with the epidemiology in the hope of finding that common link in the victims that might lead me to the virus. What I've found there is pretty interesting."

David was fascinated. No one had as yet published such an explanation. "What have you found so far? Any common link yet?"

"This is where I'm both proud and embarrassed," Kinder-Mann said. "Because yes, I've found something common, but not enough to find a common link. Not yet. I've been working with my assistant, Jack Slater, and we've identified thirty-five patients at this point who are all linked somehow."

David was wide-eyed. "Linked how?"

"Well, in a variety of ways—friendships, sexual partners, lovers, visitors at friends' houses, that sort of thing. We screened them further, and found that of these thirty-five men, there seems to be a link to seven KS patients. And those seven were among the original twenty-six that I reported to the CDC last July."

"Then you've found the link?" David was excited. The puzzle was unraveling and falling into place, and for him it had only been a matter of a few minutes in this office in San Francisco.

"No, there is no link," Kinder-Mann said. "I mean, we've boiled these thirty-five men down to being connected to these seven men, but so far we've not found anything to link the seven men, except, of course, their homosexuality. This is what frightens me, because it lends such strong evidence to the theory that the disease is sexually transmitted...."

David cut in: "But I thought that was foregone..."

Kinder-Mann nodded. "I know, but we've not been able to prove it, yet. Without proof, what can we say? What can we do? I mean, from my work and from these epidemiological data, I am confident that the disease is sexually transmitted, or to be more precise, that it is transmitted by contact with blood or semen."

David was frowning. "But if you know that, or at least suspect it with such conviction, hadn't you better issue warnings to the gay community to avoid those sex practices? Get the baths to post warnings or hand out leaflets or something?"

"No, no, no," Kinder-Mann said, emphatically. "I won't go pontificating until the facts are in; the jury's still out, and what if we're wrong? Then we'd have compromised years and years of political work to achieve this sort of freedom."

David was alarmed. He had liked this man instantly, but now, seemingly out of character, the man had turned medicine into politics. There is no escape, David told himself silently, thinking of Art Maguire and Walter Branch and the few gay leaders he knew in New York who also felt as

Kinder-Mann now did; don't rock the boat until you have to. "I think," David began, uncertain how to begin without insulting the doctor, "that perhaps there's a confusion here. On my part. I mean, medicine is one thing, politics another. Right?"

Kinder-Mann smiled, so genuinely and with such great concern that David was moved; he liked him again. "Well, it is both in this case," Dr. Kinder-Mann said. "You must understand that already, if you've been seeing what your lover's going through. *And* covering the epidemic. But, out here in San Francisco at least, you must understand how important gay business is to the city's economy. Gays don't have nearly the integration here that they do in Manhattan. Things are highly segregated, yet a third of the city is gay. That means that there exists 'an entire set of separate gay institutions to serve the gay community— medicine, dentists, bookstores, clothes stores, restaurants, baths, sex clubs, even a bank. Now if I go around stating that everyone must stop having sex, what about the economy? What about all those institutions whose very existence is predicated upon sexual freedom? It's a trade, I admit, but one that must be made, at the moment. We just don't know enough."

David said nothing for a moment. He was weighing the doctor's words in his mind. Finally, he said, "But if you wait, if people keep fucking and sucking all over the place, won't the disease pool be growing larger and larger?"

"We don't know that; we don't know anything about how it works. Only that it's sexually transmitted via semen and blood. But there may have been specific ports of entry—those seven men for example—and the disease may be working its way through the population now, creating antibodies in most men who come in contact with it."

"I've heard that before," David said. "I've also heard your argument about destroying institutionalized gayness by suggesting chastity. From gay leaders in New York. Nobody wants to take a stand. It seems negligent."

"But it's not," Kinder-Mann said with great conviction. "Because we truly have nothing to take a stand on, yet. As soon as we do, believe me, we'll yell it from the rooftops. I'd like to encourage you to tone it down when you report on this interview, if you will."

David didn't answer. He didn't know how he felt about it. Suddenly he was preoccupied with Andy, with worries about his being in New York alone. Just then, David wished he hadn't come to San Francisco; it was proving to be too difficult. The information on the nature of AIDS was useful to him; no one had yet published that explanation. But the rest, the political jabber, he could do without. Particularly since Andy lay at home, very close, David suddenly felt, to death.

Kinder-Mann watched the shadow cross David's face, saw his interest in the entire interview drain away. He knew it must be something about the young man's lover. Kinder-Mann decided to change the subject. "How is Walt Branch?" he asked.

"Fine," David answered quickly. He wanted to stop thinking about Andy. "Although he's worked up about no funds. The hospital won't fund the research."

Kinder-Mann frowned, the tan skin around his eyes crinkling into tiny folds. "Art Maguire?" he said, looking directly at David.

David nodded. "Yes, exactly. Stopping it all the way."

"Don't like him," Kinder-Mann said. "Not anymore."

David didn't say anything. He had been given to understand that the breach lay between Walt Branch and Alfred Kinder-Mann; he didn't know that there was also something between Kinder-Mann and Maguire.

"Not many people seem to," David finally said, deciding to let it rest at that. He was weary and irritated; the politics of AIDS was too distressing. He decided to end the interview. He made arrangements to come back in the morning to get a picture of Kinder-Mann and his assistant Jack Slater, as well as to tour the research labs.

Right now, it was twilight already, rather dim and cold. The rain had stopped and left a damp, harsh chill. David went down to the bright lobby, the glass walls now framing the dusk. He stopped at a phone booth and called for a taxi. He wanted to get to Castro Street—gay mecca, they called it—and have himself a drink. He needed it before he called Andy.

*

Back in New York, Walt Branch was furious. One of the nurses on the evening shift had told him a bizarre and cruel story. Apparently Dr. Irving Krantz had, the day before, made some joking wager about "how long that crazy fag in room 217 would last; any bets?"

The story made Branch sick. He didn't doubt that Krantz was capable of such insensitivity. But "that crazy fag," Branch knew, was Patrick Ross. And Patrick Ross had just died.

28   *Late January 1982 • Philadelphia*

An icy wind had blown steadily for two weeks, and Edna Stone was weary of it. She had, without telling her husband, bought a train ticket for New York, but he had discovered it in the top drawer of her bureau. And so, that night, he and Edna and Beth sat at dinner, a deep tension in the room.

Earlier that evening, when he had discovered the ticket and torn it into shreds before her eyes, she had vowed that they would have it out after dinner, after Beth had gone. He had never seen such defiance in his wife, but he didn't fear her; it was, to him, another irritant in a situation that was becoming more intolerable with every day.

Edna had made the mistake, she now realized, of telling Beth about the entire incident as they fixed supper. Beth had become furious at the idea of her father tearing the ticket to bits and ordering her mother to remain at home. But she had promised her mother not to bring it up over dinner. And so they sat in tense silence, eating pork chops and mashed potatoes. But Beth had promised herself that come time to watch TV, she'd confront her father and insist that he allow her mother to travel to see Andy.

After dinner Chuck went directly to the living room, sat in a recliner, and turned on a show. Beth and Edna washed the dishes, and Beth told her mother that she intended to speak to her father.

"Please, Beth," her mother pleaded, "don't make things worse. Your father is adamant about this, and I think it's best left alone for now. I'm going to drop the whole thing after all. I can't keep fighting him. He gave me an ultimatum in there this evening: either I stay with the family, or I visit Andy. He said he'd leave me if I disobeyed him. How can I argue with that?"

"How can you not?" Beth demanded, exasperated at her mother's reticence. "How can you let a man just push you around and forbid you to see your dying son?"

"He's my *husband,* Beth, you know that means something more..."

"Stop it, Mother," Beth said angrily, her voice raised. "You've got to face him and tell him what you're going to do."

"What's that?" Chuck Stone demanded. They both turned and saw that he was standing in the kitchen door, listening as Beth berated her mother.

"She's going to see Andy," Beth said to him, an edge to her voice.

"Beth..." Edna warned, but there was no stopping it now. The thing took on a life of its own at that point, for Chuck Stone became defensive and angry.

"Beth, you'll not influence your mother like that, especially not against me you won't!"

"Daddy, I can't stand by and silently let you have your way with this, not anymore. Andy's really sick, and you seem to have no conception of what this is doing to Momma. Andy's her son—yours too, no matter what you say—and she can't just sit here in Philly while he dies just an hour away. Let her go to him!"

"No!" he said firmly, stepping into the kitchen. Edna stood at the sink drying her hands. Beth stood by the stove, forming a triangle between them. "I have said it too many times already," he went on. "This subject is closed for good. That's it."

Beth shook her head. "No, it's not. Father, you cannot stand there and dictate that we must let Andy die alone, and in silence. You can't do it; it's completely inhuman."

"It's the way things are, Beth. Your mother has already agreed that we have put the subject to rest for good. You're in no position to dictate to me..."

Something in the room changed all of a sudden, and all three of them felt it. While Chuck protested that Beth mind her own business, a profound change of expression crossed Edna's face. She was taking on the look of a pained, anguished soul, and Beth worried for a moment that perhaps she was about to have a breakdown. As Chuck stopped speaking, Edna took a deep breath and spoke: "I can't lay it to rest, Chuck, I can't."

He turned on her, rage in his eyes. "You promised me it was over, that you wouldn't defy me again."

"I can't help it, not over this," she said. Beth watched in stony silence as they fought. "Chuck, you have to understand how much is at stake here. You know how much I loved little Andy..."

"I did, too..." he said, but she cut him off.

"It was I who sat up with him when he cried; it was I who bandaged his scrapes, who baked him cookies after school. It was I who sat up all night when he had bad dreams, while you slept and snored in the other..."

He cut her off. "Slept so I could get up and work to support you! And *you*," he added, staring at Beth.

Edna began to cry as she went on. "No, that's not it," she said. "You weren't the one who raised them, all four of them. You think it was easy? You think I saw them like you did? At the end of the day? Just as some evidence that I could make babies? No, dammit, I want you to see how it is, how I created these little ones, how I gave myself— sacrificed whatever life I could have had on my own—in order to attend to them, even when they were sick, crying brats.

"It's no easy thing, but you never saw that. You have no idea how difficult it has been for me to dismiss Andy all these years. Of course I detest his perversion; it's wrong and hurtful. But I can't ignore the fact that he is dying just because of his perversion. It hardly seems related."

"But it is!" he protested, but seeing the rage in Edna's face, he was silent again.

"No, no . . ." She was shaking her head. "I gave up myself to raise these children, and to stand by while part of my life dies is just an impossible request. You're asking me to give up everything in that case. Don't you see? I am submerged in the lives of my children, and if I can't be with Andy when he dies, then everything is waste."

There was a long silence in the room. Beth was shocked and hurt at her mother's words. She had never considered herself as a destroyer of her mother's life, had never realized that her mother was something beyond a "mother." Without thinking, she said to her mother: "Momma, you hated us, didn't you?"

Edna was shocked, hurt. "Of course not, what a stupid thing to say."

Chuck turned to Beth: "Don't be cruel to your mother, Beth," he said. Then, turning to Edna herself, he said: "You hate me, I know."

"No!" she protested. "How can you say that?"

He answered: "Then why such defiance? Why do you accuse me of destroying your life?"

"You've missed the point, daddy," Beth said, but a sharp look from his narrowed eyes told her to be still.

"I haven't!" Edna protested. "You don't understand, I'm so confused. How am I to feel about this? How am I to think?"

"I've told you how to feel!" he said sharply.

Beth exploded. "Father! That's horrible; it's revolting! You can't tell another person how to feel."

He pointed his finger at Beth as if to reprimand her, but he said nothing. She went on. "Father, you've always tried to control us, tried to control everyone around you. It makes me sick to think about how cold you are, how little you feel. You're about fifty years behind the times, you know. Men do not hide behind veneers of coldness and masculine pride; it's destructive and stupid. Just let go of it and relax."

"Beth, don't speak to your father like that," Edna said, shocked at Beth's outburst.

Beth turned on her mother. "How do you defend him? *He* is killing Andy!"

Edna gasped at the words. "Shocking..." she started to say, but Beth went on.

"Daddy, all I ever want from you is some warmth, some affection. When I was little I always wanted you to hug me or kiss me. Anything, really, that might show me that you really cared about me. But it was never there. Now I'm begging you to stop shutting your feelings inside; please, just let go..."

Her father interrupted. "Beth, you're out of line..."

"Wait, let me finish," she said.

"But you *hate* me!" he said suddenly, so abruptly and unexpectedly as to invite fear.

"Yes, at this moment, I hate everything you are, everything you stand for. Don't you see it?" She was highly anguished, in great emotional pain. She paced as she talked now, her hands gesturing frantically, shedding pent-up pain and emotions.

Her father was drawn into the fury. "How can you attack me? How long have you nursed such a hatred against me?"

Beth began to cry as she answered. "I don't know! I never knew I felt all these things until this moment. But my brother is dying just an hour from here, and you do nothing. Even as your son dies, you can't give anything: no emotion, no leeway for Momma to see her own son, the son you're killing with your coldness."

He exploded: "Shut up!" He took a step towards her, then stopped, shouting. "You don't know what you're talking about. How dare you accuse me; how dare you be so bitter against me. I've done nothing wrong here. I've done the right thing, always. Always!"

Edna shook her head, tears still streaming down her face. "Chuck..." she warned, but he ignored her.

"No, let me finish," he said. "I'm sick about it, you don't see that, Beth. But I am. I have anxiety; I have memories, painful and hurting now. I see Andy as a little boy, running and playing, but I can't fit it together anymore. I always did the right thing, but it turned out wrong. And I have no answer for that. *I* was *betrayed!* Do you know what I mean, Beth? My son betrayed my paternity; he became something I could never have produced..."

"He was only a little boy, Father," Beth said.

Her mother cut her off: "Don't, Beth."

But Beth would not listen. "That you could never have produced?" she said. "What do you mean—you could never have produced a man that loves men? That is not afraid to show his love or affection for other men? Is that what you're afraid of? Is that what you could have never produced? I believe it! Father, I believe it, because you cannot do it yourself. You can show no love, no warmth, towards me or Momma or Andy or another man. Why, Daddy? Can't you let go and release it? Can't you just sit down, look into your heart and find some love? What holds you back?"

He was frozen in her argument. He was filled with inertia. A lifetime of American manhood had produced a man who, in the face of direct pleading from his daughter, could do nothing but stand mute. She stood before him, looking up at her father, expecting—hoping—for an answer. But he stood there, silent.

And then the moment passed. Beth relaxed her posture, her shoulders sagging. She sank into a chair at the kitchen table, and her mother sat down heavily beside her. Chuck Stone stood still, his face twisted with unexpressed rage, but he would not speak. Beth buried her face in her folded arms and wept. Her mother put her arms around her and comforted her.

Finally, Chuck Stone relaxed his stance, let his arms fall loosely at his sides. He was defeated, but bristling with defense. "That's all I want to hear about this tonight. Or ever again," he said. "This will be the end of it." He turned and left the room.

Beth continued to cry in her mother's arms. Edna Stone comforted her child, her heart filled with regret that such an ugly scene had taken place. She now, too, felt as Chuck did: they had had enough. It was best left alone.

*

In the front room, Chuck Stone stood at the window for a moment. He trembled in his fury and pain, but he couldn't let go. He put the palm of his hand against his forehead and set his mouth in a grimace. It was becoming difficult for him to ignore his feelings: he loved Andy so very much, more than anyone knew. To think that his son was dying... under those circumstances...

Chuck Stone sobbed and choked back the tears. He was right, he knew. He believed what he said, no matter his feelings. And so he got hold of himself, wiped the lone tear from his cheek, and stared out the window.

29 *February 1982 • New York City*

David returned to New York a few days later. January had already passed into February, a cold, dark time of the year when the brightness of spring and summer seems nothing more than a bad rumor. David's trip to San Francisco had been more an exercise in frustration than coverage of the epidemic. He had, all told, been more or less favorably impressed by Kinder-Mann and his work at UCSF, and he had been touched deeply by a struggling organization, the Kaposi's Sarcoma Foundation, housed in tiny offices overlooking Castro Street.

But the story didn't have enough appeal for David, not anymore, for the repetition of the same story over and over was wearing thin. As Andy's own health diminished, as David had to face it more strongly in his everyday life, the epidemic as it related to others held less interest for him. He suddenly found that he wanted out of the involvement with the paper. He was tired of repeating the miserable story in relation to other people, because now, with Andy's worsening condition, he did not relish living it out himself. Now that he and especially Andy had reached some sort of accord, he wished only to see that it was fulfilled, done with.

David found that, as he had feared and known in his gut, Andy had worsened, terribly. There had been a new and sudden proliferation of KS lesions all over his body, and the staph infection had broken out again in his groin. Andy showed the red, pustular sores and the KS lesions to David the evening he returned from San Francisco. David had looked, reluctantly; it was approaching overload.

"This is it," Andy said to David, broaching the subject. There were facts he had to relate, and none of it could wait. "I wouldn't tell you this on the phone, but I have to go into the hospital in the next few days. Dr. Branch just diagnosed pneumocystis pneumonia."

"No!" David gasped, tears abruptly running down his cheeks. He found it hard to accept, this final and long-awaited moment, when Andy would be hospitalized. All the tension of his trip welled up and overflowed at that moment. David felt overwhelmed. "How so fast?" he asked feebly.

Andy opened his mouth to answer, but then said nothing. David accepted the silence, but he couldn't control his tears. He was filled with conflicting feelings: hope, based on the work he had seen in San Francisco; fear, that he would lose Andy soon; frustration, from the inertia surrounding the epidemic's resolution; and anger, that the world was simply not fair. David was tired, weary. He looked blankly at Andy, inquisitive.

Andy spoke softly. "This is it, David. I have to go into Mt. Zion, so they can treat the pneumonia and the staph and the cancer, continue the cobalt and chemotherapy."

"No..." David sighed the word, hardly spoke it.

Andy spoke even more softly. "I may refuse treatment. I haven't decided. It may be best at this point to accept it and press on..." His voice trailed off as he watched David's suffering; he had not known he would inflict so much pain, but then, of course, what could he expect?

David's mind was working denial and hope, but his conscious mind brought him round again and again to the facts. Couldn't Andy stick it out just a while longer, until, perhaps, Kinder-Mann found the virus? But no, that wouldn't do, it wouldn't happen. Andy would go fast now; David knew the pattern. The onset of a serious decline in the condition signaled the start of what David knew to be a death sentence for Andy, for all so far. He would have to face it, somehow.

"David!" It was Andy shouting, standing before David and yelling his name. "David? Snap out of it! Lord knows I never expected to have to be the strong one at this point..." He didn't finish the sentence. David looked up at his lover, so pale and thin, so dignified as he faced the severity of his illness. And David realized that he had no right to behave as he was, to draw away into his own world of selfish cares and fears.

That he should be the strong one, David said to himself. That he should be the strong one... David was filled with a sudden strength, a vitality borrowed from Andy's dignity. What had seemed so pathetic only a moment before— Andy's ghastly gray pallor, his thinning hair, the hideous lesions on his skin—what had seemed so pathetic now seemed the inverted symbol of Andy's strength.

He *has* stuck it out! David told himself. He's been strong and faced it at every turn, while I ran and hid in my fucking press coverage of the damned crisis. It was nothing new, really, but it was, for David, one of those rare and triumphant moments of crystal clarity, when the tragedies, as well as victories, of the world somehow fit, a moment when David saw that what had already been accomplished had been good, had been real.

He stood and held Andy close, saying nothing. It was a moment when the whole of Andy's illness became a true reality, when both of them saw together that they had weathered a storm, and, moreover, that there was more to come: they accepted Andy's illness. And they gathered their strength for what was left.

30

The next morning, when David awoke, he went in to Andy's bed. David had slept on the couch; he couldn't bear to hear Andy cough on and off through the night. He sat down beside him and gently touched his shoulder. "Andy," he said, "wake up." He leaned over to kiss Andy on the cheek and realized how very still he was.

David shook Andy by the shoulder, but there was no response. David leaned in close, his own heart pounding. Andy was breathing, deeply even, though unevenly. David started to panic; he felt frantic.

"Andy!" David spoke sharply. But Andy lay still, breathing quietly.

David stood and paced around the bed, then back again. He was unable to collect his thoughts. What to do? he asked himself, trying to clear his head of the panic. In a moment it subsided, and he hurried to the phone, his eye trained on Andy. He phoned Mt. Zion, asked to be put through to Walt Branch, it was an emergency. David told Branch that he couldn't awaken Andy, that he must have lapsed into a coma. Branch, sensing David's panic, told him to calm down and pack some of Andy's things for the hospital; Dr. Branch would send an ambulance around at once.

The wait was neary terminal for David. He tried twice more to waken Andy, but nothing. He packed an overnight bag, then paced and smoked, waiting. Finally, after what had only been a few minutes, the ambulance arrived. David rode in the ambulance with Andy, nervous, completely uncertain. Branch admitted Andy to intensive care and then asked David if he would please calm down and wait for him in his office. David walked slowly to the elevator, his mind a jumble of thoughts and feelings. He knew that Andy was to be admitted to the hospital, and that his condition was extremely serious, but he hadn't expected this, not so sudden.

He got to the office and told Meg what had happened.

"Yes, I know, dear," she said. "Walt told me they were bringing him in."

David went into Dr. Branch's inner office and sat down. He stood again, walked to the window, and looked out. It was a brilliant winter day, bright, sunny. David sat down again. The day had already been too long, far too long. He closed his eyes and somehow managed to doze off.

He awoke when Dr. Branch walked into the office. "David," he said simply. "Andy is stable now. He's in intensive care. The pneumonia is much worse than I thought. We're fighting it with antibiotics, but it's difficult to treat..."

"I know," David said. He was far too familiar with the disease.

"I need to explain Andy's special situation to you, though," Branch went on. "Because of the nature of AIDS, it's necessary for us to establish certain isolation procedures for him. It's as much to protect him as it is for us, because in his weakened state, any infection could be fatal. So we isolate him, requiring that nurses, doctors, and visitors wear a mask, gloves, shoe coverings, surgical cap and gown. This keeps our bacteria away from him, as well as whatever is infecting him away from us."

"I understand," David said, not fully comprehending the extreme measures. "How long before I can see him?"

"Oh, you can go down now, if you like," Branch answered. "But first, I need to know if I should contact his family. I remember he told me that he wasn't certain he wanted them to know..."

"Yes, that's right," David said. "He told his sister, you know..."

"Yes, I remember, but what about his folks?"

"Well, I know she told them," David went on. "Andy doesn't know that, because when she called again last week to talk to him, he was sleeping after chemotherapy, and I decided not to tell him what she told me. Apparently when she told them what was going on, they said they didn't care, didn't want to hear another word. They've never approved of his gayness, and especially not of his living with me. As far as they're concerned, Andy's already dead."

David's eyes brimmed with tears. Dr. Branch put his arm around his shoulder, the only comforting thing he knew. There was nothing he could say. He looked across the room at the window, shaking his head. He knew that many felt as Andy's parents did, but he couldn't believe it.

"Why don't you go see him now," Dr. Branch said gently.

David only nodded and left the office. He saw Meg smiling at him and managed to smile back. He walked the long hall to the elevator, got in, and pushed the button.

He got off at intensive care and asked to see Andy Stone.

"I'm sorry," the nurse said. "But Mr. Stone is in critical condition and in isolation. Only family may be admitted."

"But Dr. Branch just told me I could look in on him," David said, incredulous at the nurse's coldness.

"I'm sorry, sir, but the patient is asleep and couldn't see anyone, anyway," she said. "Only family can go in. That's the rules."

"But I'm his lover," David protested.

The nurse fixed him with a sardonic smile. "That's not family, now is it? You're not his wife." With that she turned away.

David was furious. "Listen to me." She turned around, her eyebrows raised. "I said I'm his lover. His family knows he's dying and they don't care. Do you understand that? They don't care! I'm the only family he's got, and that's based on the fact that I love him and he loves me. Do you understand that? Do you understand that we're in love? Or do you understand his family's attitude?"

David turned and walked away. The nurse stood still, all color drained from her face. She had not expected a confrontation. David decided to return to Dr. Branch's office. He was furious, but since he had vented his anger at the nurse, his fury turned to hurt. But he knew that that was the way it was. He had no legal right to be with the man he loved, even if he were lying in a hospital bed, dying. David got to Branch's office and explained the situation to Meg.

"Oh, for chrissakes!" Meg said in annoyance. "Just a minute. Dr. Branch is in with a patient for a minute, but I'll get him to call that nurse." And then, leaning close, she whispered: "Don't mind her, anyway. She's a bitch."

A few minutes later Branch was on the phone, demanding to speak to the head nurse in intensive care. He told her that David Markman was to be allowed to visit Andy Stone, at any time of the day or night, regardless of visiting hours or stupid rules.

David was grateful for Branch's intervention, but it didn't satisfy him. Not only did he feel cheated and abused by a cruel and discriminatory rule, he felt anger, a deep burning rage, a rage that hurt. That nurse had slapped him in the face, had slapped four years of a good relationship right in the face. Yet his response had only vented his anger on the nurse; the situation was not changed.

The situation was changed only when he had "got permission" from the authoritative "doctor" to see *his* lover! Dammit! he shouted in his heart, what will it take before this love is recognized? Why must this minor difference orient an entire world toward madness?

David passed the nurses' station. He smiled disingenuously at the nurse; she cringed and sent a nurse's aide to assist him.

The aide showed him how to put on the gown, mask, cap, and gloves, then left him to enter Andy's room. He looked at his lover lying there, deeply asleep. The hurt of the past few minutes was intensified by the sight of his dying lover. Andy looked terrible, worse than David had expected, yet there was, in Andy's face, a certain calm.

David sat down in a hard white plastic chair near the bed and stared at Andy. He wasn't sure what he felt. He wondered if he would ever feel again.

*

Later, when David had resigned himself that there was nothing more to be done, he went home to their apartment. He felt the loneliness wash over him. His family was gone; the apartment was empty. David went to the living room and stared out into the street. It was bitter black, the street empty. David lit a Winston and stood smoking by the window, his hand trembling, causing ashes to flicker onto the sill.

He thought of all they had been through, of the suddenness of this moment, when he should be alone in the apartment, unknowing, expectant. He thought of the cruelty of the nurse, refusing him admittance to his own lover's room. He remembered his words, indistinct, raging. And then, in a rising swell of anger, he decided to call Andy's parents, to tell them that their son lay dying in the hospital.

It seemed late, but he realized it was not yet eleven o'clock. So he found their number, dialed it, and waited. The line was engaged on the fourth ring, and David identified himself to Andy's mother. She met his words with silence at first, then prompted him to speak. He told her of Andy's condition, and David could make out that as he spoke, she was covering the receiver with her hand and repeating the news to Andy's father.

In a moment, the phone was seized by Andy's father. He interrupted David loudly, exclaiming in wild tones that David should not have called. He launched into a litany of obscenities, called David a fag, a fucking queer. He blamed David for it all: "You did it, you dirty little faggot; you gave my son that fucking queer disease from your filthy sex practices and I hate you, I want you dead, too, all of you..."

David hung up, the adrenalin causing his body to shake all over. He lit another cigarette and dialed Rita's number. He simply could not take it all alone. She answered, a little groggy—she had been sleeping, obviously—and David related the story of what had just happened. She was sympathetic. "Oh, god, honey, you should have known they'd be that awful, but how dreadful for you to go through that. You know, you did the right thing, anyway. They had to be told."

David felt better for her support. "Thanks, Rita, I thought they had to know, too."

"Of course they did," she said.

"But I fucked it up, Rita," David said. "I should have asked for Beth, because now I'm afraid she's not going to get the message about Andy. I can't reach her except through their folks. She might not find out in time to get up here..." His voice faltered.

"Now listen to me, David Markman, listen close. This is real life. Got that? This is real life." She let the words sink in for a moment. "Now what most folks don't like to know or think about, and what they should always remember is that real life is tough, damn tough. Okay? Got that, David?"

"Yeah," he said.

"Good," she said. "Because honey, you've got the toughest stuff left to get through yet. At least you're not sticking your head in the sand like Jim, just dropping Andy like a leper or something. You're right there with him, fighting for his life, for your life. You just keep fighting, honey, 'cause something's got to give here, and it's not gonna be you or me. You're okay, David, you're okay. And remember, it's tough, and you gotta be tough as nails yourself."

David hung up and lit yet another cigarette. Rita had done it, had turned the tide for him. He sat by the window and smoked.

*

In Philadelphia, Chuck Stone watched his wife crying as he slammed down the phone. His fury was unbelievable; the whole thing was revolting him. But he couldn't bear to see Edna crying like that. "Stop crying, honey," he said, trying to control his rage that Andy's queer friend should call them and cause such pain. But she couldn't stop crying; the news was too much. Chuck knew then that he had been right all along. It was this sort of a scene—all this pain and trouble—that he had been trying to avoid. If only they had left it alone as he had ordered.

He looked at Edna and remembered their argument of a couple weeks before, when Elizabeth had attacked him so cruelly. That, coupled with tonight's episode on the phone, confirmed his conviction that the matter had to be dropped altogether. While he didn't want to add to Edna's suffering, he knew that this was the moment to set things out straight.

"Edna, I know you're upset," he started. "But you've got to remember that I tried to warn you all along about this. This is the kind of heartache I've tried to spare you. Let's just stop all this now and consider that Andy's already dead, as I did long ago. And we won't tell Beth. Okay? Will you do that? Will you forget about it all and assure me that you won't bring it up ever again? That you won't try to contact Andy or this friend of his? Will you promise?"

She looked up at him with a hatred in her eyes that he would never forget. And then he saw it leave, saw her eyes soften and sort of glaze over with tears. She nodded, making no sound. She knew, as she nodded her head and agreed to his demand, that she had no choice. He had made that clear two weeks ago; it was either the family life or Andy. And so it was over. She started to cry once again, because she realized as she nodded her head and capitulated, that she would never see Andy again.

31   *Mid-February 1982 • New York City*

Carolyn Branch was resplendent in a black-and-white gabardine and silk suit. Minutes before, she had gotten off the phone with Mrs. Dr. Sakowitz, who had informed her with absolute certainty that the federal grant—in the sum of three and a half million dollars—had just been bestowed upon Mt. Zion Hospital's Division of Biomedical Research. And, after quickly checking with her husband, she realized that he had been given no notice whatsoever in the matter.

And so she stood before her mirror, admiring herself as she prepared to pay Art Maguire a surprise visit. She appraised her image: stunning. Her suit was exquisite in design and execution. The left shoulder piece and sleeve were fashioned in white: the balance of the suit was darkest black, cinched tight at the waist by a black silk sash. Small, thin stoles of glistening ermine cascaded from her left shoulder down across her bust. The hemline, well below her knees, was cut at an angle and gave way, finally, to black stockings and heels. Her hat of black felt tipped violently sideways, its wide brim plunging dramatically across her face, lightly concealed by a thin white veil.

As protection against the weather she slipped into a full-length black mink, and, once finished, admired herself in the mirror. She knew she cut a striking figure; she hoped to throw Art Maguire off his guard. She took one last glance before leaving the room. She smiled, tossed her head, and told herself: Carolyn, you really know how to put on the dog!

For this occasion she had summoned a limousine, which was now waiting in the street at her door. She pulled on her black gloves, picked up her white leather clutch, and went down to the car. The doorman of the building tipped his hat as he held the door, and she pulled her fur tight at the throat as she felt the biting sting of the cold February air.

It was bitter cold, the sky a flat gray, casting a dull gray light over Manhattan. She hurried across the sidewalk, smiling and thanking the chauffeur, who held open the door to the limousine. Once inside, she was grateful for the warmth and comfort of the car. She sat back and looked out at the city. To her left was Central Park, looking rather cold and bleak, she thought. As the limousine pulled away and into the street, she sat tapping her fingers against her lap; she was anxious to confront Art Maguire, anxious to put in effect the plan that she and Walter had hoped would not be necessary.

She shifted and looked out the window as the limousine turned off Park Avenue onto East Fifty-seventh. Just a few more blocks to Lexington Avenue, then a right turn and down a few more blocks. She drummed her fingers against her clutch. It was time.

The limousine pulled up in front of Mt. Zion. She looked out the window at the enormous brick building, dingy with soot and grime. The chauffeur opened her door and helped her step out. She made her way quickly across the tiny plaza and up the steps to the doors. Once inside the lobby, she was thankful once again for the warmth; it was terribly cold out.

It had been several months since she had been inside Mt. Zion. The lobby was jammed, as always, with every imaginable type of person. She crossed the lobby and waited beside the bank of elevator doors.

In the elevator, people eyed her costume conspicuously. She held her head regally and awaited the proper floor. Finally, the doors opened on Art Maguire's floor and she made her way along the bright halls to his offices. As soon as she stepped inside, she knew she could work her way past the secretary in a flash.

"Yes? May I help you?" the young woman said, her eyes moving from head to toe of Carolyn's outfit.

"I'd like to speak with Dr. Maguire for a few minutes if I may," Carolyn said.

"Have you an appointment?" the secretary asked.

"I don't need one," Carolyn answered. "I'm Carolyn Branch."

A look of surprise crossed the secretary's face, and she nodded and immediately rose, going into Maguire's office. She emerged a moment later, holding open the door and beckoning with a graciously extended hand for Mrs. Branch to please come in. Carolyn nodded and made her entrance.

As usual, Art Maguire was perched on the edge of his desk, as though ready to attack should something untoward enter his office. Carolyn noticed his size first; he had gained another thirty pounds or so since she had last seen him. How *does* he do it? she asked herself, marveling at the immensity of his belly. Next she noticed that he was not looking at her, but rather down at the floor. How very odd, she thought.

Art Maguire was staring at the floor for a moment, trying to suppress the deep heartburn that he felt. He knew he shouldn't have put all that salsa on his eggs that morning. He pushed his fist against his solar plexus for a moment, in an attempt to alleviate the gas. Then he saw her shoes, black and white leather, the arches swooping down at sharp angles from the high white heels. The body of the shoes was scant, the tips of the shoes revealing just the beginning of the cleavages between her toes. His eyes moved up from there, taking in the black stockings, the elegant dress, the ermine stoles. As she slipped off her mink, he saw the dramatic white sleeve and shoulder piece. She threw her clutch and mink coat onto a settee and sat down.

"Have a seat, Art," she suggested, indicating his place behind his desk. He got up—rather dutifully—and sat there.

"How *are* you, Carolyn my darling?" he suddenly exclaimed, his hands rising imperiously as though to bestow a papal blessing. "It's been such a while, hasn't it?"

She indulged a saccharine smile. "Hasn't it," she said flatly, her tone incongruous with her facial expression.

"When was the last time, anyway?" he asked, now scratching his temple in an effort at thought.

"Your birthday party last year," she answered. "Don't you remember? I spilled champagne on your davenport; you had to get the houseboy to clean it up."

"Oh, yes, indeed," he said, chuckling. Carolyn raised her eyebrows in surprise; she had never seen such a tremendous belly jiggling like a bowl of jello.

"How is he, anyway? Such a cute one he was," she asked. Maguire frowned. "Who?"

"The houseboy," Carolyn said icily. "Your houseboy."

"Oh, him!" Maguire exclaimed, again throwing his hands up, then settling them, palms down, on the desktop. "Had to let him go."

"I see," she said, suddenly sitting straight and saying nothing. He smiled, the hollow insincere smile of habit. She said nothing, just stared at him. He shifted in his seat. The silence widened. Finally, just when she sensed he was about to say something, she said: "Congratulations, Art."

He was taken aback. "How's that?"

"On the grant. From Washington. Three and a half million dollars will go a long way."

His face became blank, guarded. He squinted his eyes, genuinely perplexed that she should have knowledge of it. "How did you know that?" he asked, very curious. "The phone call only came through this morning."

"Oh, Art," she said with a disparaging tone. "I've been in this game as long as you. Don't you recall?"

At her reference to their past, he shifted again. She detected a swallowing motion in his throat, surely a sign she was getting to him already.

"Well, that's that," he said, his meaning unclear.

"Yes, it is," she said coolly. "Tell me, Art, how much of that three and a half million is earmarked for Walter's research into AIDS?"

He gulped again. "Well, now, Carolyn, these things take time, you know that. We'll have to draw up budgets, and the hospital board will meet to examine avenues of possible research..."

"Shut up and cut the crap," Carolyn commanded. "Don't give me that claptrap. You don't get budgets *after* an award; that's all drawn up as part of the proposal. And the hospital board hasn't a damn thing to do with it at this point. Let's get to the point, Art."

He sat still, his face turning a rather deep shade of red.

"How much of that grant is slack? How much is discretionary? I want to see a copy of the proposal and its budgets from you, with every slack, every discretionary fund, every overestimate highlighted in yellow marker, along with a total of those figures. Because that money, Dr. Maguire, is what will be going into AIDS research at Mt. Zion."

He held up his hands. "Whoa, Carolyn, that's just not realistic. How am I supposed to do that? It's all settled..."

"Oh, stop whining!" she said venomously. "I'm so sick of the way you whine about everything! And you know when I started to get sick of it? About twenty-five years ago, when you whined and moaned about my leaving you for Walter."

His face registered terror. She was crossing into dangerous turf. "Please, Carolyn..." he whispered.

She went on. "It's not such a tough thing to do, Art darling. Just cut out the excesses in the budget and shuffle it over to Walter and Max in infectious diseases. That's all I'm asking. They've got to get a start on the AIDS problem."

"But Carolyn, you have to understand that there are political implications to that sort of research, even if I were to shuffle the funds around. Mt. Zion could lose important benefactors. What about these rich old Jews on the board? They don't want us doing that kind of work at Mt. Zion..."

"Or the rich old Episcopalians? Or the rich old Roman Catholics?" she cut in. "Or how about the rich old fags?"

There was a sudden and stunning silence in the office. Carolyn stared into Maguire's eyes with clear, cold honesty. She intended to do it, and he began to see her plan.

He spoke slowly: "Carolyn, you wouldn't think of doing something rash?"

"Rash?" she said. "I've been thinking of doing something rash ever since you used me so long ago. How do you think I felt when I discovered you were gay and using me as a cover? I *cared* about you, at least I felt something. And when I told you, you begged me to keep up the front, not to become involved with Walt? Oh, Art, you've made a mockery of your life, of everything that you are. Well, I'm going to help you out, drag you right into the dirt for all your lies."

"That's blackmail," he said, trying to sound as if he were warning her.

"Oh, yes, indeed," she admitted. "But a very fair form. All I ask is for that slack money to go to AIDS research, and in exchange, your secret need not leak out. It's really too bad you made a secret of it, that you lied to so many people for so long. Because if you hadn't, this little scheme of mine wouldn't work."

He was perspiring. She had him backed into a corner. She was right; her threat was a real one. Certain members of the board and the administration would never tolerate a revelation of his tastes, even now. He was beat; he would have to maintain the lie.

"All right," he said quietly. "You'll have those papers by the end of the week."

She smiled, ecstatically. "Wonderful, Art; I'm so glad you saw it my way. You'll see that besides saving yourself, you'll feel good knowing that something good is being done with that money."

He nodded. "Sure, sure. Would you leave?" All pretense of civility was done.

Carolyn did not like his tone. "All right, I'll be going. I feel sick about this, worse than you, I'm certain. What I've had to do just now—unbelievably—it spits in the face of all the decent people who'll work hard to solve this thing; and they'll do it just because they know it's right—or because they're dying. But look at what I've done here; at least now we have the money we need to start to fight a situation that was brought about largely by the kind of unnecessary dishonesty, fear, and shame which you and too many others have adopted as a lifestyle." She gathered her coat and clutch. "Good day, Arthur."

He made no response.

32

That night, like so many others in the past week and a half, David stood outside Andy's door and prepared to go in. He slipped on the sterile hospital garments, the gown and shoe coverings, then the cap and face mask. The apparel made him a stranger to Andy, who could see nothing now of his visitors but their eyes. But there was no choice. Both Andy and those around him had to be protected. Finally, he slipped on the rubber gloves and went in.

Andy was asleep, deeply asleep. David just stared as he stood by the side of the bed. He could barely recognize Andy now. In just a few short days he had broken out with herpes lesions, in addition to the staph lesions and the Kaposi's sarcoma. The herpes blisters covered a good part of Andy's face and neck, red, running.

Andy was terribly, unearthly thin; a dull, gray pallor showed on the good side of his face. David reached down with his gloved hand and touched Andy's small hand, so fragile now. Andy stirred, opened his eyes for a moment. he smiled at David. David smiled back, touched by the fact that Andy remained true to his commitment: he held himself well; he was, despite the agony and the disfigurement of the cancer, still a human being, a man whom David loved.

"Hi, Andy," he said. Andy opened his eyes full and opened his mouth to speak. A great fit of coughing seized him for several moments, and then he spoke, very softly, his voice rough and gravelly.

"Hi, David, I love you."

"I love you," David said. "How you doing?"

"Never better," Andy whispered, closing his eyes again. It had become a routine joke between them the past few days. The nightly vigil was tense and painful; levity helped. Andy coughed, then asked: "How did the ordinance do?" He knew it had been on the council's agenda for that day.

David swallowed hard. He said simply, "It failed."

Andy looked straight into David's eyes, a cold, expressionless stare. He said nothing, betrayed no feeling about the matter. "I'm not sleeping so much now," Andy said. "These sores hurt too much. The medicine doesn't help. I've been thinking a lot."

"You're doing okay," David said, uncertain what he meant.

"Yeah," Andy said. "I've had a lot to think about. There's a lot I've got to say before I go."

David swallowed back the tears. "Don't," he said. "Not now."

Andy nodded. He didn't have the strength, but he knew that very soon he would have to let his thoughts out. He had tried for three nights now, but each time, neither of them had the strength to talk. Andy knew the moment would come, soon. He closed his eyes again, overcome with fatigue.

David stood there for a while longer, watching Andy rest. His mind was more or less a blank, but over and over he had the recurring image of the medical center in San Francisco, of Dr. Kinder-Mann's lab. Thank god there are some gay doctors who care, David said to himself, for the first time in years truly thanking God. Lately, it had seemed necessary to believe; there was nowhere else to turn. Dr. Kinder-Mann was working hard, David knew, but there would be many months before any break-throughs. And in the past two weeks, Dr. Branch had briefed him on Mt. Zion's intractability. It mattered little at this moment; David would fight soon, and it would be the fiercest battle he would ever wage. There would be a reso-lution to the epidemic; he and others would force it. There was no other way. But now, in these last days, or maybe weeks, of Andy's life, David placed his strength in faith, in love for Andy.

And in that quiet moment beside Andy's bed, David closed his eyes and whispered a prayer, to whom he didn't know, but he focused his thoughts for Andy, for himself, for Dr. Kinder-Mann. And for all the other gay men suf-fering with the strange disease.

33

Across town Carolyn Whittier Branch presided over the dinner table like an empress at a state event. She wore an expression of secrecy and delight. Branch ob-served her as she cut into her lamb chop, wondering what was up. He knew she would speak in good time. Finally, the moment came.

She lay down her knife and fork and refreshed her palate with wine. "Now," she said, setting her glass down, "I have something to tell you."

"Yes, Carolyn?" he prompted, anxious to hear.

"I had that little meeting with Art this morning, the one we had hoped not to have to have."

Branch nodded. Oh, my god, he thought to himself.

"A piece of cake," she said, instantly relieving him of worry.

"You know," he said, "I hadn't heard a thing about the grant. Not one word!"

"I know," Carolyn said. "Naomi called me right before I called you and told me that the thing had come through.

I didn't let on when I spoke to you, though, because I didn't want you to know that I was seeing Art about it. The tension might have ruined the plan. So as soon as I confirmed with you that you'd had no word about it, I marched into Art's office and laid the cards out on the table. It was only a matter of minutes, really."

She went on to describe the meeting in detail, and Branch delighted in the story. They both laughed at their own skulduggery; it had been a real coup. As they toasted each other, the phone rang. Carolyn answered it. "It's the hospital, dear," she said, handing over the phone. She stood and smoothed her dress and went into the den. Another evening at home alone, she thought to herself as she heard her husband say that yes, he'd be there as soon as he could.

He came into the den in a moment. "I've got to go to the hospital," he said.

"Of course, dear," she said, rising to pour herself a drink. Nothing else to do, she resigned herself, coming down from that plateau of triumph.

"Andy Stone's lung has collapsed from the pneumonia. I've got to be there."

"My god!" she gasped. "How awful." She was shocked and concerned. He kissed her and hurried out the door. She sank into the davenport and sipped her drink.

34

Branch arrived at Mt. Zion and raced to the intensive care unit. He found Stone unconscious and in critical condition. He examined him, studied the chart and tests as ordered by the emergency physician. There was nothing he could do now but wait. He went out to search for David.

Branch found Markman sitting in the waiting room, trying to look strong, assured, but Branch could see the strain in his eyes, the tension of waiting telling in the weary, worn expression of fatigue.

"Dr. Branch," David said, standing.

"Sit down, David. I've just examined Andy. He's okay for this moment, but I'll be frank. It doesn't look good. This is the pattern too often."

"What happens next?"

"We wait," Branch answered. "We're using the strongest antibiotics, but Andy has refused most serious treatment; he's really too weak to hold out this time."

"Oh," David said hollowly. "I talked with him for a minute, earlier this evening; he said he had things to tell me before he dies."

"Go sit with him," Branch said, realizing how important it would be for them to talk were Andy to awaken, if only for a few minutes. "Go in and be there."

"Thanks," David said. Branch put his arm across David's shoulders and walked with him to Andy's room, helped David put on the sterile garments.

Branch returned to the nurses' station and studied Andy's chart once again. There was really nothing more he could do. He knew that it was most likely that Andy would succumb to the pneumonia, probably that night. None of the KS patients in a similar condition had survived it yet. He sat down heavily and read the chart and waited.

35

Andy felt the hospital door open and someone walk in long before he opened his eyes. He lay still, thinking that it must be Dr. Branch, the nurse, or David. He tried to bring himself alert, but the pain in his chest nagged at him, dragged him down. He kept his eyes closed and drifted into sleep, or semi-consciousness; he couldn't distinguish which. He dreamed of David coming into the room, of the early evening, and then he sensed that David was standing beside his bed, and he realized that he wasn't dreaming after all, that someone had come in. But he couldn't judge how long they had been standing there. He tried to concentrate on the moment, tried to forget the harsh pain in his chest, tried to force himself fully awake. He had to talk to David; there were things that must be said. The sleepiness had to be overcome, had to give way to a minute or two with David. But the pain shot through him, pulling him down again.

Then he felt the brush of David's hand against his cheek. He forced his eyes open, happier than he had ever been to see David standing there. David whispered, "I'm here, Andy." Andy smiled, closed his eyes again. He concentrated on finding the strength to raise his hand. David found it and held it tight.

Andy wanted to talk, to summon up those things he needed to release. He knew now that he was dying, but somehow, the effort seemed too great, too much a burden after such a long journey and difficult evening. He wanted only to rest, to lie still with his hand in David's.

David sat on the edge of the bed. "Dear, dear Andy," he whispered, bringing the hand to his face. "I love you."

The power of David's voice raised Andy from his slumber again. It is such a struggle, Andy thought, looking to David for some response, then realizing that he had not spoken the words, only thought them. "It's tough," Andy finally said, opening his eyes fully and suddenly becoming aware of the white hospital room and David, there on the edge of the bed, draped in sterile garb.

David didn't say anything for a moment; he was at a loss. But Andy was tapping his reserve once again. "Funny," he whispered, "but somehow it's also very easy. I feel at peace in a way." He closed his eyes and then opened them again. "Still, David, if I had a choice, I'd go home."

The moment was more difficult for David than he had imagined it would be. Where was his strength? Where was *his* reserve? It was as though Andy were feeding on David's energy in these last minutes.

"I was awake for a long time this afternoon," Andy said, "Before you came to visit earlier." His voice was hoarse, raspy with the pneumonia. "I tried to put the pieces together, to see some meaning in it all. That's been my only thought since I came in here, but I don't know..."

Andy stopped and trembled; he couldn't understand the sudden pain that would pass through his body, then, just as quickly, pass away, leaving him shuddering in a calm relief. He didn't want David to see his pain. It was his own, and this seemed to him the only thing he had left; a cruel possession, he thought, but it was something, something that imparted to him a persistent, enduring sense of life.

He looked across the room, towards the window. The blinds were shut. "My question has boiled down to one thing," Andy went on. "Whether or not—if I had the chance—I would choose not to be gay." And there was the pain again, coursing through him, exploding in his chest and then fading quietly. David could feel Andy's pain through their joined hands. It was almost more than he could bear.

David didn't try to stop him. He understood that for many, especially those afflicted by the disease, this question posed itself as seemingly central. He didn't care, at the moment, if it were or were not relevant or politically correct or logical. He knew that he, too, had found the question in the back of his own mind too many times.

Andy lay still again, looking back at David. "I've thought back to childhood, to my high school days, college, and all that came after... It seems so brief now, all of it. Could I have taken a different path, David? Could I have changed one thing, made some conscious decision to be more conforming? Thousands of men do it, and they don't—and won't—have AIDS."

"But are their lives real?" David asked.

"I don't know," Andy said softly. "I wish I knew that answer. But it doesn't matter, not at all."

David felt Andy's grip tighten. "Because," Andy went on, "I did it the way I am, no apologies. I don't care, I don't regret it. It's too late to regret it now, anyway. But I know this: the answer to my question is that no, I wouldn't have chosen not to be gay. It has been the most compelling force..."

"You know, David, we were there! We were at the forefront of something new, something hopeful. How many people can say that? How many people have been out there—in the parades, in the papers, in the political offices—doing something that makes it easier for others to come out, to be fully gay and fully human, to have men like you to love..."

Tears brimmed in their eyes, but Andy would not cry. He was done with that, he was done with suffering. He wasn't sure, but he knew that he was infused with a great harmony, a consonance. He had made his armistice with the world.

"I wouldn't change it," he said, finally.

David held the hand tight, watched as Andy closed his eyes and rested once again. After some time—Andy couldn't judge if it were minutes or hours—he opened his eyes, saw that David was still there, holding his hand.

It's all so simple, so plain, Andy thought to himself. He watched David looking at him, wondered what he might be thinking. He saw David's lips moving, forming the words "I love you." That's good, Andy thought, but he couldn't answer. He was ready to open his mouth and whisper the same, but something small and magnificent deep inside him had loosened itself, was growing larger, expanding, releasing itself. Andy could hear David crying, but it didn't matter. It was done.

Published in paperback.
There is also a special edition of ten numbered copies,
handbound in boards and signed by the author.